The Invisible Realm

Rachel Hammond

BALBOA.
PRESS

A DIVISION OF HAY HOUSE

Balboa Press books may be ordered through booksellers or by contacting:

Balboa Press
A Division of Hay House
1663 Liberty Drive
Bloomington, IN 47403
www.balboapress.com.au
1 (877) 407-4847

Because of the dynamic nature of the Internet, any web addresses or links contained in this book may have changed since publication and may no longer be valid. The views expressed in this work are solely those of the author and do not necessarily reflect the views of the publisher, and the publisher hereby disclaims any responsibility for them.

The author of this book does not dispense medical advice or prescribe the use of any technique as a form of treatment for physical, emotional, or medical problems without the advice of a physician, either directly or indirectly. The intent of the author is only to offer information of a general nature to help you in your quest for emotional and spiritual well-being. In the event you use any of the information in this book for yourself, which is your constitutional right, the author and the publisher assume no responsibility for your actions.

Any people depicted in stock imagery provided by Thinkstock are models, and such images are being used for illustrative purposes only.
Certain stock imagery © Thinkstock.

Print information available on the last page.

ISBN: 978-1-4525-3173-1 (sc)
ISBN: 978-1-4525-3174-8 (e)

Balboa Press rev. date: 11/23/2015

For

Chloe and Bianca, you are my dreams come true.

Thank you
Elaine Williams, for providing your eyes and your ears
Russell, for having my back
Jesus Christ, for the greatest love affair of all time.

Introduction

At the beginning of all things, one great land spanned both the seen and the unseen. The invisible dimensions were first, then the substance of the invisible fashioned the Tactile. The Invisible Realm, teeming over with goodness, yearned for new expression. So, out from the artist's longing, poured the form of the Tactile Plain. This Plain was intended to bring enjoyment to all those given a place on it.

No detail was passed over as something insignificant. Recognition of a pleasing perfume, for example, pored over until its beauty was full and unique. Sweet smells wafting up from its source, and its transition through a tactile body. Nostrils, mildly flaring out, receive the pleasing interruption. The chemistry of the body, lighting up like a roadmap, linking many receptors on its path until, finally, the collation of information connects to the brain part that deciphers its genesis. Then, with eyes widening at its remembrance, all other preoccupations, arrested for precious moments in the acknowledgement of the beauty of scent.

Unprepared Lips pull swiftly to horizontal tensions; sweet, exhilarating tickles arise from the belly and travel upward causing muscles to contract and then release, repeatedly, to their staccato rhythms. Cheeks draw upward causing eyes to squint and vision to blur as tears fill the void. Noses wrinkle at the flushing heat that rises through opening capillaries, expressing their plump pink hue until, the crescendo, the explosion of audible release through now open lips.

This unexpected expression, this mixture, this union of fullness from both the tactile and invisible was always part of the original intent. However, something dreadful did occur. The seen and the unseen were given cause to divorce in one single day. The breach activated by the use of trickery, administered to the naïve by the dastardly. I will not tell you any more about that just yet as it would cause a whole other book to be written, and as we well know, time is short, and history is very, very long. Even so, please take my word that things could not continue as they had been.

Over the passing of Time, both worlds began to suffer the consequence of such an event. The second world to exist, the Tactile Plain, now recognised as the Cambrae Sphere, began to forget all about the Unseen Places and presumed that its existence was for itself and out of itself. With the initial union absent from memory, the Tactile Plain did not remember what it was missing.

The unseen world, however, yearned for its companion. He felt her loss so deeply that his tears formed mountains and oceans across the unseen lands in her memory. Fixing his eyes upon her, he watched. The entrapment of his love could clearly be seen. He called out to her, but he could not be heard. For, how could he communicate with the world that no longer desired to accept his existence?

When the right time became, one called Victor who sat in most high esteem from the unseen realm, changed form to become visible and was sent to the Tactile Plain to heal the dis-ease of separation forever. He, in three long days, challenged the system that became of the separation and restored everything so it could return to its original state. He fought bravely a fight that no one else dared, or could. Now, it would seem the matter entirely rectified, but it was not.

More were sent from the Invisible Realm to remind the Tactile Plain of what Victor had accomplished for them so thoroughly. They were taught how to demonstrate the reversal of the infraction. This, though, was not an easy task and had many unique challenges of its own.

The beings chosen to perform this task were picked from the Invisible Realm. They were to be born in the Tactile Plain and developed upon the Cambrae Sphere. The power given them was mighty, but, in the transition from realm to the plain, they did not remember who they were.

Throughout the lives of the ones placed upon the Tactile Plain, beings from the Invisible Realm came to bring them back to remembrance and stir out memories embedded within their DNA, until; finally, the understanding was released.

Our journey does not begin at this point however; it begins with the Chosen in the Invisible Realm.

Chapter 1

INVENTION

Isabella sat upon the verdant hill and looked out toward the horizon. Though she supposed she had viewed it a thousand times before, this occasion felt like the very first time. Such a magnificent sight lay bare before her eyes. *What an extraordinary light,* she pondered.

The light that shone so gloriously bright was made up with flashes of brilliant colour sparkling through the expanse of sky. Its intensity crowned the subdued backdrop of emerald green that frothed and bubbled with a life of its own.

Though the panorama rang out with such vibrancy, it was, in fact, immensely peaceful and inspiring to the imagination. With its many dimensions of colour, Isabella imagined that she was able to climb upon the skies surface and look below at the flourishing leafy ground with its mineralised pathways of living stone that outlined three separate destinations.

Isabella, treasuring the view for a few moments longer, deeply inhaled as though she could breathe in the very atmosphere, and then, standing up, she continues her journey. Walking down the pathway, Isabella quickly connected to the junction that defines the three great provinces, each one containing three diverse kinships. The first turn in the path leans to the right, and leads on to the Province of Chosen, the second turning, a little further on, veers off to the left and leads to the Province of Kings, while the third, facing straight ahead, leads to the Province of the Eirtherol. The Province of Chosen was Isabella's destination for that day.

As she walked, Isabella contemplated the beauty of the other two provinces, their feasting celebrations, the richness of each community, and the exclusive beauty of every home. The differences were vast in taste and character, even within the inflection of their speech, yet, she could not choose the province with superior beauty. Her mind kept drawing comparison and parallels between them, never managing to draw any conclusion other than all were perfection.

At the end of her ponderings, another, more perplexing thought occurred to her. *How could I possibly know all of this?* She could not seem to recall her beginning at all. As quickly as the thought entered, it disappeared as the balmy day took over her senses once again.

At precisely the same time of Isabella's contemplations, one named Eleneke was considering the ages ahead. Although she knew there was no way to predict the coming events, she enjoyed marvelling at its mysteries. Eleneke, previously involved in a myriad of similar journeys, and each one was quite different from the last.

The consequence of a decision made by one of the tactile kin did not offer the same conclusion as when another chose in the same way, for, there were many variables to each being that are not apparent to the typical observer, even if this particular observer happened to be many thousands of years old.

Eleneke's insides smiled, *Victor had decidedly more wisdom and forethought than I could ever begin to understand or imagine. There is nothing ordinary about any one of these little creatures; they were each fashioned from a unique design.* Eleneke had been given a particular tenderness toward the ones not of her kind, as did certain other Eirtherol, who were given the same commissioning.

A wave of excitement flooded Eleneke at the thought of her getting to meet and know more of these peculiar and exotic creatures. The Eirtherol so enjoyed the little creatures, fascinating in the level of depth and unpredictability that they carry. *How could they harbour so much quality?* She thought. With these notions echoing throughout her being, she also sets off down the path that veered right, to the Province of Chosen.

There were many ways available for Eleneke to get to her destination, but she chose to walk and enjoy the living, breathing picture that surrounded. Time was of no consequence to her, as the currency of time does not exist in Invisible Realm. The only gauge that she held was that of her heart; that was their way. Eleneke knew that when her desire to be in a place became stronger than her desire to be anywhere else, that was the occasion in which to proceed. The Eirtherol did nothing from sheer obligation; even so, the paths they chose to walk in were their intended pathways. Eleneke cast her eye over to her destination.

As it drew nearer, she saw a body of water stretching further than the sharpest of natural eyes could see. It appeared both still and inviting with an occasional ripple caused by a gently blowing breeze teasing its surface. The breeze carried with it a matchless fusion of scents from both the land and the water. These blended scents made the most delightful of perfumes.

The skies above Eleneke's head held such clarity that, if she looked at its reflection on the lake, and then back up toward the sky; she would have difficulty in knowing whether she stood upon her feet or hung upside down. That is if it were not for the many types of birds adorning the open heavens.

The airborne creatures speckled the skies as paint holds to a canvass, quiet, still and sustaining this suspended motion for long intervals. Then most unexpectedly, they took to flight at an exuberant pace, playfully chasing brightly decorated insects without any intent to ingest.

Clusters of mature trees stood tall around the grounds, their enormous branches bearing weight from the generously proportioned and ornate wooden chairs that adorned them. Each one of these chairs, prepared in the Province of Kings, handcrafted from the finest imaginations, each one a distinct work of art.

As she continued walking, Eleneke remembers the strange and magnificent creatures that potter about on the lawn lush areas ahead. Thoughts of them always increased her joy. Slowly moving from place to place, the beasts simply delight in their existence. One particular animal, a gentle and affectionate creature by nature, spends its time seeking out any nearing Eirtherol or Chosen. It carries around its considerably hefty body without much grace, though obviously relishing the hilarity of its clumsiness.

The happy creature, dressed in a velvety fleece, lay its great mass down at the feet of any Eirtherol or Chosen that desired to sit in the beauty of the meadow. Once received, the creature nestles in close and envelops the seated one with its full silken tail. Then, when satisfied that his guest has settled, it bestows yet another pleasure. Rising from deep inside its body, a giggly purr forms and enhances the experience with its lulling vibration. Eleneke finished with her musing, laughs loudly and continues her hike.

In between the sky and the waters tiny particles of light flash and dart about. They shift from random pattern to random pattern, obviously in control of their own movements, yet, when somebody approaches, those lights appear compelled to follow the one walking; being free to move individually, but apparently not disconnected from their surrounds either. Birthed from the parent, new tiny energies frequently explode into the scenery, intensifying the colour in their presence.

Parent lights hover in the background of these little illuminations; larger and more concentrated, the size of a torch glow though their shape unrefined, they stay close to the infant lights, and continue to invest their supplies. Both kinds of lights add generously to the tranquillity and overt beauty of their surroundings, yet, this attribute is just a by-product. Their primary purpose becomes evident the moment a being starts to talk.

The large lights congregate around Chosen and Eirtherol while the smaller lights nestle within. A connection is formed between two beings, and in conversation, words are birthed. Quickly, bursting out of their larger host, the infant lights connect themselves to the freshly delivered phrases. (As words are released they linger in the air around the one who spoke, and the one who listened. This can be seen clearly in the Invisible Realm). The tiny seed and the connected word permeate the body of the willing receiver and becoming part of their very fabric, add to their constitution.

That is incredible thought Eleneke. The Eirtherol remembers back to the time of innocence, before the 3-day battle, when she was a much younger being. With others of her kin, she was taken aside and given the indulgence of watching these very lights at their commencement.

While still in incubation, these tiny seed lights were prepared in a unique way. Impressed before their own beginning with innate abilities to capture actual physical words, they were trained to collect each thought, every feeling and every morsel of learning that led a speaker to arrive at a conclusion, then finally, to deposit the enriched word into its beneficiary, and most effectively so. *If someone had studied vast quantities of text, and reflected upon the content for a considerable while, they would still not receive the same quality and completeness that is so easily grasped with the help of the lights*, Eleneke continued her remembrance.

So, the grateful recipient receives the word and the light into its being, where the qualities, upon impact separate. The word that is heard stays within their mind, but the enhancements of the word, the accompanying thoughts and feelings, delve deeper, feeding the enlightenments into the host's makeup, leaving an un-intellectualized memory, an impression, and a deeper understanding. At the right time, the little seeds contribution releases up and out the body, revealing the full meaning, to the expectant mind, which can now begin to understand and rely upon the unearthed wisdom.

The lights also shine upon the orator, illuminating any point spoken of but from a distinctly different perspective from the hearer. Each time the words are related, the truths develop in richness, depth and brilliance, thus inspiring the one sharing the wisdom as much, if not more than, the one listening. Suddenly it dawned on Eleneke, and she laughed at her slowness to understand, *it is precisely these little lights making Daraketh – The Position of Gathering, a perfect place for instruction, preparation, and profound guidance for within.*

★

As Isabella walked the narrow path that curled through the Province of Chosen, she approached the first Kinship, Daraketh – The Position of Gathering. Looking at the seemingly unfamiliar signpost, she remembers her previous and unresolved thought. *How is it that I know of my destination, even though I cannot recall ever being here before? If I search my deepest remembrances, I am not aware of ever being told about it either. Why Daraketh Isabella, and not any of the other Kinships? Why do I choose this way?* Her thoughts were somewhat more remarkable than disturbing. After a short period, Isabella caught sight of someone in the distance, and her previous deliberation dissolved as a new one endeavours to occupy her mind.

Up ahead, stands a structure of ancient stone surrounded by moss of green and purple with colourful wildflowers and shrubbery bordering that. This feast for the eye nestled in among numerous lazy looking weepy trees with their long branches brushing against the ground. The fragrance that pours out from this uncultivated vegetation is gloriously dizzying and Isabella could have fascinated in them for hours. Instead, she chose to fixate upon an unfamiliar figure that leant up against the stone formation.

As she nears the figure, it becomes quickly evident that the character has been expecting her. With a wave of his hand, the male motions for Isabella to join him. Isabella, pleased with the thought of company, felt no need to hesitate in her decision. She had enjoyed her walk with her own thoughts, and now she would enjoy her time being shared with another.

Isabella had almost reached the ancient stone when the handsome man takes steps toward her. Without any utterance, he met Isabella's intended route and they both continue upon the path that she has been travelling.

His smile was unguarded as he introduced himself. "I am happy to be making your acquaintance, Isabella. I am named Aaron," his slow and soft drawl compelled Isabella's full attention. Raising her eyebrows in surprise, she replies in amusement, "Well there is no need for me to introduce myself as you already know my name," she playfully poses her thoughts with a questioning tone. Aaron smiles and promptly presents an explanation, "I knew you would be coming, an Eirtherol had told me all about you. I was also told to wait here for you, but I didn't know for how long. Then I became completely distracted by my surroundings. I was wholly taken in by it. It's a good thing I looked off in that direction when you came by or I may have missed you altogether." Isabella grins without parting her lips, allowing herself to be lost in the beauty of her surrounds.

Aaron was the same as Isabella in that he did not remember where he came from, or how he knew to go to Daraketh, but his consciousness had been awakened for longer. His essence was like the other Chosen in the Invisible Realm, innocent, unaware of pain, embarrassment or shame, and filled with gentle anticipation. Each Chosen, however, still had many combinations of quality that made them quite distinct from each other. All were intrigued and all were intriguing.

As they walked together, Isabella felt impressed upon by a profound sense of peace encompassing Aaron. Even though she was not found lacking in this attribute, his presence was arresting, and, as she conversed with him further, with words and without, her own awareness of this beautiful sacred quality was heightened.

In no time at all, the new acquaintances caught sight of Daraketh – The Position of Gathering. The signpost was obscured by distance, but it was clear that they were entering into a new part of the Province. For the air ahead had become deeper, more defined; almost as if someone had drawn an outline across the sky, and filled it in with other shadings. Variant hews of greens, blues and oranges layered upon the colour that previously dominated, giving everything the appearance of more depth and animation.

It occurs to Isabella that it is these little lights hanging in the air that cause the distinctive change. They seem to reflect upon themselves the vibrancy of colour around them. Sometimes the illuminations mirror a single orange hue from a spray of flowers, throwing that colour across the luxuriant landscape, while other times they gather a collection of shades from varying sources, mixing the palate to create a unique and generous display. Isabella easily envisages that the lights are operating together to create a new masterpiece every few blinks of the eye or so.

Not only did the colour change, but so did the atmosphere. It was electric, resembling sparklers popping and bursting throughout the open skies. This electricity gravitates toward the Chosen and resonates within their own bodies. Its sensations suggest the promise of answers to weighty mysteries and subdued secrets that floated just below one's level of awareness, profound questions, affecting their own existence. With anticipation building upon the vigour of the already eager pair, and pace taking on new speed and purpose, their eyes survey the grounds ahead.

A few steps on, the element of wetness adds its idiosyncrasy and merges crispness into the ether. "Water ahead," Aarons calming voice echoes with charged anticipation, "I can smell it but I cannot see it." An exuberant smile overtakes his face as he continues sharing his enthusiasm with Isabella, "I find affinity with its movement, I can't explain why." Isabella giggled inside at the intensity of her companion. "I will help you look for it," replied Isabella with joyous voice. But, it was not water that they observed next.

Others, similar to Aaron and Isabella were wandering around, exploring the unfamiliar territory while enjoying the company of others. They were amusing to watch in their newness, stopping sometimes to stand still and take in their surroundings with a look of wonderment etched upon their faces. Isabella supposed that both she and Aaron did the same things.

Isabella's eyes were drawn to others that were of similar proportion to the Chosen, but much taller. These ones were brighter in countenance so Isabella examined their faces to understand the cause. As she did, a strong impression rose up from within and presented unearned truth. "Aaron, when I look at their faces, I am convinced of why they glow. They agree only to peace and allow rule by the most gentle of wisdom. See how they laugh," Isabella whispered.

"Their displays of light-heartedness can only be possessed by ones confident of the outcome of all things, sure that it is full of incontestable favour. They are decidedly regal, and extraordinarily graceful in movement. Look at the way they carry themselves. Though their faces look no older than ours, their expression transcends the very idea of age. They are proved and have existed much longer than we," Isabella's amiable voice sang out her impressions a little louder this time. She had never seen Eirtherol before, but had heard from Aaron all about them and could instantly recognise them by these immense qualities. They were an impressive sight to behold.

As the travellers draw closer, their eyes begin adjusting to the changing light and things not seen before become evident. They notice tiny little people with pudgy faces, short arms, supple legs and rounded tummies scattered about, rolling around in the thick grasses. These little ones were having a marvellous time playing; the sound of their laughter filled the air with good nature and frivolity. It looked as though an invisible force was tickling them, rolling them and tossing them upward, only to catch them and place them back on the lush, velvety grasses. They were completely enthralling to watch.

As Isabella and Aaron observe the novel creatures, a broad sense of repose settles upon them; in response, they seek out a place to sit down and indulge. Once identified the two travel toward their separate idyllic locations to settle in to enjoy the tranquillity. Aaron moves toward the grasses near a tremendously fragrant tree. He is soon joined by one of the large downy animals. It curled up behind, and wraps itself around his seated body, giving perfect comfort, while Isabella takes a swing seat near the still water's edge and reclines slightly.

Isabella now settled in, notices a sense of euphoria that appears to cross the entire land. It has almost an edible, breathable quality that transfers toward one's insides as well. She realises that this effect has taken all of her companions also, and they, like she, had found a place to rest. Some seated on garden beds of flowers while others are sitting in and amongst the trees. One other lay upon the grasses in the approximate centre of the land and gazes at the show of lights occurring above her in the sky.

The little ones, still frolicking around though now collected up by the Eirtherol and held tightly in their plentiful arms, two small ones to each Eirtherol. The little ones, nestling into the Eirtherol's neck, close their soft and glistening eyes. The Eirtherol also close their eyes and an aura of gold radiates out from them, surrounding them all momentarily. A notion enters Isabella's mind, but it is not her own. *Love is the highest currency and gold is its representation here.* The thought sounds deeper in pitch than Isabella's usual ponderings and it carries an unfamiliar accent.

Isabella's eyes hastily open as she realises she is not alone. Eleneke stands before her, a tall and dark skinned Eirtherol with curls of ebony framing her extraordinary face. Her chiselled features are exceedingly serene and her movements both valiant and graceful. She is holding two cuddling little ones in her arms. Both small beings open their eyes and much to Isabella's surprise and delight, the little male speaks out, with a sweet and rounded sound. "We are here for you to tell you of many things, and to establish in your heart a purpose. I am a Chosen Who Chose Not to go, as is my sister Janity," he points toward his little female companion and then continues on, "I will be your advisor in many things here, as will Eleneke," his chubby little fingers drumming upon the Eirtherol's collarbone. This action causes the Eirtherol to laugh in amusement. The little male went on, "Janity is learning to do as I do. Oh," he chuckles to himself, "I did forget something of importance, I am Wesley; Wesley is my name." With a nod of his head and contented smile, he continues. "I will only be with you while you are here, but Eleneke will be with you wherever you go, whether you are aware of her presence or not." He smiles a gummy open smile and giggles from his bouncy rounded belly. Eleneke smiles widely as she meets the gaze of Isabella.

Isabella, out of the corner of her eye, is sure she had seen more golden light glimmering out from Eleneke, but this time, it showered over her. *The currency of love*, she thought, *to know, and to be known, to receive and be received*. She is drawn into her own thoughts for a time, running across her mind, stealing her attention, but only for a short while.

Behind the elegant frame of Eleneke, some of the lights begin to gather and hover with a definite purpose. Isabella senses that something new is approaching.

The Eirtherol smiles again at the young Chosen and then places her generous hand upon Isabella's diminutive frame. Isabella's instincts tell her that she is receiving something from Eleneke, but could not pinpoint what exactly. All she can confidently recognise is clarity of definition coming to her, but a description of what she could not say.

Eleneke spoke into Isabella's curious heart with a knowing look, "Do not be unsettled; you have not missed my meaning, you contain it. It has become a part of you, and when you need it, it will rise up and be obvious in its presence. Your very being will witness a safety and understanding that is not visible, nor obvious, because of this moment." Eleneke looked deeply into the vulnerable and questioning eyes of Isabella and Isabella's heart was again contented.

From nowhere, the sounds of tinkling little bells fill up the crackling skies. Thousands of small blue-tinged white birds circle around, then settle over a little area of the grounds next to the waters. It quickly becomes evident to the Chosen that these little birds are the bells. It is also obvious that the birds want to draw the attention of the inhabitants upon the land. So, the Chosen comply with their veiled request and draw closer to the animated choir.

Arriving at the place of much excitement, the Chosen look up at the noisy assembly, then down to the ground on which they stand. A platform, slightly raised, lay just before their feet. It appears to be made of a thick, yielding substance that is both dark with colour, yet still somehow subdued.

A few Eirtherol carrying little ones step upon the platform, walk to the furthest point, and then release the Chosen Who Chose Not To Go upon its surface. As the little ones roll and coo, the Eirtherol crouch their tall bodies down to sit. The Chosen, now feeling confident of their requirements, follow closely after. The platform pushes up from under them, filling even the spaces between their toes, though not rigidly so. Its pleasant tickles invite curious hands to touch and experience the peculiar wonder also. The Chosen quickly sit down, intending to play with this new material, when the platform suddenly begins to rise, and hovers above the waters toward its destination.

The deep blue still waters gently ripple around the platforms porous edge as the skies dazzle with its shows of light and crackle. Each Chosen, yet again, unable to distinguish their separateness from the surroundings is silently drawn into the beauty of it all. The Eirtherol, familiar with the spectacle, grin in amusement and settle back to observe as each Chosen remains drawn into the complete and unfathomable satisfaction until the end of the journey.

As if with a sense of humour, the platform rapidly reduces to an abrupt halt. With destination being met, the passengers take hold of their own senses yet again. One of the Eirtherol untangles his long body and hoists himself up; claps his hands and draws all eyes to himself. With mouth agape, the Eirtherol prepares to release new understanding towards the occupants of the boat, when a small number of bell birds begin to chime, distracting his intention. The Eirtherol pauses to see what the interruption is all about. The birds, now swooping over his head, cause him to lose balance and he is plunged into the sweeping blue waters.

The airborne nuisances disappear quickly out of sight, yet their clanging tones still linger. "Were they laughing?" splutter one the Chosen before they all fall about in fits of laughter. This action from the tiny troublemakers left everyone with the sense of being wonderfully out of control. The merriment stops for a brief moment as the waterlogged Eirtherol re-boards the platform but soon recommences at the sound of his own laughter.

The vehicle begins to lower, touching the water underneath it. The water reciprocates the touch, reaches up inside the platform and releases its fluidity, filling up every empty and parched space. As the elements combine, what had been one form of beauty is now quickly transformed into another. A magnificent array of vivid colour becomes evident all over and through its surface. The texture of the platform is changed, becoming softer and lighter.

It is now quite clear that they have travelled not on a platform at all, but on the back of a living being, a magnificently formed creature not resembling any animal that Isabella has ever seen before. The minds of the Chosen begin to race with excitement as they start to perceive that there is so much more inspired life to explore.

Wesley turns to Eleneke and asks her to place him on her shoulder. The little being begins to address the now attentive crowd. With his head held high and his proud little arms resting on his chest, he speaks. "We have now come to a place where we can share our experience. There is some learning, only for you; for who you are, and for what you would need, and then, there are other learning's that are equally applicable, one to another, and do not need to be adjusted to anyone but stand as they are for all. This second learning is the learning you are all about to receive."

Isabella pondering upon the words of Wesley, experiences a sense of being prepared for something. Having no other point of reference than her current circumstances, she allows questions in her mind to pass by unaddressed and makes a choice to trust in the nature of these incredible beings.

"The one who is expected has now arrived," called out Janity using the loudest possible voice that her small physique could muster. Each passenger looks up to meet the one to be introduced. Someone was being carried upon the back of a large and exquisite bird with dewy black feathers, long neck and powerful wings. The bird finds a place to perch, settles, and then opens its beak to release a greeting in the form of song, arresting the audience with its charm. The passenger it carries, slides from its back quite inconspicuously, tidies his appearance and waits for the bird to finish its tune. Once finished, the newcomer thanks the bird for its offerings and, sitting on the edge of the water creature, makes himself comfortable.

Isabella looks at the one who has joined them. His size is the same as the Eirtherol, yet, it is clear that he is a Chosen. It is also clear, by the sound of the whispers from other Chosen, that they have drawn a similar conclusion. An Eirtherol, understanding their curiosity, quickly replies to the inquisition. "He is a King, a Chosen that has returned. He has been where you will go and now has re-entered the Invisible Realm. Usually, when a Chosen has returned, their appearance is somewhat altered, though still recognisable from the Tactile Plains. See, they display a more robust level of form."

"So the Tactile Plain is where we will go Eleneke?" Isabella looked into the face of Eleneke. She was happy to understand an answer to at least one mystery. Eleneke smiles her open warming smile and places her hand upon Isabella's shoulder. "Now is the time for you to know this."

By this one single touch from the hand of Eleneke, the history of the separation between the Invisible Realm and the Tactile Plains is revealed in great detail. Victor and his accomplishments are also shown, along with other things, critical things for a sent Chosen to know. Other Eirtherol, seeing Eleneke's action, take her lead and begin to release the same physical transfer to each of the other Chosen.

With wide eyes, the younger beings absorb the information and begin to process these new ideas in their thoughts. Ideas of failing, the concept of pain and difficulty enters their thinking for the very first time. As the Chosen grapple with these new concepts, their readable faces disclose that they have become quite overwhelmed.

Wesley cries out loudly to attract their attention and then speaks with the greatest of confidence, "We know the path that is laid out ahead of you and we know how it is that you finish," His emphasis was defined. "You have all been given a powerful bravery so don't fear now. You are loved so greatly, and because of this love, you are well provided for."

Those words of comfort are accepted by the Chosen as the beginning of their destiny is implanted into the deepest part of their cores. They realise their futures are intertwined with each other's, but also, connected to something much larger than they. They were attached to a destiny that encompassed a broader span than they could even begin to understand.

As they share a reflective thought with one another, and in their own minds, it becomes apparent that in cooperation, they are, without question, powerful. With this new and intriguing information, the Chosen's appetite to understand is expanded, and a deep silence falls among all the beings as the enormity sinks in.

A short time passes, and attentions are once again placed toward this Returned Chosen that sat with them. He was clothed in fabric finery, detailed yet simple. A crown made from precious metals and studded with gems adorns his head. Every facet embellished exquisitely, as though one with very minute hands had prepared it. Finally, he opens his mouth to speak and as he did, all eyes were drawn to him once more.

"I am Michael, and I am a King." His articulation precise, his discourse well-spoken, and his words sweet as honey; a sense of high authority and sincere kindness abides within them. "I come to you from the Province of Kings. It is an extraordinary Province, one that you will all come to know. There, we host the most extravagant feasting celebrations." A broad smile overtook his face as he continued, "I did not want to come to you without evidence of the impending festivities, so I have bought with me a token."

Michael quickly leans across the giant bird and runs his hand down its neck. This action pleased the bird, and it releases a silken cloth pouch from under its wing. Michael whispers his thanks to the bird, takes hold of the bag and releases its contents to the curious audience. The colourful glass-like orbs that it contained now quickly placed in the mouths of all who are aboard. The taste was delicious and good for both food and drink.

After the refreshment had been relished, Michael continues. "The first thing that I need to disclose to you is simply this. You were crafted, purposefully and precisely, to be exactly as you are. You are intended to differ from each other, from all others; there has been no lack of ingenuity as you were contemplated into being, and so rest assured, that you are a unique expression, a powerful and distinctive work of art. However, you will not often recognise these qualities within yourselves, and indeed, most that you encounter will not; even so, in time, you will come to trust this truth.

There will be some, in times to come, that hold influence and power over you, some with legitimacy and some, well, fraudulently. They will provoke you to doubt in these truths. Their questions will resonate throughout your being; desperately trying to persuade you that you are indeed, no one of consequence, and in doing so, they undermine your very purpose. You need not adjust yourself under this improper influence.

There is room for you to enter fullness, a place that no one else can fill. You each contain something of significance, something needing to be revealed upon the Tactile Plains. You can never be too much, and you are not too little when you are true to whom you were created to be."

Michael scanning the faces of his listeners continues, "You cannot take anyone's place, nor can anyone fit your own, you that are valuable beyond measure. So do not try to diminish yourself to make room for others, for there is no need, there is plenty of space for the full expression of all."

Michael slowly and deliberately points his ring dressed fingers to each of the enthralled Chosen, "You will all find your proper place." He smiles. "This is truth and does not change regardless of thinking's or fashion. When you are stronger in this understanding, you will become guides to help release those held captive with these same reasoning's too."

Michael, deep in his heart, knew that this was just the beginnings of understanding and he desired to share so much more, however, he also understood that timing is a crucial and even beautiful truth, when administered without wisdom or concern, can damage beings so new.

Michael continued his address; "I have a question for you to ponder. Through unseen eyes, you will observe things that are not yet, but will be beautiful and amazing things. However, at the very same time, with your outside eyes, you will see it look broken, maligned, or useless in some way, yet it is the same thing that you see. My question is this; in which eyes do you trust?"

The Chosen look around to see if anyone will answer this conundrum, but no one volunteers. Michael continued, "Remember, if it does not contain hope then it is not the truth. Even so, everything you experience, pleasant or not, can be used as a tool in your hands if viewed with the right vision. In fact, if you keep in mind that those things that are most valuable are often those that appear to be the most damaged.

Even so, your outside eyes will be the stronger of the two, especially when you encounter the Barren-slick, deceptive weaponry of our enemy. It will find where you are weak in minds sight and cause illusions of thought to be fused over your external eyes, making discernment of truth...well...difficult. However, over time, you will learn to purposefully disregard anxiousness, and halt the seemingly unending barrage of open-ended questions that assault you. Then, you will begin to hear and trust your other eyes, your invisible eyes, developing them to become more dominant. Then, you will have increased in authority and dominion over the Tactile Plain, causing it to take on nature of the Invisible, as it was in the beginning."

Something, at that precise time, opened up within the Chosen, something that had not been encountered before. A sense of danger combined with tremendous excitement rested upon them. Michael instantly recognises what had just taken place. "That feeling new to your experience is called adventure my friends." He laughs as he reminisces from his own memories of the same encounter he had many, many ages before.

The Chosen had a lot to talk about, and the Eirtherol, along with the Chosen Who Chose Not, were eager to join in. These long anticipated conversations were thrilling for the experienced every time.

Michael satisfied that his task done well dismisses himself with a smile and bow of his head. "Till next time we meet," he turns to leave. "Wait," cried a voice from one of the Chosen. Michael and the other passengers turn their heads to study the one who speaks. Dark wavy hair frames the male's angular face while glistening ebony eyes reflect intelligent curiosity. "My name is Wry and I would like for you to tell me something," with a confident and pronounced voice, he continued, "When do we come to meet with you and have the feast in your land?" Michael laughed. Previously informed about the qualities of each Chosen, he was aware of Wry's candid appreciation for cuisine and community. "Well Wry, you will have to live in that anticipation, for it does not happen until you all come back again. You will see Victor before you leave." Michael quickly boards the elegant winged creature and they take off into the endless skies.

Afterward, there were no further commitments and the Eirtherol regard the Chosen's need to rest from all the cerebral stimulation.

Countless hours were allocated and spent exploring possibilities and delving into the learning's of the social kind; skills were practiced, abilities noticed and all senses participating. After considerable time, Darién, the Eirtherol in the company of a Chosen named Cara, called for attention. Placing his hands to encircle his mouth, he releases a hulking yodel.

"We will take you to another Kinship in the Province of Chosen where you will be refreshed. You will eat and drink, walk and explore, then you will rest in your private chambers at your own leisure. Then the following is another time of learning and preparation where we will tell you more of the barren-slick and prepare you for what that all means. Until then, however, have a thrilling and peaceful time." The living platform rises up and takes them to dry land.

Given the choice, the group could be bought by carriage, ride a horse or be carried by the winged creatures; alternately, they could use their own feet and walk, run or meander along the picturesque and exquisitely fragrant pathways. Each Chosen selects according to their desires.

As the Chosen decide, the Eirtherol play games. Taking great pleasure in guessing who would choose what transport, they laugh heartily at their incorrect choices, and present false explanations as to why the Chosen chose that way until the last of the Chosen had picked their intended form of transportation.

Some elected to go alone, allowing for space to listen to their thoughts and explore the stillness around them. Others decided to travel in the company of another Chosen, enjoying the newness of enriched fellowship. While various others, drawn by their unique and established wisdom and a tremendous sense of peace and power that they exude, prefer the companionship of Eirtherol.

It is impossible to say how long their journey took, as there is no phase, no watch, no hunger, in fact, nothing pressing in on the Invisible Realm to make any demands on time whatsoever.

★

Aaron was one of the first to arrive at Ralley – The Rivered City. He had travelled by carriage with other Chosen and a few Eirtherol. The city was breathtaking, as anticipated, but what had not been expected was the long lengths of waterways running throughout the colossal city like liquefied veins flowing through its streets.

Even the few paths made of stone were dripping with water. Around the stable pathways, numerous grandiose fountains positioned about, tossing about their playful waters out onto the street. They hummed and glowed and deposited hazy condensation droplets into the air, filling up any of the lands dry warmth.

Just behind the city stood an expansive waterfall that extended across the horizon and cascaded down from out of the magnificent skies. Aaron could easily see all the froth and bubble caused by the friction of the waters hitting the rockery from above it, but where the water poured out from, he could not see.

As the mysterious waters fell toward the ground, it continually refreshed the cities healthy rivers, streams and waterway. The expression of sound that exuded from it was supremely peaceful. Also, being released from a high and unseen source, were thousands of tiny scented flowers that accompanied it. They caught the light from the skies and glinted like minuscule diamonds. Delicate in structure, their upbeat fragrance filled the entire land. *Experiencing the beauty of these falls*, Aaron decided, *is like having my very soul massaged and attended to*. Once the waterfall was thoroughly taken in, the next sight to catch his attention was equally beautiful but held a definite subtlety as compared to the falls.

The skies, though primarily indigo, flashed with swirling colour around and throughout. As oil spread thinly, then split with water, the light reflecting off to reveal thick layering of colour, drawing attention to different hue at various intervals.

Swirls of white regularly appear in no particular pattern or order, superimposing over the top of the constantly changing shades of the sky. There is no concentration of brightness to be seen, no sun to blaze through the day and no moon to shine throughout the night though the land is not lacking in light.

The waters and skies, in all complementary adornments, make a stunning backdrop to the exquisite stone built resting quarters, lively eateries and other places of entertainment. Situated towards the back of the city, each building was made ready to receive. Ralley – The Rivered City is alive and thoroughly prepared to host its new guests.

Meanwhile, Isabella had made her own decision. Having walked for as long as she could remember, she willed to experience something else and the majestic beasts, the horses, drew her curiosity. With their sturdy legs and tails, and fiery manes that did not burn, how could she not be fascinated with them?

"Eleneke, will you join me in our travelling? For I would like to be in company with you," Isabella presents her request to the Eirtherol in her gentle manner. Eleneke surged with happiness as she anticipated the favoured connection to be shared with this Chosen; "I will accompany you," Eleneke turned toward the horses, and called out for them to come near. The beasts were glad to be chosen and quickly trotted closer.

Eleneke held out her hands and rubbed the chin of each horse in greeting, "Which one would you take Isabella?" The Chosen quickly picks the mottled black and white animal, leaving the Auburn horse for Eleneke. "You have picked Sir Cedric. I will ride upon Nancy," revealed Eleneke. The newly acquainted duo mounted the horses.

"Then we are ready Eleneke. So let us ride," squealed Isabella with glee.

The pressure of the wind on their faces is exhilarating as they travel along at utmost speed. For a while, all four beings fascinate in the sensations and head directly toward their destination. Then, with mutual agreement, they experienced the same level of delight, but at a much slower pace. Isabella and Eleneke direct the horses to zigzag, jump, chase, intentionally adding length to their journey. At other times, the new companions slide off the fiery horses and walk beside. Either way, the bond between Chosen and Eirtherol was being sealed.

After a time, their destination was in sight. Isabella gasps as she tries to take in the intense prettiness of it all. "Ralley is a visual masterpiece is it not," said Eleneke with pride. Isabella now dumbfounded, is unable to reply. "Thank you, Isabella. I have treasured our time together," with that, Eleneke and Nancy ride off into the city.

Isabella dismounts Cedric and takes a seat on the small wall that extends around the majority of the city. The horse whinnies and trots off in the same direction that Eleneke and Nancy took. "Thank you Cedric, for the ride," was the first words that escaped from Isabella's lips, but by this time, Cedric had trotted too far away to hear her. Isabella still intoxicated by her surroundings, watches on as the last Chosen arrives at the city.

Growing sounds of laughter compete with her dreamy state, and Isabella is drawn back to her senses once again. The noise is coming from two of the Chosen. With their infectious giggles multiplying, Isabella reverts to reflection *the sounds of laughter present such a delicious oddity.* The very thought of it falls down from her head and runs deeply into her belly where settles to pulse and tickle, causing similar sounds of hilarity to escape from her lips. The merry Chosen take notice of the sympathetic noises escaping from Isabella and move in her direction. The regal female calls out, "Wry and Cara," she indicated with a pointed finger. "Come and join with us," and with that, Isabella delightfully accepts.

As the trio walk along the dainty paths and spiralling waterways, attachments begin to form. They hold lengthy vocal contemplations, and with limited understandings they concoct stories about the situation they are in. The longer they speak, the more ridiculous the theories become, making room for humour; then from light and humorous tales new curiosities are birthed, and the Chosen return to seriousness; over and over, this cycle is repeated.

Each time Victor is mentioned, silence follows. The impressions of him quickly transform into high emotion, overpowering any need to speak for extended periods. At other occasions, they discuss their beginnings, and the slightness of memory that they seem to possess. To all three beings, it was a quandary worth pursuing.

Each time the trio stopped to enter into a meaningful discussion, small droplets of water collected close to their feet until tiny and refreshing pools develop. The blue and mauve wildflowers adorning the pathways mix with the fresh, damp air and released their heady scents. Their perfumes enhance the senses of the trio and encourage longevity in their conversation. Once the Chosen finish and begin to walk again, the pools quickly evaporate and travel to join the massive waterfall. All life that surrounds the Chosen is indeed, genuinely interested in their happiness and wellbeing.

Up, Further ahead, and nearer the back of Ralley – the Rivered City stands its central building. It is the largest of them and stands three stories high with fountains and waterways adorning. Like the many other buildings nearby, it is made of hand carved pale stone, but upon closer inspection, the stone is scattered with flecks of gold, silver and crystal subtly strewn through both brick and mortar. It stands quietly elegant in front of the spectacular falls.

Sounds of boisterous banter escape from the grand doorway; immediately Isabella recognises the voice of Aaron. "That my friends, is the sound of Aaron." Isabella smiled as she gestured for Wry and Cara to enter the building containing the voice. With speed increased with enthusiasm, the trio navigates the grand doorway and enter the giant vestry, quickly following the sounds up the great stairway and on the second floor. With large strides across the landing, they enter an exceedingly large dining room.

Aaron is seated at an expansive banqueting table with Chosen, Eirtherol and the tiny Chosen Who Chose Not. The smaller of the beings were propped up on their chairs with pillowy cushions, accommodating their size. The table was presented with the finest fare. Cutlery and plating, made of pure moulded gold, glasses and goblets of crystal, encrusted with colourful gems and decorative vases holding invigorating flora on display.

The ceiling above them has many tiny lights strewn around in a seemingly haphazard way, like clusters of miniature galaxies in suspension. The lights continue down the walls and emit a soft glow that aluminates the room, without vexing the eyes.

Generous piles of food, spread out on the table, displayed with a remarkable presentation. Delectable and exotic fruits lay upon the hand carved wooden trays, spice heightened dishes of grain and pomegranate stand near hot and cold cloches waiting to reveal their wares. Jars filled with pickled vegetable, condiments sweet and savoury, and carefully made chocolates placed in particular positions upon the delicate cloth.

Sweet and spicy aromas waft around, enticing appetites where previously, none existed. This overpowering desire to feast overtakes all who are present and Isabella, Wry and Cara, chose their chairs.

Those seated indulged every culinary passion for any morsel of food that takes to their liking. The extraordinary buffet hummed at their taste buds, creating curiously beautiful sensations, immersing bodies in total and complete fulfilment and pleasure. Each flavour contrasts and compliments the palate, in both taste and texture. As these elements combine and mingle, the newly formed liquid velvet caresses both cheek and tongue.

Other dishes, being only vaporous, are taken into the body through the nose, causing a different sensation altogether. The full bodied vapour slowly creeps into the nostrils, caressing them with gentle tickles. These mild tickles make their way down into the deeper parts of the beings, increasing in impact to an unexpected crescendo. Both Chosen and Eirtherol alike explode into an avalanche of laughter. It was in this way that the individuals spent a considerable while.

After much time passed, and vast quantities of food consumed, the visitor's appetites became suddenly satisfied. The Chosen, overwhelmed with contentment, laze back, look around and take note of their gratifying surroundings.

The days that followed are filled with playful exploration and enigmatic discussion, yet a peaceful tranquillity undergirds their conjecture. Like wide eyed children with curiosity insatiable, the mystery of not knowing is a pleasure equal to the resolving of the unknown.

In the season spent at Ralley- The Rivered City, four of the seven Chosen would gather in the feasting and communal rooms at the same time, quite incidentally, or so it would seem. At each meeting, Isabella, Aaron, Wry and Cara deepened their newly formed connections toward each other, and each one's sense of well-being and belonging heightened at every gathering.

Isabella's disposition was more restrained than her companions, though not from withholding, nor from shyness; for Isabella considered things for a very long time before revealing them, her current notion included. Intent on sharing her theory, she set out to find her companions once again, and once again, there they were, hoping to find her. Isabella began her address immediately.

"I have been thinking about mysteries again; where we come from, our beginnings. I have turned it upside down, and inside out, looking from any angle that comes to me, yet, I still cannot make sense of it, though there is one conclusion to which I am continually drawn. We, and all life that surround us, as far as our eyes can see, and further, are held within the grasp of something very fine, and much more complex than we are. So, whether we find the answers we seek or not, we are held firmly within its safety."

Wry, Cara and Aaron stood in silence listening to their precious friend, regarding her words. Cara, excited by the opinion, replied, "Isabella, we are drawn to each other for a reason. In your absence, we have been talking about the very same things, and have reached the same conclusion." All four, further increased in connection, exuded happiness.

Eleneke, Asher and Darien, standing near to the Chosen, watch with great interest. It is clear that the little beings are developing and increasing in understanding. It is also clear that their bonds for each other are settling into something quite concrete though one thing is not clear. Eleneke speaks out the curiosity, "We may well be part of the same company in the coming while. Though one thing I do not understand. They are four, and we are three. I have not seen it done this way before." Darien nods, "hmm," the befuddled sound falls from his lips, "I look forward to understanding it."

Years, centuries, even millenniums have passed by; the time for the next learning has now arrived. The Chosen, given the opportunity to do any final things they have an inclination for, are called back to meet at the city gates. This time, their return journey to Daraketh, made all together, except for the Chosen Who Chose Not. They would re-join later.

Back in Daraketh, every being gathers in the one place closest to the water's edge and takes a seat on a round grassy knoll at its edge. Soon the tiny lights move their form and congregate rapidly around the much-rested group. The energy above is fuelled with anticipation as the Chosen understand; a teaching of much consequence is about to take place.

The Chosen prepare their minds to retain as much information as possible, the atmosphere around them catches and reflects their burden, and the Eirtherol hastily intervene with a reminder. "It does not depend on your minds, little ones, to capture all of this information," Eleneke soft tone broke through. "It is a receiving of a knowing, not a memory. It will settle in your very beings, and one day, when you have an experience that leaves you in need, the knowing will make its way up through you and only then, will your mind know how to receive it."

Darién continues on from where Eleneke left off, "Many times, you will feel a tiny fluttering in your bellies, and it is there that your answer is contained. If you rely too heavily on your minds, disregarding the other knowing's, this slight indication will be overpowered, and rendered almost, undetectable. So hold to the confidence that all you need has, or will, be provided for you; your mind will then rest."

"Even we, the Eirtherol," gestures Asher, "will be experienced mostly as a knowing once you inhabit the Tactile Plains. Our presence, our whispers, our gifts, will often be hidden from your external sights and received only as a sensation of lightness, inside or out, that is, until your inner vision becomes more developed. Then, you are capable of seeing us enter into the Tactile Plain in a more tactile way, without the aid of disguise. Until that time, you must learn to subdue all fears and trust that you are indeed in the hands of something finer and more complex." Asher smiles at the Chosen, and knowing their earlier drawn conclusion, is assured that his words bring added security.

The Chosen, filled with anticipation for the time ahead, wait in silence. The essence of their collective anticipation escapes their being, combines, and then climbs high into the sky until it takes a new shape. Its transformation, both visible and audible, forms an effervescent firework display in the now changed and darkly coloured skies. Popping loudly and sparkling bright, the energy increases and spreads out far beyond the area of teaching. Bursting up and over like the contents of a champagne bottle opened in celebration.

While the suspense still builds, a luminous figure enters into view. Walking along the water's edge is another of the Returned Chosen, one of the Kings. She is a spectacular being, easily comparable to the beauty of the atmosphere surrounding her. Her garments pulsating with light made it impossible to precisely define her outline. An electrifying figure, the matter of her body jumped and bounced around with unexpected jolts and behaviours that act quite contrary to the expected.

As she comes closer, the appearance of her features gain structure, and though she still radiates with this moving light, her deep green eyes are now, clearly visible. They are extraordinary, meekness personified, power under complete and gentle control, and this gives them the appearance of a most unusual kindness.

All eyes are transfixed upon this beguiling King. Others begin to join the group, other Kings, other Eirtherol, other Chosen, and lastly, the diminutive Chosen Who Chose Not. The larger group now poised, waited with baited breath for what was about to be disclosed.

Isabella barely noticed the new Chosen, who had taken a seat next to her that is until he takes her hand to offer an introduction. Isabella, quite taken aback for a moment, quickly regathered herself. His soft brown eyes look straight into hers and with mouth turning upward and teeth bearing; a candid smile overtook his mellow face. Isabella, quite glad of the break from the weight of the occasion, gratefully reciprocates his gesture.

Turning her attention back to the Returned King, her hand remained laying in the hand of this unknown Chosen. However, now, her attention divided. *There is something about this new one*, she thought, *holding his hand leads me to feel ridiculously happy.* The joy of this thought pulsates throughout her body, escapes her lips, and impacts the environment around her. Its form, accompanying the anticipation, hovers in the air, and displaces any growing tensions that these ones of little experience began to feel.

With external weight calmed, Isabella's regarded the new Chosen again. She felt both apprehensive and wonderment, for his presence took away all consciousness of her own, something she was quite unaccustomed to. Yet, her hand remained in his.

As the gathering waited for the King to draw nearer, Isabella's awareness was now, exclusively given to this Chosen of much intrigue. Studying him in silence, she took note of his quality. His intense eyes drew her into his world and the serenity that covered him fell upon her and embraced her with its stillness. Isabella causes an internal decision to eclipse all external realities and focuses solely on her newly realised desire. *I join myself to him completely; we will never be parted.* It was certain. The Chosen King, now only steps away, drew her wandering thoughts back to join with the others.

The king, very tall, and still vibrating with light, sat down upon a seat that was placed facing the gathering at the water's edge for her by two Eirtherol. She took a moment to prepare herself to speak. Knowing that there had been much anticipation for her arrival and the delivery of her darker message, she chose not to hesitate.

"My name is Eliza, and I come to bring education to you, one that you cannot yet understand. Trying to will be of no use now, for you have seen nothing of what I will tell you, nor anything similar. But rest in the assurance of your making, for, out of high intelligence you were brought into being, your body willingly holds it for you." Eliza pauses, displays a gentle smile, and continues, "I am here to familiarise you with the Barren-slick, the sly poison from our enemy. This treacherous weapon of theirs is what you must learn to conquer."

Surveying the engrossed crowd, she carries on. "Something will be whispered to each and every one of you, something insidious though it feigns insignificant personal banter. None of you will experience this in quite the same way, for the whispers have been meticulously prepared, just for you, and will be delivered in such a way for you to best receive it. Laden with attachments such as shame, fear and the like, it is planned in such a way, to bring about your isolation, and so inhibiting its detection, thus, allowing its continual growth.

The barren-slicks first purpose is to prevent remembrance of who you are and from where you came. If it fails in this first purpose, it will be used to attack your advancement instead. For some pitiable Chosen, it is severely paralysing. With whispered tales of hopelessness going unnoticed for a considerable time, a foundation is built, one that cannot easily be rectified. Upon that foundation, every thought, every vision, every word is built in to fit tightly, bringing validation. The targeted Chosen senses something, but cannot hear clearly enough to heed the wisdom of it for, overshadowing, is the volume of the barren-slick. Knowing it to be right, yet unable to understand easily, the Chosen's frustrated effort tires them, and in their weariness, they refuse to challenge the barren-slick any further." Eliza's focus is drawn from her message to the faces of these small and inexperienced beings.

There is deep sadness in her voice as tears spill out from her downward facing eyes. With voice slightly higher and lighter, with emotions overflowing she continues, "Over and over again, these ones speak of the whisper and all the connections that they have made to accommodate it. The barren-slick becomes an insurmountable barrier for them that they will never see past. Indeed, they are still Kings, but they are now stilted Kings.

Even their bodies are affected, their soured faces, unable to see past the tactile places. They go round and round in circles to these insidious melodies, and never let go. When you have gained understanding, and you meet one of these ones, do not despise them, for they have enough troubles. Instead, show them what it is that you see and offer some comfort, but do not take their counsel for they will try to put out your own light, believing it to be for your good. The barren-slick is of an extremely infectious nature and will attempt to grow upon any doubt or fear that you have not yet disarmed or realised."

The King, quick to notice her detour, returns to the original subject. "Throughout your season upon the Tactile Plain, the barren-slick will be your primary opposition. But, do not despair, for you are given an authoritative defence, and eventual attack."

With lightened heart, Eliza laughs, "Oh yes, the tables can turn and it will be you that is the hunter. You have been given an internal alarm, a small but persistent feeling that will grip you deep inside your bellies and help you to identify and bring the solution into the dangers of any situation that you must face. Once you have learned to pay attention to your inside eyes, you will focus upon the unseen with more ease, and gather your truth from this source, thus quickly dispelling any fresh onslaught against you, and eventually unravel the Slick all the way back to your beginnings. The Eirtherol will be there to help you in all this too, though, most of the time, you will not know it."

The King stopped talking and again looked around at her audience to see what had been ingested. The tiny lights busily depositing themselves into the Chosen was evidence enough to the King that her delivery was successful. "Looking upon your gallant faces, I am sure that you will do well."

Turning her face upward toward the sky, Eliza's face lightens up with an enormous smile. With a jovial tone, she speaks. "Yes, I think he has joined with us." The Chosen begin to whisper amongst each other, looking eagerly around to see the one that they wanted to see. Though, to the puzzlement of the Chosen, the Eirtherol and Returned Kings did not demonstrate the same reverence. Instead, sounds of laughter escaped their noses as they clamped shut their mouths, attempting to contain the avalanche of hilarity that wrestled them from within.

The new Chosen seated next to Isabella, released his hand from hers, rose to his feet, and stepped away from the others and toward the water. As he did, he grew taller and wider and began to shimmer with light. The further away he stepped, the bigger and brighter he became until no one could see an end to him. The brightness surrounding him kept getting brighter and brighter until the Chosen could no longer bear its intensity. Each one covered their eyes with their hands in protection, though; even then, the light still permeated their sights. Eliza, the Returned King, spoke out loudly, "This, oh lovely ones, is your Victor."

Victor was by now, absolutely everywhere, nothing was left empty of his presence. As he grew, each being became increasingly aware that they were actually inside of him themselves. Joy, peace and power buzzed through their helplessly overwhelmed bodies and minds until no separation was between themselves, each other or Victor. Their existence was now entirely contained within. They had entered into the perfect union.

★

The Eirtherol and Chosen are not the only forms of sophisticated life to exist within the realms. For another race of beings hold a great, but unfortunate significance. These figures, once considerably elegant and distinguished, had now taken on new forms.

From a distance, their handsome and strong shapes appear as striking as they had ever been, but, upon closer inspection, another truth is quickly evident. Twists and buckles occurring throughout their person disfigure their previous frame. This diminishing of handsomeness continues to deteriorate their form over the course of their existence. These ones are the Lesser Princes of Barren.

The Lesser Princes, at one time, enjoyed immense and pure abilities, similar to that of the Eirtherol, but over the course of the three-day battle, these beings were quick to fall into error. Choosing to side with the Barren Prince, they now suffer under the same consequence.

The outcome of their choices had led them into places of limitation, something unaccustomed to. Once, they had seen without limit through the eyes of all known realms, but now, they can no longer employ this virtue. Their gift of seeing out from the Invisible Realm was hastily withdrawn, and along with it, the power supply that accompanied.

Without the use of these powerful gifts, the Princes invent new ways to survive. Now relying purely upon the cognitive, the experiential and the predictive, these beings encouraged their vision to distort with bitter and vengeful thinking. It was by this practice that they happened upon an alternative power.

With much experimentation, the Princes discovered that if they used rules designed by the Original Power and applied them to the variant root of crafted and hostile thought, they could wield a lesser but still adequate force. Though successfully resolving the dilemma, there were still more obstacles to overcome.

For the Lesser Princes had suffered another significant loss through their ill-fated allegiance. As completely free beings, they had travelled at will to any realm, and to any location within it, settling wherever they pleased. No place was exempt from them, but this freedom applies no more.

With everything removed from their ownership, these now vagrants, these migrating squatters, scour the span between the Tactile and the In-Between Places until they find areas that had been forgotten by those that exist. The Lesser Princes vigorously camouflage their new positions to look like their own. All resemblance to what was being quickly covered over, so anything of beauty or comfort, and all form of original expression, now concealed until no remnant of the previous occupant remains.

These otherworldly creatures, substantially steeped in a military tactic of a unique sort from the earliest of times, trained extensively in mind mastery, deception and division. The beings plead convincingly to naïve minds and manipulate situations using peer coercion as one of their allies. Their instruction was for one very distinct purpose, cold and calculated retribution.

A trio of these creatures, seated face-to-face in a cramped and dark room with only a minimal amount of light dribbling in through a tiny, high placed window painted over in black. It was barely enough to make out even the vaguest of silhouettes from their associated faces, though perfectly adequate for their needs, for they did not require looking at the countenance of their companions. Details of that sort were of no use to them for their purposes.

The air around them lay heavily, hanging densely about and pervading every space. Sliding up and into their nostrils and down throats, it coating every porous thing, asphyxiating any surfaces that it lay upon; its concentration quickly suffocated anything of natural quality, but the Lesser Princes were anything but natural.

No movement of air was felt throughout the entire building structure, except from what the three beings caused. Every window, vent and fracture in the environment, now carefully covered, that is, aside from the dribble of light that seeped through the high window, much to the silent irritation of the Lesser Princes.

The room overall, pleased the beings, for the practical purpose of its design was very effective. Should any movement be sensed on the premises, any entrance of freshness or breeze clearly indicated an intrusion, which would be remedied with severity and haste. There were highly pressing issues at hand and no distractions would be tolerated.

All three beings, Avril, Harshaw and Calamity, were well versed in the weaknesses that their enemies bore. Their gathered experience made them a powerful force to be reckoned with, and this meeting brought proof of their current situation. Called now, to the same place, at the same time, it was evident that the recognition of their status was now acknowledged. They were ready.

"Summoned," exclaimed a proud feminine voice from a position void of light. There came no reply to break through the silence, though she was not alone, for two other Lesser Princes sat nearby.

Avril, Harshaw and Calamity adjusted themselves until they faced the lone entrance to the room. The archaic-looking door left slightly ajar so that the Princes could adapt to the experience of tension that resided in the In-Between Places. These complicated souls began intensely conversing about the detail of the season that had come upon them, reflecting upon the sizeable door that their formidable foe seemed to have left open wide.

All three had collected many a lifetime of expertise and were not prepared to waste even one tiny portion of it. They could not afford to, as their enemy was indeed powerful, and seemed to hold on to all advantage, always. He had demonstrated this to them, over and over again, much to their silent dismay. At one particular time, when the Princes thought their foe had been completely dethroned and incapable of any type of recovery, it turned out to be their most miserable failure, a failure that almost entirely crippled them. They knew time was short, and their demise was inevitable, unless.

"Almost inevitable," voiced Harshaw. His words as usual, start on a high pitch and end lower, with each phrase clipping at the end; his particular displeasure evident through his acrid tone. Haughtily, he continues, "We know of his peculiar penchant for things and beings of such little consequence. Although we consider them nothing, useless pieces of vain rubbish, we will place all our energies into their slow, painful distortion. Let them resemble us, be our sons and our daughters, instead of his little kings, for this will bring our great enemy to his knees."

Even with much bravado in his statement, Harshaw knew in the deepest part of his being, as they all did, that these ones their enemy cared for so much were not as insignificant as they might like to acknowledge. After all, time and time again, these beings, once awakened to their invisible eyes, could open up and hold any power that was ever possible to hold.

Harshaw continues, "Everything we have done, all that we have learned, and everything we have trained for is about to assist us in our current and only motivation. Remember continuously how many ages this knowledge has taken to develop. Do not let us forget, do not let us waste even one droplet." He paused to emphasise his point, then expressed himself further. "There must always be a reason for our every action; no detail can be forgotten, no word spoken in vain. Remember how we purged ourselves until any breach within us had been wholly dissuaded?

Remember also, how we buried ourselves in deep observation of our own mighty conquerors, and also of those unfortunate wretches that had failed. For millennium upon millennium we have studied, we have practiced, we have developed. Do not forget that we want to leave nothing, nothing to the control of any external forces. This way, our plan cannot and will not fail. Let no weakness in our minds have any voice, let them say nothing except that, we will succeed, and we will do it in such a manner that it will never be forgotten."

Avril's directed her face toward Harshaw's, and then turned toward Calamity, and, silencing Harshaw with an inward breath, she spoke, "The Barren Prince would not have afforded us the notable advantage and high privilege of entering the fortress had we not been of the same opinion as him on the subject. He is confident of our success, so there is no doubt in my mind. That being said, we must have no complacency. We must hold to remembrance the great favour, the higher ranking and extra authority that has been granted us."

Avril took a long slow breath, rising to her feet at the thought of her own power, and continued, "We have been given the use of as many subservient as we request and every resource that is part of our weaponry has been made available to us by order of the Barren Prince. None of our kinds may contradict or interfere with the choice of direction that we have designed. Our plans are all mapped out, both blueprint and detail, and the process of application is just about to be received."

The conversation carried on, with each statement designed to fortify their resolve. With their machine like reasoning and unshakeable focus, they would be cold administers for the Barren Prince. With no movement, nor expression, or look of anticipation whatsoever, all three stood to their feet and began to journey out from their hollow, toward the start of their assignment in the brighter places. They headed toward Realms End.

Sun, nor the moon, or even stars lit up the firmament that the trio stepped on. Instead, the brightness that surrounded was caused by billions of whirring and flashing particles, opening and closing at giddying speeds. This light was unlike any other lights in any other realm though it contained the source that lit them all.

The hybrid of atmospheres caused an incredible tension, not completely tactile, not completely invisible, the laws collide and the meshing of difference sit uncomfortably. The Lesser Princes felt the push/pull intensely, and even though they had prepared well, they were still ill-equipped to accommodate the pressure though none complained.

Only moments later, they were again assaulted by their surrounds, but this time from a different angle. An aroma, a spiced yet mild aroma, mingled in the air and took its turn at agitating the Princes. It was the fragrance of Victor. The combination of light and odour overtook their senses, leaving self-composure near impossible.

Calamity broke the silence, "ugh," with childlike voice, she complained, as she attempted to conceal her heaving stomach. She quickly regained her composure in efforts to dismiss the moment. Harshaw, however, was quick to identify with her. "I think it repellent that he will not take himself from this environment. I would rather he stick to his own realm and let us be on our own."

Avril glared sharply with her intense eyes. Something in them was immensely frightening. Her voice sounded with strict correction and rage as she spits out the words, "Do not waste your time on those things that we cannot do anything about. Do not waste my time or concentration either."

Calamity and Harshaw heeded the reprimand and nodded their heads to acknowledge agreement with their astute associate. "This is no time to display weakness, not at the beginning, not ever," Avril's words were clipped and harsh, as her point was made plain. All three resolute beings forged quietly forward with every bit of vigour they could muster until they reached their destination.

Realm's End, the point of greatest tension was soon arrived at. Avril, Harshaw and Calamity moved into their appointed positions facing the Tactile Plain. Each being standing upon the edge overlooks the line where time begins and new laws take hold. A large net, defined by governing mathematical equation, outlines clear boundaries upon the plain by its thickness or thinness at that point. Camping upon many of the borders are Eirtherol, or Lesser Princes, or in undecided places, a combination of the both, with much larger beings shadowing far over them. The net, conscientiously strewn across the entire span of the Tactile Plain, throbbed and groaned out a haunting dirge across its span.

At this sight, any other creature would have gasped in wonder, letting out a cacophony of sounds, commending the inventor of such a concept, but for the Lesser Princes, the unstructured within the structure only perplexed them. Muddy, uneven, untidy, whiffy, tactile, yet guarded by predetermined rule. Each time without fail, and without consent, the creation, its fragility and complexity, momentarily silence their minds. Avril's first returning thought pours unguided from her tightened lips, "Peculiar." Each Lesser Prince takes one step forward; stepping into the same space, yet, each one appears in an entirely different location.

It was here, within time that Avril, Harshaw and Calamity will watch and wait in solitude, looking out for particular Eirtherol, who would, quite obliviously reveal the Grovel that will suffer from their severe and menacing plan.

★

Meanwhile, having fully attended their duties of preparation, Eleneke, Asher and Darien leave the Province of Eirtherol to wait in patience within the boundaries of the In-Between Places. The beings, temporarily freed from any mission, bask in the beauty of the dazzling light and delicious fragrance that this realm contains.

Mesmerised by their surroundings they drift about the air, in stillness, and without speech, wholly submerged in the pure delight of just being.

Out from nowhere, this sweetness of being dramatically gives way to a commanding sense of occasion, raising the Eirtherol's anticipation and convincing them of imminent change. The beings quickly move concentration away from their immediate surroundings, and place it toward the expression of their unseen eyes, eager for what was to be revealed.

There stood Victor; hand over his heart, with a knowing smile on his face. He nods his head to find a rhythm, and once satisfied with a pace, he releases a song of words unrecognisable to the Eirtherol. The melody is simple, but the content of tone is not. Kindness, gentleness, peace, all manner of good collaborates within his tune, swirling, combining, fortifying. Victor is singing his signature song, his song of approval, his admission of kin.

As the melody develops, Victor pushes his hand into his chest and pulls out an article jealously guarded within. His fingers, wrapped tightly around the precious object, are opened to reveal its content. A small dark seed, barely visible, is lifted toward Victor's mouth. Locating its position, his breath directs his melody toward it. The tiny seed cracking open, receives the sound and takes on all its potency.

Victor, looking upon the seed, carefully releases it into another position; a pre-prepared receptacle stands by, assuring the perfect environment for nurture. Victor, now silent, stands to smile, assured of his good work.

Transfixed in the artistry Eleneke remarks of the one she holds in sight, "He is substantial in all that is good, and all his ways outstanding. Continually I am fascinated, regardless of how many times I have seen it. Those little ones, they had seemed so real, so complete, yet, they did not exist. While we watched, they had tried so hard to understand the questions that presented to them, yet they could not have even imagined the truth." She breathes out a humming, closed mouth laugh through a gentle smile, and continues, "Their place in my heart has already been established, once they come into being, this love I hold for them will be matured."

Eleneke and her companions, again quieted by awe, stand silently upon the surface of the In-Between Places. Breathing in, breathing out, they transfix upon the Invisible then pull back to observe the In-Between, waiting for their next movement to reveal when something unexpected takes a form within their minds.

A scroll sealed with red wax and bordered with golden flecks falls into sight. The seal cracks open, the scroll unravels and its contents are revealed. Eleneke, Asher and Darién are requested to join the most highly seated within the deepest place of Absolute Beauty in the Invisible Realm. Though this invitation is the utmost desire of any Eirtherol, the host does not assume acceptance and requests for confirmation.

With the greatest of delight, we accept your proposal; and consider it a high honour to be invited. The response, not verbalised, is drawn from the hearts of the stately beings, and observed in that same instant by the one who sent the invitation.

Asher takes a long, deep inhale, savouring the moment. *I am standing on the precipice of my greatest excitement.* As this thought consumes his head, his being fills up with free energy. Jiggling around from foot to foot, he shakes himself vigorously. Overwhelmed with passion, Asher tries to calm his overtly eager state. He lifts his arms above his head, stretches, and releases all of his breath.

Then, quite abruptly, Asher is pulled from this inner tension by an external pressure felt sharp upon his ribs. The powerful beings automatic response is to fall on the floor in surprise. Now strewn about the floor, Asher develops his vigilance, and in doing so, is alerted to the cause of his tumble. Darién!

"Darién, you have been over-endowed with frivolity and mischief," he stated loudly. "I was expressing my own excitement, just as you had been." After a moment's silence, Asher and Darién began to snigger and hoot as Eleneke shakes her head with a broad grin adorning her bright face.

With perkiness subsiding, a great door slides down below the grounds surface and swings up again behind them, introducing the place of Absolute Beauty. With attentions toward each other dissolving, the Eirtherol's feasting eyes scan the much-anticipated spectacle. Just as they had been told, everything that surrounded was living and moving and in constant metamorphosis. Some things are subtle and slow to change while others are quick and easily discerned by even peripheral vision.

The sights release sounds and the sounds, having wispy colours and shape rise into the air, becoming new and living entities too. Each one of the colourful resonances holds to the next and they combine to produce fresh and light symphonies of delicate quality. The measured tones dance alongside the crescendos of sustained notes and these important calls takes shade beneath the brighter and brassier inclusions. "It is quite clear that this is the birthplace of all musical instruments," reflects Eleneke aloud.

The waters, stones, plants, creatures, sounds and scents, everything that the Eirtherol can take in through their senses, filled to capacity with life, yet always being fed more life and more light. This expanse of realm displays exhilarations not possible in any other place. For the Place of Absolute Beauty holds no memory, nor knowledge of anything other than spectacular displays of beauty and attentive, personal adorations.

Darién, thoroughly taken by the experience of goodness that surrounds him can no longer hold his tongue. He releases his poem of praise, "To be here in this place, is like taking in of the oxygen from a time forgotten forest, but instead of inhaling through the nostrils and mouth, every pore, every part, drinks of it deeply. New life stirs from its powerful freshness. Though my body is healthy, I feel an irresistible and unusual vigour entering it." Eleneke gives only a broad smile, for her experience is far surpassed by mere words.

Eleneke perceives something quietly understated and her attentions are drawn to its root. This undercurrent, flowing around the realm, grows more dramatic and emerges to prominence. Eleneke wonders if its growth is caused by her attentions, or whether her attention is attracted by the growth. Asher and Darién notice too.

With the undercurrents continual increase, a billowy blanket of transparent substance falls out from nowhere cloaking both Eirtherol and surroundings. The sheet covers everything, yet strangely, reveals more, prompting the level of ecstasy to arise. As levels continue to rise, the inundated Eirtherol surrenders all bodily control and drop down, first to their knees, then upon their faces to experience it. With minds packed with sound, light, colour and fragrance, understanding opens.

From arrival, their experience of the place of Absolute Beauty was only a partial expression, purposefully muted by the generosity of the host. *Eleneke, Darién, Asher, I wanted you to delight in these sights before fullness was revealed to you.* A much loved voice ran through their beings, telling the pure truth. Now, under no disillusion, the Eirtherol stay face down, splayed out with no need or desire for any other thing.

Lying powerless, but blissfully contented on the aromatic, springy floor, the Eirtherol find they are unable to utter even a single intelligible word. Their playfully gargled attempts now quickly abandoned as an impressive figure walks toward them. With each step forward, their ecstasies grow stronger, and though thoroughly dazed, the Eirtherol still recognise the approaching figure.

Victor finds much amusement in the Eirtherol's position and watches them as they vainly attempt to acquire some sort of composure. "Impossible," he teases as he stands amid the curiously placed guests.

The utmost desire of any Eirtherol is to bring their deeply felt respect to Victor. Over the ages, much time is spent rehearsing songs of honour, sometimes alone, sometimes in collaboration, tunes constructed and lyric generously deliberated upon. For Eleneke, Asher and Darién, the time of fulfilment had arrived, thought now, laying near him in Absolute Beauty, their songs felt lacking in substance, contrived even, and could not release from their mouths. "Your praise in Absolute Beauty can only be a spontaneous response to this glory. For yes, your songs are honouring, but they carry a past glory, one revealed at the moment of their conception." Victor's jovial voice throws out words that are entirely obvious, though only after their hearing.

Settling into this certainty, the Eirtherol relax, completely immersing into the environment. Peace flows through their minds as never experienced before. The receptive beings witness two separate and continuous waves crashing left and right within their minds. Its sounds lull them to stillness until they became one with their surrounds, unaware of boundary, form, or size. This very act of acceptance, for Victor, was the honour song; the gratitude that he had been hoping for and the enjoyment of this provision became his own bliss.

Holding to this perfect state, the Eirtherol still hear the words of the highest seated, "As you have already seen from the In-Between Places, the time for those little ones has come, so you are released to them; bring them your aid." He lays a hand upon the shoulder of Eleneke, and continues to speak, "As you have lain folded upon this floor, much light and life has entered you and increased your capacity and understanding of goodness. You now carry more, both for yourselves and for the benefit of these little Chosen, which in turn is for my sake also."

"Go now, in my favour and my blessings." With that, Victor could no longer be seen.

Chapter 2

THE SEED

The area around the Eirtherol quickly changed into a fusion of atmospheres where the Unseen and Tactile places meld into a convex and hybrid world; in only moments, the trio finds themselves in three entirely separate locations upon the Cambrae Sphere.

Eleneke now stands in a warm and sterile room, amidst some of those from the Cambrasian race. The atmosphere around her pulsates with a brighter light and the airs property sweetened and denser, yet the original occupants remain unaware of her presence.

They would have noticed the lightness in their being, and a strange lack of apprehension had their attentions not been fixed entirely upon a woman with a swollen belly lying upon a tidy and hygienic birthing table. Blips and bleeps, coming from the basic yet adequate machinery, cut through the otherwise quiet area.

A fit woman wearing a simple and neat uniform brings welcome announcement to an exhausted looking couple, "Congratulations to you both, all that hard work has paid off, for you have poured forward a vibrantly and healthy female child." She hands a wriggling infant over to the eager and overjoyed parents.

"The time is 3.29 of light, on the turn of Acar in its 5th day. Write this down," the woman snaps her fingers to obtain the attention of a young girl gripping a large book. The overwhelmed father, with tears glinting in his eyes proudly bellows, "We have both decided on the name of our girl child, and shall now confide, that her name is," he pauses, draws in a deep breath, and continues. "Isabella, our little one is named Isabella."

Eleneke, thankful to be present at such a moment, sends ripples of joy into the atmosphere of the room. A mixture of cheer and relief thickens throughout the area and, received with ease by all those present.

Eleneke continues to watch the careful proceedings that follow the birth. Both Mother and child are looked after well while the father is guided toward a quiet room allocated to them for the first few light cycles of their little girl's existence. Confident that all was well, Eleneke reacquaints herself with the strange and fascinating land that she finds herself a part.

Eleneke was thinking about the three Greater Lights, Numa, which was red, Acar, which was orange, and Ento, which shone violet, and how they moved around in a slightly askew elliptical motion. It was as if they were reeling out and then reigned back in again to a central point of a pivot. She considered the light and colour of the Greater Lights, and how they profoundly affected the three seasons.

Next, she envisaged the Greater Land and the Islands, the waterways and the high places, and everything that resided within it. The Cambrae Sphere was definitely one of the greatest masterpieces of physical substance. Speaking aloud she continues in wonder about her situation. "How incredible it is to me that I would be selected to aid one of the Chosen in this remarkable place, and at this particular time."

Isabella was born on the Volcano Island, a preserved land where the air is moist and warm and the vegetation lush and thriving. A large volcano is situated very close to the centre of the Island, simmering away, releasing its potently mineralised cinders to the four winds. The winds distribute the ash all over the Island into the waterways, enriching the vegetation and bringing healthiness to the land and seas, then onto the creatures of all kinds, offering them well-nourished and long lives.

It has not always been this way for these people. Eleneke deliberated. *Many a courage-filled soul has held vigorously to their heart impression and then given all of their lives to achieve this freedom for their lineage.* Her thoughts plagued with emotion as she considered the brave souls from a previous time.

Eleneke glances at the precious child she is to aid and senses the need to revisit the girl's forefathers. So, with no further persuasion required, the Eirtherol opens her mouth and releases a song without words, calling out to her kindred in the In–Between Places, advising them of her intention to partake of their talents. In the next moment, she was with them.

★

The Party shining with golden beams hang together in the atmospheres just outside of the Tactile Plains. With surrounding light glinting and gleaming, the impressive figures fastidiously attend to their task. Eleneke closes her eyes to receive while her company begin to impart the song of the history of an ill-fated king and the nation that he profoundly affected.

Entering sharply into Eleneke's mind, the catalyst to the identity of Isabella's people becomes apparent. A good looking and intelligent boy of young age was sitting upon the city wall, looking out over his homeland. Eleneke watched on as some Lesser Princes begin to take wagers on the boy.

They were wagering as to whether he would achieve greatness because of what they were about to subject him to, or whether he would be reduced to an ineffective pile of rubble like so many others they had previously distressed. Either way, he would be a source of their amusement for a time.

The Lesser Princes gather about the boy and begin to whisper a great fear into his heart. The unrelenting force in which it was applied would have been enough to unnerve even the most gentle and stable of men.

Eleneke watches as her kin attempt to intervene but their access is denied. For the boy offered over the fertility of his mind solely to the voice of the Lesser Princes. Eleneke moves in closer to the Lesser Princes to listen to the soundless words gushing forward from their ferocious mouths. Though inaudible externally, the voices could be heard as a shrill and constant gnawing in the mind of their victim. It was a sound that refused to be ignored.

Eleneke, aghast at the harshness of the onslaught, interprets their soundless provocations as she continues observing. "There is a great failing in this Sphere that can be easily recognised if any cretin would take the care to notice. The source of all things is entirely inadequate and cannot," the Lesser Princes pause to snigger at their own cunning then quickly continue, "no, will not, offer to you those things that you most greatly desire."

Another gleeful looking Lesser Prince adds his contribution, "There is only lack waiting for those that do not grasp and strive and then procure a portion. There is a lack of currency, lack of honour, lack of position, lack of ground and lack of invention." The Lesser Princes persistence presses the fear deeper into the boys mind. "There is no friendship, no love, and no brotherly affection that will part with anything of means. One must take as much as one can, and share it with no man unless it profits."

Eleneke watches on as the young man, out of self-preservation, acquires a taste for great power and position. To accommodate his motivations he begins enhancing his skills and develops a convincing veneer of charm and a staggeringly flattering way in his speech. Then, using his newfound deceit, artfully secures himself a place in ultimate control. He is crowned sovereign before his 30th birthday.

The new king was remorseless, taking all that is of value from both land and people, and trading it for profit. For the kingdom and its people, there was much lack, but for the king, his own pockets were lined with enormous financial advantage.

Suddenly, in the mind's eye of Eleneke, a new focus takes hold. Downcast in their appearance, a group of people from the same land are thrown lifelines of courage from a great number of the Eirtherol. These people readily accepted the lines and used them to support themselves and one another.

Between the whispers of the Eirtherol and the prudent persistence of the people, a plan was soon developed. Combining their meagre resources, the group purchased a vessel that would take them across the seas and on to discover the Volcano Isle.

The aiding Eirtherol were in great anticipation for the freedom of this people and watched over their pathway to provide safe passage. When the weary but liberated passengers arrived upon the shores of their new land, the Eirtherol sustained them further by passing peace, rest and life into their inner beings.

With renewed vigour and unseen inspiration, the sojourners made their plans to build homes under the ground, ensuring the rich vegetation around them were both their hiding place and their nourishment. Many generations were faithful to this vision and now, the benefits to the lineage were many.

Tears flood Eleneke's eyes as she pieces together the information. *From a place of poverty, these brave souls have risked all for a hope and for the love of their children, with hardly any reassurance from circumstance. They paid dearly for the emancipation of their line, rescuing them from the young king and his greed*, continuing to ponder, the Eirtherol fills with elation, *But their hope has been realised. Isabella, you have lived out their dream, and surely you have inherited their strength also.*

Eleneke thanking her companions left the In-Between Places to re-join Isabella upon the Cambrae Sphere. She carefully discerns the atmosphere around her to see if any of the Lesser Princes had taken residence in her absence. They had not. With this reassurance, she turns her full attentions toward the small family that would become a large part of her life.

★

Isabella's mother and father had desired the arrival of their own child for the longest of times. They were undeterred by the long list of important requirements needing fulfilment before their request for a child was granted. Nor did they hold any expectation for more than the single child that was permitted them. Being rational people, they understood the logic and reasoning of their land. For, as the Volcano Isle tradition dictates, the position of the child is to be the same situation as that of the parents, and for that position, just one child is required. For, in this way, the governing bodies wished to sustain all types of life, not just the life of Cambrasian's.

Now, was the beginning of Isabella's turn to bring her own precious contribution to this well-maintained land, this newest girl child would have much to offer. She, from her very first understanding, would be trained in the sciences about the Palatability of Sustenance. She would be taught to hold her position in high regard and learn to take pride in her work, (as each person is trained to believe about their personal work, and rightly so.)

Isabella would be well-meaningly convinced by both parents and community, that her position was indeed her future destiny, a respectful destiny of importance. If she were to explore other possibilities and leave her fate, she would inadvertently be robbing her close community of the richness that she contained for a selfless and futile pursuit. The child would also be steeped in the rich history of her people from the old land, and much else that she could take personal pride.

Her cultural and family history, however, was not the only influence on the life of Isabella. She, though completely unaware, is also being groomed and guided with the delicate whispers and the subtle touch of Eleneke, her constant companion.

★

Eleneke watched on as the tiny child blossomed into an exceptional young woman with high character. Isabella was slight in stature with a lovely face and dark blonde hair; as a child endowed with reflective disposition, she was not afraid of her own company, spending much of her free time playing about in the higher land amongst the tree's and waterways. Isabella was the greatest source of joy for her parents.

The Eirtherol had grown to love this sweet child deeply as she deliberated long upon her compelling nature. Eleneke understood that she could never predict Isabella's thoughts or actions just by knowing her, nor could she ever read her mind, but, what she did know was that, over time, she would begin to understand the motivations that drove Isabella's heart.

Eleneke's influence upon Isabella's life was profound, yet subtle. In fact, Isabella would remain unaware of most of these interactions until her return to the Invisible Lands. For, over time, Eleneke had warded off many barren-slick episodes that were fashioned to detain or derail her.

The weaponry that the Lesser Princes chose to forge against Isabella was common. Used upon the seemingly unremarkable, the tool generally resulted in near flawless effectiveness. This weapon was, most always, quickly accepted as truth by the perplexed target, who unwittingly allowed the infection to breed, leading to immobilisation of the tragically taken one for the term of their natural life.

This common barren-slick was directed toward Isabella to convince her that she was most insignificant and quite powerless, thus pointing her toward a state of permanent and doubtful delusion. Eleneke, no stranger to this form of attack, positioned herself to discourage any meditation upon it, diluted it with whispered alternatives, ones that Isabella would readily accept. Therefore, though the seed of the idea was present within Isabella's mind, neither being permits the Slick to germinate or to fester.

In the experience of Isabella, barren-slick appears as a secondary contemplation. Taking less than a moment to receive, it slides behind other more prominently positioned thoughts, intent on establishing a quiet place to grow. Isabella, unaware of the barren-slicks message, notices an unease tying knots in her stomach, the internal alarm talked of in the Invisible Realm. Now uncomfortable, she listens for the source of distress but instead hears the salvation songs whispered by Eleneke. The seed of barren-slick, permitted just a short while to take root, dies for lack of attention and Isabella carries on quite unaware of the exchange.

To the ones that can see from the In-Between Places, this slick looks like small glass nails with corrosive centres and sharply pointed ends. Blown from the Lesser Princes lips, these well-aimed needles plunge hard, stabbing into the core of their target. Newly pierced, the tiny cavities magnetically attract thin shards of darkness into the usually luminous body, instigating weakness to that point in all realms known, and unknown.

Eirtherol in attendance, release songs of deliverance over the Chosen at this point, offering gentleness, peace and promise to dislodge shards, both new and old, with their power. The Chosen, accepting the alternative, dispels the darkness and returns to light by singing the new lyric repeatedly, healing any unfavourable change within body or character.

This was daily life, as they knew it from the birth of the girl child, although framed among an everyday existence of any Cambrasian from the Volcano Isle. Eleneke looks on with elation as this now young woman continues to resist the Barren-slick assault. *Tenacious; Isabella has gained a high degree of resistance toward these assaults, quite unusual for one her age.*

Isabella's progress causes great excitement among other Eirtherol also. For they consider her equipped to entertain less conventional ideas, ones that do not appeal to the sensibilities of most. For they are constructed with a foresight that Isabella does not yet understand, therefore appearing to present a significant risk. However, now that the Chosen recognises and accepts their tone of voice, the Eirtherol believe her ready to host the dreaming from the Invisible Realms.

The three Greater Lights radiate their brightness throughout all of the lands from the Cambrae Sphere. The light from Numa and Acar had collided to produce a pleasant faint ripple of scarlet in the predominantly orange skies over the Volcano Isle. Isabella, now having left childhood, was absorbed in her trade, taking exceptional attention to all her usual duties, and simultaneously, pondering upon their improvement. She moved her hands deliberately, pairing different foods with herbs, spices and flora, and then presenting them elegantly on rose coloured platters.

Eleneke, feeling again very proud, poured a quantity of her goodness toward Isabella and all those that accompanied her in the open, spacious room. She stilled her spirits to deem the risk in leaving Isabella for a time correctly. Quickly, it was determined that Isabella would be adept at holding to herself if the Barren-slick should be flung out against her in the absence of the Eirtherol.

Just then, with this surety still reverberating throughout her being, Eleneke's kin summoned her to the Invisible Realms. This summoning was an art form to a spectator, as the beings from the

In-Between Places called and cooed with voiceless sounds that rippled a pathway through the atmospheres. As the ripples fell upon Eleneke, the environment around her began to tremble quite rapidly. Colour and sound collided, and melded together as ripples of the hushed tone grew wider. Understanding its meaning, Eleneke took a step back out of the Tactile Measure of Time and was instantly transferred to Daraketh – The Position of Gathering upon the Invisible Realms. It was in that place that she re-joined with her company.

After moments of affection toward one another, the residents of the In-Between Places express aloud what Eleneke had just captured in her own being. With excitement, they announce that Isabella is prepared enough to accept a new direction designed uniquely for her. Eleneke was to rouse Isabella in the vehicle of a dream.

Isabella was to be informed by the notion of her freedom to choose a new path if she so desired. Should she listen, she would hear of a purpose greater than what she could conceive of in her own heart, for now It was her time to take a stride across the threshold and through the door that was about to be opened up to her. She was not to worry about anything, as just a small step into the directions she needed to head would suffice for now. Eleneke was to give this direction into her heart the day following the night vision so Isabella would be freshly prepared to hear it.

Eleneke reminded of the skill and experience that Isabella had gained from rejecting the Barren-slick though still needed for this defence; it now served an additional purpose. These same skills are required to protect her destiny from well-meaning people who would see her only for what they believed her to be, also, from any Cambrasian that sat under the subjection of the Lesser Princes, for their words were almost as cruel and ensnaring as the skilful Lesser Princes themselves.

A small hand tugs at Eleneke's robe. It is Janity, one of the Chosen Who Chose Not. "Janity, how long have you been there?" Eleneke lifts the little being up and cradles her in an arm, "You look as though you are bursting with a secret to tell me." The Eirtherol stares intently at the bouncing little being and caresses her cheek in tender affection until Janity lies back peacefully. "I do Eleneke; I do have something to tell you," her sweet cooing voice causes the doting side of the Eirtherol to rise. "Well then, if you have something you want to tell me, I have something that I want to hear, go ahead Janity."

"Victor came and gave me a message for you," feeling the importance of it all, Janity's cheeks, lips and eyes lift upwards. After savouring the moment, she continues, "It is about Isabella. Her journey, for the next times upon the Tactile Plain, will be marked with signposts, sending clues for what is to come. These signposts will be the Greater Lights. Victor wants you to think upon Acar, Numa and Ento, their qualities of colour and all the change they bring when it is their turn for prominence. As you do this, you have a greater understanding of how to prepare."

Eleneke lifts Janity up out of her arms and kisses her forehead. "Thank you sweet one, you did well. I now know what I must do now so I will get right to it." The Eirtherol throws Janity up into the air, catches her, and then tickles her plump belly. The little one explodes with joy, triggering Eleneke and others present to laugh with her in happiness. After hugging the Chosen Who Chose Not one more time, Eleneke hands her to an awaiting Eirtherol. She thanks her friends, and with eyes closed, presses her cheek softly against theirs in love. With contact sincerely relished the meeting parted company.

★

Eleneke took a short stroll towards an exquisite and tall tree adorned with billowing ruby blossom and jade coloured fruit. There, making herself comfortable, she begins to reflect upon her history with the Chosen. She recalls that Isabella was most susceptible to receiving and remembering dreams. Eleneke appreciated the wisdom of her colleagues in the choosing of this medium.

After a while of careful consideration, Eleneke spent a generous while constructing the dream. With her slender hands drawing pictured in the skies all around her, she attached and overlapped the small images to each other, rearranging them a little, until they fit together. Finally, after the design was complete, Eleneke was satisfied that this dream was able to incite Isabella into a place of deep thought once she had awoken from it.

Eleneke took her embroidered work into her hands and added to it an essence of hope that she always carried with her. She closed her eyes, and released the piece into the atmosphere where it broke down into gleaming little light filled fragments, and then disappeared altogether.

★

It was the ebbing of the Greater Lights and Isabella's thoughts gravitated toward the pretty bed–sit that revived her spent self every evening. She looked forward to the time that she would spend, engaged in her own company when an appealing and unpredictable idea struck. She would quickly leave the lower district, make her way from under the earth, and to the higher land to watch the tide gently wash over the shore, leaving its deposit of tiny sequin–like beads of sea life in its wane.

She walked the many steps upward onto the surface. Though her day had been long, she enjoyed the additional employment of her energies and felt the life within her become quickly vigorous again, despite the late hour. She reached the pinnacle of the stairs, took in a wisp of crisp, fresh flowing air into her lungs, and then made her way to her favourite part of the coastline, intending to stare out over the seemingly endless seas. Peaceful and alone, she allowed herself to enter rest.

Unbeknownst to Isabella, however, she was far from alone, for some Lesser Princes who had taken assignments upon the Island, gathered around to watch. Some, who often frequented the area, had taken notice of the particular attentions of Eleneke, a high-ranking Eirtherol, toward Isabella and, being wary of the situation, alerted as many of their affiliates as they could manage to do. The Lesser Princes began to speculate upon the curiously early ripening of Isabella and the current absence of Eleneke.

Could this be the beginning of her release? And if it was, what was the intended outcome? When the deep uncertainty they felt could not be undone by conjecture, the Princes decided to investigate Isabella's state of strength by throwing her their most cutting barbs. When they witnessed the total futility of their influence upon her, they quickly sent some of the Lesser Princes back to their authorities, so the proper higher ranker could be warned.

Isabella did indeed feel the barbs though she believed them to be tensions from the day's efforts trying to pilfer from her private time. So, quickly dismissing each one with great ease, she quickly reconnected her focus to those things she had purposed to think on.

Isabella further reflected upon the day, allowing herself to feel the full satisfaction of her labour. She had worked hard and well, bringing about near perfection from her craft, and then displaying her work, for all to experience at the common time of sustenance, where she enjoyed the company of her dearest friends. She felt the warmth of satisfaction take her body into deeper repose.

With a large breath, Isabella turned her attentions upon the wandering ocean with its chippy and moving surface. As her fleeting glances turned to a firm fixation, the sea began to prompt the uncomfortable notion of uncertainty. It was at that precise moment that Eleneke returned.

Eleneke noticed the sweet fragrance of intuitiveness hovering all around her naïve companion, so to help; she places a steadying hand on Isabella's abdomen. Though Isabella does not feel the touch, she definitely experiences a change. A sensation, a softly unnerving feeling, lands upon her heart. It contains an epiphany of the impending new walking toward her.

Isabella, wrapping her arms around herself, reflects upon her bewilderment for a short time. As she watched the Greater Lights vanish from the opulent skies, she hastily drops from her introspection and begins her short journey home.

Glad to be back in the comfort of her cosy dwellings, Isabella took in a small chapter of a book about her trade before extinguishing all the lanterns. Eager to lay down that evening, she jumps into her resting compartment and closes her eyes tightly. After pulling the blankets up to cover her mouth, she quickly falls into a weighty and long sleep.

Isabella, immediately taken up, out through the skies, past the clouds, over the Lesser Lights, and further into a dark blackness that contained no sound and no sensation. Regardless, Isabella knew she was traveling at a marvellous pace, and yet, still picking up speed rapidly. Had she not felt so exhilarated, the terror would have taken over her.

As she travelled, a young man came into her view, only slightly older than herself. He quickly matched pace and moved alongside her. He had a tear running down one side of his face and a chart in his hand. His smile was sincere as he repeated a phrase, "I will take you as far as I can go," and then he disappeared out of view, leaving only a slim trail of light behind him. Isabella, looking downward, noticed that she also left a thin trail of light. Holding onto that light hung two other people, who in turn, caused their own path, making a thicker strand in their own wake.

The astonished young woman, looking to her side notices a gentleman's timepiece made of a valuable material. Its face was black opal and its hands were made out of light. The timepiece was vibrating and buzzing. A voice came from the skies near its whereabouts and said, "It can wait no more."

Looking to her other side she saw a reproduction of the greater lands. Isabella felt compelled to stare at it, and as she did, an unseen hand-scrawled the word Deficit over the surface of the sphere. She saw many people with their arms lifted high as if they had been overthrown and were not surrendering. The voice again said, "Well, which way will you go?" The voice of another questioned, "But, is she free to choose?"

Isabella answered, but not aloud. She silenced the second voice, and to the first she replied, "The entire length of the journey." Isabella was then immediately placed side by side with the two people who had been following after her. All three Cambrasian's increase in speed until their bodies could take no more. Then, all of a sudden, they were pulled up, and out, through something resembling a thin curtain. When they were through the curtain, everything around them had changed. All had turned to light. In fact, the light that surrounded them made the light that they knew seem like darkness.

At this realisation, Isabella and her companions spin around in rapid velocity to face the direction from where they had come from, and then thrust forward and down. This time, the trail of light moved ahead of them, though not the same light that had followed them; instead, it was a new light, the light of lights. Then, instead of continuing as a thin trail, brightness rolled out like a tidal wave before them and touched everything in its path.

Isabella woke abruptly. She could still see the light in her mind's eye and felt a strange familiarity with it, but could not think why. She lay on her bed, watching as the Greater Lights chased away the

Lesser Lights seeping their dark violet glow through the window above her head. Slightly weary, Isabella begins preparing herself for the day ahead.

The dream had affected Isabella quite profoundly. She made many attempts to dismiss it as nothing more than a night disturbance caused by an apprehension that was yet to be recognised, but could not fully convince herself of its insignificance. All throughout her waking hours, she replayed its message, both consciously and unconsciously. By doing so, Isabella allowed her heart to become open, enabling her to receive something that she could not have previously entertained.

Eleneke smiled with great satisfaction as she witnessed the impact of her embroidered imagery upon this small being that she loved so dearly. The Eirtherol did not tire of nourishing Isabella's thoughts with whispered guidance and securities. As the Greater Lights again made their way underneath the horizon, Eleneke gave Isabella a hope-filled whisper and then left the Chosen to her own contemplations.

Eleneke sang out to those of her kin from the In-Between Places, bringing them an awareness of the success of their plans. In return, the Eirtherol called and cooed with their voices resounding in celebration of the accomplishment. Their voices gathered, causing large pools of vibration to gather outside of the Tactile Measure of Time, to shimmer, vibrate, and send their goodness into the time-governed atmosphere.

At this very same time, Eleneke placed her face to the face of Isabella and, looked deeply into her eyes until she felt a connection. She then began to sing into Isabella the land song from the Greater Lands that had been the place of Isabella's ancestry.

The sound was a deep, rolling sound that was rich in resonance, not overtly drum like, but with a low pitched and dull thud at certain intervals. This phrasing frequently repeated, each time with more or less overtone. The sounds flooded from the stomach of Eleneke, and then, passing through to her lips. It was both beautiful and eerie, and though only lasting a minute or so, it had touched Isabella to her very core.

Isabella knew in that first instant of the refrain that she had heard her lands cry (though she could not perceive the sound, nor the singer.) Her heart reverberated elatedly with the history of many generations that had contributed in fashioning her very fabric. After all, did not her face still resemble theirs even though there had been a significant separation? She comes to understand part of her night vision and now is clear on at least one task. She is to go back to the place where her bloodline began.

Eleneke carefully took from her garments a delicately ornate and small decanter. It was made from ruby like material that had been rolled so thinly that it resembled coloured glass. She threw the decanter into the air above Isabella, where it dissolved into tiny droplets of incredible fragrance. The droplets started to spin in little circles, and then reconnect to each other and depart, skyward, leaving a trail of its content behind it. This fragrant trail transformed into a thin line of concentrated light that could be seen from all the other realms. It broke through the Tactile Measure of Time and left a permanent opening over the head of Isabella.

★

Meanwhile, Avril had been jumping in and out of the Tactile Measure of Time in her attempts to locate the Grovel that she was assigned to keep, when summoned by one of great eminence, Superior Ranker Denken: The Keeper of Knowledge.

Denken was the highest in command of all the Lesser Princes; He was the Barren Prince's chief assistant. Denken endowed with access to significant power and knowledge and had oversight of all critical activities among the little beings on the Cambrae Sphere.

As soon as she was made aware, Avril wasted no time in attending the meeting with Superior Denken. The profusion of knowledge and ability that he would impart inspired her haste.

The formal greeting belied the emotion of the two authorities. Denken, severely curious to view the Lesser Prince who had been newly promoted by the Barren Prince and was quite impatient to sum her up to see if she was capable of threatening his position, for promotion was not something given out often. Whereas Avril, with no thought that she may be considered a rival, was churning up inside at the idea of receiving anything that Denken had to offer.

Denken took in all that he could see of Avril from his big chair, and in his arrogance, decided she could not now, nor ever, overshadow him. Unbound from that fear, Denken prepared to release a little off the wealth of knowledge in his possession to his subordinate. Yet still, he would put on impressive displays for her, with all the expected bravado, to ensure that she did understand her place. Avril girding her cowering heart was very careful to contain herself as was fitting for a Lesser Prince of any means.

Denken stood to his feet rather unexpectedly. Avril's body flinches as her instincts cried out to depart; yet, by sheer will, she remained. Without warning, Denken's form fell out from view, leaving menacing questions playing upon her mind, and though she knew well of this particular parlour trick, she did not know her superior well. Avril steadied herself by recollecting her training and recited quotes in her mind, "A master in his standing would never allow one to feel any safety, and so would change his position, his mood and his command at unanticipated times."

Denken, impressed at her standing, re-emerged only a hand span away from her face. Avril, for some moments, was taken aback, then taken in by his beguiling appearance. His face once handsome was now melting downward like a spent candle. She followed along the ridges and lines of his face in complete fascination. Denken allows this admiration for a time while he gazed through her with unyielding eyes.

Suddenly, Denken started to talk loudly and rapidly with his shattering voice. "The one that you have an assignment with is named Isabella, from the Volcano Isle. You have seen her already and noticed her unexpected early ripening. She is accompanied by the one they call Eleneke, in a manner, a formidable foe, yet soft and weak like the rest of the inane Eirtherol. She had held to Isabella's side since the Grovel's birth but now has parted from her.

Though it remains uncertain, the Eirtherol was most likely summoned to the Invisible Realm to be given information about Isabella's journey. The information must be of high importance, as they did not risk any possibility of interception by the choosing of that location. The Barren Princes personal assistants are still working on ways to hear into that realm, but are so far, unsuccessful."

His voice drops to a flat and monotonous pitch as he whispers of weaknesses in Isabella that were currently untouched, and some little know failings of her current culture and the culture that her forbears resided in. He spoke of plans that were most likely to be played out, and also of the greatest strengths of Eleneke.

Avril was careful to fix every word into her mind's eye, not treating anything Denken said as unimportant. Denken noted this and quietly decided to take Avril into his confidence further if the correct situation arose.

Finally, when Denken finished his divulge, he walked to a corridor of drawers that was located just behind his seat. He motioned for Avril to join him. Avril remained silent as Denken pulled out from a drawer, a small, and then a larger book.

The little book was a detailed history of the influence of the Lesser Princes upon Isabella through both direct and indirect means, whereas the large book had predictions on the future and the likelihood of their occurrence. Denken then informed Avril of her own weaknesses, and what she would need to do to resolve them.

Knowing they had concluded Avril lowered her entire body to the ground and placed herself flat on the floor, as a sign of her willing acceptance that Denken was indeed her superior. Then, while lifting her eyes toward him, she picked herself up and stood to her feet, body erect, head lowered.

Denken was not at that moment inclined to acknowledge her existence so he continued on as though she had not been there at all. Avril held her gaze just underneath his eyes, and waited silently for her dismissal; to leave sooner would be a dire mistake on her part. He, after some moments, scowling with annoyance, raised his left eyebrow, dragging up with it his wilted face.

Avril, being well versed in the power of intimidation and domination, recognised this sign and quickly complied with its instruction. She knew that this was her time of release, and hastily departed his company to attend to her new assignments.

By the time Avril returned to the In-Between Places to observe her subject on the Cambrae Sphere, Isabella had been busy preparing herself for a journey of unfamiliarity. The newly enhanced Avril saw that the time was ripe, and, pulled upon the atmosphere with her extended fingers, calling for Harshaw and Calamity to join her. They came quickly to her call and then, they did not speak, they did not move, they just watched.

Chapter 3

A stream of light pours out from the Invisible Realm and into Eleneke's being. She ponders.

Acar now dominates the skies. Her vibrant orange spray brings forward new life while the comfortable warmth of her glow reveals cheer, hope, and promise. She, the gentlest of the Daystars extends the time of light, allowing room to receive any possibility.

Indeed, the possibility will be conceived, nurtured and followed, but not without challenge. Chosen will meet and friendships will blossom, but the wrath of the Lesser Princes will be severe as the reign of Acar ends.

An entire season had passed since Isabella made her significantly life-altering decision to leave the Volcano Isle. The wait was enforced upon her, as only a few passenger bearing charters ever left the Islands in one full round of Greater Light Cycles. Isabella was glad for the opportunity to wait and used it wisely to tie up all her loose ends and study about her impending travels.

Though thoroughly convinced of her decision, when it came time to book a passage on the large ship, she recognised, deep within, a growing pang of uncertainty, though she could not understand why. Nor could she discern if its recognition was a help or a hindrance to her. This haunting retreated each time she returned to any other part of her preparation, but quickly returned the moment she thought of the ship.

"I cannot constantly doubt my way. If it is wrong, then it be wrong, but if it is right, then let it not be hindered," and with that thought, it was decided. Isabella no longer lingered upon her uncertainty and, from that time onward, as she continued with her plans, the haunting became so dull that she no longer even cared to recognise it.

Finally, the day of her departure had arrived. Alone, Isabella stood upon the highest cliff face on the Island where the only known wharf had been positioned. The dock, strategically placed underneath the overhanging cliff for reasons of defence, and could not be viewed from the top. She took in all of the sights and scents around her and thought again of the possibility of never returning. Carrying just one large satchel upon her back, Isabella walked towards the winch and pulley mechanism that would lower her down directly upon the ship's deck. It was manually operated, as most of the equipment was on the Island, and just large enough to take a couple of people at a time.

As the Cambrasian drew nearer, she felt her heart again being pulled into uncertainty. The feelings this time were so intense that her stomach begins to churn. At that precise moment, an arresting thought made its way to her mind. It was an impression that would not accept dismissal this time though she tried. The thought just kept on spinning and whirring around the inside of her mind. Isabella knew for sure that, if she wanted to go any further in peace, then she must entertain the idea for a while to solve it.

Amidst the inner upheaval, Isabella's eyes were continually drawn to the left side of the cliffs face, much further away from the winch and pulley that she felt comfortable in attending. She knew the ship would depart without her rather than fall out of its schedule, and Isabella would not be able to acquire another ticket for a further two seasons. Even so, it was obviously apparent that her need to appease the thoughts was greater than her fear of missing the craft.

Isabella quickly settled in her heart that she would entertain this perspective and took a brisk walk to her left. On arrival, her eyes drawn yet again, but this time downward to the side of the cliff face. Looking all around the area, she was just about to dismiss these inklings as complete absurdity when a glint of light caught her eye. She followed the light as it moved down the face of the cliff further. There, she saw a rustic spiral stairwell partially obscured by leaves. It appeared to lead all the way down to a pebbly beach, which was also mostly concealed by foliage.

Something resonated within Isabella. She wanted to abandon her journey and travel down those antiquated steps. She wanted to step upon that pebbled beach to see where those ideas took her. "But", she spoke aloud, "What would result?" Not willing to take another chance, Isabella makes her first decision concrete within her heart. She would ignore these impulses, race back to the winch, and board the boat as planned.

Eleneke, her constant companion, looks upon her Chosen for a moment, with an awareness that no further aid would benefit Isabella at this time. She knew well not to force her position even though it was for the utmost welfare of her subject. After all, it was within their creed that all are given the basic decency of self-containment, even though not many ever realise it.

Isabella fled with all her might toward the winch and pulley. Though she knew well that the distance was too far for her to make it, sheer determination carried her forward. She was further spurred on by the sound of a blowing whistle that told her the ship had already taken its leave of the wharf. With no time at all to take captive a thought, she jumped upon the elevated platform and quickly began to lower herself downward.

Isabella's heart struck with dread as she peered beneath to see the nearly impossible challenge that awaited her. Her next move made with no thought, and no hesitation. She leaps, with all of her strength, forward, off the platform and toward the slowly moving vessel. Isabella instantly knew that she had made a mistake and was sure to, at the very least, devastate her body. There was nothing more that she could do now but hold her breath.

Eleneke took grasp of the ill-fated Isabella, pulling her beyond the Tactile Measure of Time and into the In-Between Places. Isabella perceiving the sensation of her body coming to a complete halt notices a bright light seeping through her tightly closed eyelids. The light reminded her of the night vision she had taken direction from and now wondered if the dream had actually been a warning.

Isabella begins to feel somewhat disorientated, as most certainly, her body should have crashed upon the deck by now. Now utterly perplexed, she opens her eyes, one at a time. A light greets her; it is almost blinding, though surprisingly not painful, even so, she can still vaguely make out a face that presents in front of her. Upon the face was a concerned gaze. Though Isabella had not seen this face before, it appeared oddly familiar. Isabella had heard stories of near-death experiences from time to time and now assumed that this was her end.

Eleneke held the frightened girl and gave her a reassuring smile that lingered for some time. As she smiled, a powerful peace enters into the heart of the young woman. "Take my courage little one, for it is well," said the face. Then, Isabella was carefully placed back into the Tactile Measure of Time, right at the point of her landing. So, without even the slightest impact on her grateful body, Isabella had boarded.

★

The boat was almost full with both Islanders and residents of the Greater Lands. Most of the passengers aboard were seated below the deck, organising themselves for the three light cycles trip that lay ahead of them.

Of the handful of people situated on the deck at the time of Isabella's arrival, most were looking out onto the open seas and had missed the spectacle altogether. Of the three that had observed, two felt their eyes insulted their sanities so strongly that they chose to ignore the incident altogether. However, one other did see and did not refuse the observation, for he was a man that had experienced strange happenings before.

The man stared over at the shaken figure of the girl that had, by this time, collected herself up from the deck. Isabella felt exposed as the weight of the strangers glare fell upon her and lingered longer than either politeness or concern would dictate, and though she pretended not to notice, the onlooker ignored her feeble façade and motioned for her company. Isabella felt a deep apprehension rise from the pit of her stomach, and further into her throat bringing its warning to her person. However, this was not the only alert she observed.

"Take caution," was the whisper that entered into the heart of Isabella. Eleneke stood close, veiled in the Invisible. Though holding confidence in the progress of the Chosen, the Eirtherol knew that this man, well trained by the Lesser Princes, operated within the same parameters of sight that they did. One shown much from the In-Between Places, he possesses a wicked cunning that innocence could not often discern.

Keeping the alert in the front of her mind, Isabella quickly evaluated her circumstance. It appeared impossible to avoid the intrusion of the brazen passenger as he was located right next to the access hatch that led to the lower decking. With his eyes still firmly fixed upon her, she also realised that he was unwilling to allow her smooth passage. Isabella raising her head, takes a deep breath, and walks purposefully toward the hatch.

Isabella studies the insistent man. He is dressed in a cream, linen suit, slightly ill-fitting, and entirely unfamiliar to her, or indeed to any from the Volcano Isle. His face is well lined, and though apparently weathered; he is not as old as the creases indicate. He is sitting on a bench with his suitcase pressed up to the side of his leg. Again, the man motions for Isabella to join him.

In a jaded manner, the man speaks, "Your name is Isabella is it not?" He pulled his lips to the sides of his face, mimicking a smile, widens his eyes, and then continues. "Well, that is your name isn't it? I am asking you a question dear. Are you looking for your manners?" His face, though set to a smile, is apparently seething with malice, and his tone rings out in sarcasm. Isabella looks at the impertinent man, unaware of the gathering of Lesser Princes that are all around him.

Resigned to answering, she chose to reply in a concise manner, "That is my name though I do not recall having met you before." The man sighed through his nose, retaining his fake grin, "Oh cut it out Isabella; I saw what just happened to you. Here I sit, minding my own business, and there you are, out from nowhere." The man lifts his hands, palms up, feigning surprise. Isabella's tears well up into her eyes as the confusion of the incident returned to her mind. She looks up and presses her fingers into her tear ducts, stopping the flow that threatens, and looks back at her aggravator. He seemed irritated, yet is clearly enjoying himself.

"Do you believe in an order Isabella? That everything has a purpose, everything has an allotted time?" Isabella lifted her eyes a little higher to indicate that he had her audience, but she did not speak. He continued, "It was your turn to be dispelled from this rotten place. I will state it another way to make it perfectly clear for you, it was your turn to die Isabella." With the words released, the man twisted his face into some sort of grimace, as though he had pity upon her.

Isabella flinched at the words presented to her, then stood in disbelief at the candour of the man. She opened her mouth to answer but could find no words, she tried to continue forward and past him, but her feet were stuck down with fear.

"But, Isabella, you did not die, you averted death, it was a curious sight, odd. You see, when you jumped from that lofty height, I thought you were sure to become a ruddy pile upon the deck, but, you disappeared from sight for a breath and suddenly, well, now you are here, not a scratch on you." He chortled to himself in amusement, "What a peculiar thing for one so unremarkable."

The Lesser Princes that surrounded the situation became unusually excited as the strange man poured forward his hurtful words. The Princes used the invisible substance of his prose to carry their darts into the struggling mind of Isabella where the painful lyric circled, looking for a place to settle. Spinning around and around inside of her mind, it causes her much confusion. Isabella, too appalled to speak, continues to bear this verbal attack.

The darts of barren-slick keep firing, "Do not think that this has happened because you have a life of importance?" He pauses, quickly looking her up and down, "For indeed, you do not. Believe me, I can tell. Instead, I suggest that you have fallen into a cosmic mistake, a happenstance that seems in your favour. Now, quite unwittingly, or should I say dimwittedly, you Isabella, have changed the order of things, and that shouldn't be, should it?" he pauses and points toward the sky, "Oh wait, I can see it now, the reason this Sphere wants to wipe you out. Nourishment expert I think, was it? You left your post. You should be purged from this Sphere for leaving your post." Isabella felt sick to her stomach, but still, did not move.

"Up for more are you, well, when you pull your wits about you again, and regain the composure that you were hoping to hold on to, you will come to the understand that you are now a thing of repugnance." His sneering amusement could not be repressed as he added, "What will Isabella do now? Now that she knows she was supposed to breathe no more breath from that point on?"

Eleneke was watching this cruel onslaught from a place that concealed her from the gaze of the Lesser Princes. *I can see that you need my assistance, Isabella, for you have entertained this maliciousness for too long now.* Eleneke held her hand to Isabella's shoulder and pressed forward her potency into the Chosen.

As the strength poured forward into Isabella, Eleneke's form could be seen emerging from her place of concealment. Her splendidness, warming even the natural air around the Chosen, was a clear sign to the Lesser Princes that they were severely outranked. One by one, the involved Princes took notice, and, with no resistance, each one retreated.

With the Princes departure, their influence left also. Yet, the Cambrasian marionette continued to speak, only now, his words did not sting like before; though Isabella's body was still filled with adrenaline, she could now resist the spinning words that tried to lodge into her mind. With senses speedily returning, Isabella concludes that what she had entertained was just the ramblings of a man, completely disconnected from reality.

Glaring at him, partly in anger, partly in pity, she gathers up her concentration and brusquely pushes past this foolish character. Springing down the steps, Isabella retreats into the small cabin allocated her, near the end of the way.

Once the Lesser Princes saw that the Eirtherol had left with Isabella, they returned to the miserable marionette. They knew full well that he would always go too far with the information they related, but they settled on the understanding that, at least he was an outlet for their guile into the tactile plane. They would ride with him until they found another, more shrewd being, going their way.

Isabella, now alone, sat upon the divan meant for her sleeping. She laid her head in her hands and cried, and, even though her mind had stopped spinning, the cruel words of the man remained. *He was most certainly mad* she concluded in thought, *though he knew my name, and many other things about me that he should not have. He was right about the fall too; I should have died.*

Isabella contemplating the grave words presented her, wholeheartedly battled their sting. Firstly, she questions the input of the intruder then, she questions herself and finally, she searches deep within for answers. As she does, she happens upon a dilemma, for the words of the stranger connect to words that she has heard many times before. For, his words had newly exposed the lyrics chanted to her by the Lesser Princes over the duration of her existence. The rants of this lunatic threaten to usurp the confidence she carries, the very confidence required to make the bravest of decisions.

Eleneke knew that the fight that fell upon Isabella was not a fair one and sat down on the divan. Laughing as she thought of how the

Princes had overstepped their hand, *barren-slick holds more power when it is not realised. You have given yourself away.* At her laugh, the room fills with an unexpected lightness, slightly lifting the spirits of even the forlorn Chosen.

Eleneke understood what she had to do. Throughout the long night, she would speak truth into Isabella, truth that refuted the claims of their common enemy, and in doing so, replenish her body with fresh vigour. "Isabella," she whispered, "To be called Chosen is to be placed in a very high position, and to stand in that location, and walk to its very pinnacle, will take the courage of heroes."

Eleneke stared intently at the Chosen, who is still softly weeping. She takes from her clothing a red silken purse covered with purple embroidery. The Eirtherol drew back the ribbon that held it secure and released the content. A watery and colourless solution spills out on her open hand. The moisture gathers into tiny balls, and starts to bounce, slightly at first, and then higher as it gathers momentum. Eleneke whispers something into the substance, and then places it upon Isabella's shoulders.

The tiny leaping balls bounce deeper and deeper, entering into Isabella's frame, and then plunging further until they stay held within her body. Though Isabella did not initially feel anything, she most certainly would. For, this enthralling substance was none other than the actual courage of the highest measure. It is the substance of the courage of Victor.

Isabella felt lighter within her being, kicked off her shoes, and gratefully lay back upon the soft blue bed sheets. Surprised at the sudden calmness in her mind, she closes her eyes and relishes each moment of peace. After a short time of enjoying the tranquillity, she falls into a weighty and satisfying sleep.

Early morning came and went and Isabella had not opened her eyes. By late morning, she entered that unearthly place between asleep and awake.

Isabella sat in a warm rock pool, surrounded by lush greenery and delicate blossom sprays, listening to the splashing sounds produced by tiny dancing waterfalls. She sits face to face with Eleneke. "I know you: you saved my sorry self from great dismay," her voice was quiet. Eleneke replied with cheer in her voice, "Much more than you know." Isabella quickly jumps up from her place and throws her small arms around the reciprocating Eleneke.

After a short while, Eleneke excuses herself from Isabella's firm grip, gently positions the smaller being further away until their eyes could meet, then releases from her mouth a tone that is both soft and confident. "We will meet like this, you and I, and in other ways too, with more frequency as time goes on. Each time we do, you will know me better. However, for now, I want you to remember your thoughts before you left the shores of your land. What were you looking for before you leapt from the solid land and onto the sea-vessel? I want you to bring it back to remembrance, and take a look back soon after your waking."

Isabella awoke. Cautiously, stretching her body out upon the comfortable divan, assessing any damage acquired from the stressors that presented the day before. Isabella was astonished to discover that there was none; in fact, the contrary was true. So, Isabella stretched further, and basked in the wellness of her body. It was as though the best healers upon the Cambrae Sphere had attended to her form and addressed each of her needs and desires.

"What is more," she whispered, "my mind sits in the same state as my body, and I am most pleased to have found myself in this way." While continuing to lavish in her good fortune, the shining face of the one who had saved her dropped into the forefront of her mind. "In my dream we spoke, you and I, but I do not recall our conversation."

Although the memory of the words spoken had vanished from the mind of the Cambrasian, they still remained. For now, they are entrenched in her heart.

Isabella decided to take a walk on deck to look out at the unspoiled Island that had been her home for so long. She supposed that, though it was later in the day than she first anticipated, the land could still be viewed using one of the telescopes situated upon deck. With spring in her step, Isabella leaves the cabin and climbs the stairs.

The day is breezy and the skies filled with brilliant light from Acar and Ento, two of the three Greater Lights. Isabella looks up into the brightness and set her eyes upon the two lights to locate their position. As the Daystars move closer together, Isabella's excitement increased. *The Crossing, I will finally see the Crossing.*

This phenomenon occurs two times each cycle, within the first few days, then approximately one-third the way through, as two of the Daystars stand together in exactly the same locality at precisely the same time. The hue from each star colliding, their splendid crystalline surfaces briefly surrender prominence. In these few short moments, laser-like beams of colour, both familiar and unnamed, shoot out over the waters to reveal secrets of its anatomy. This glimpse, having wider implications, sets wonder in motion throughout the atmosphere of the entire Cambrasian Sphere, causing all spirits to lift.

Isabella had not witnessed this spectacle before as her employment required full attention while the Greater Lights shone. *I have wanted to see this since I was very young, and now, as I follow my night vision, I finally see. It is more breathtaking that I had imagined. This is no coincidence; in fact, I hold it as proof that I have indeed chosen the right path for me.*

Feeling more exhilarated than she could have ever had hoped, Isabella races toward the back of the boat, placing her hands on the sturdy railing, leans forward and experiences the rushing sea breeze in all its tumultuous glory. Closing her eyes tightly, she inhales the freshness that leapt straight from the ocean and draws it into her lungs. Opening her eyes, she sees something that she does not expect.

A small wooden boat is making its way toward the Island shores. Greatly concerned with the intention of this unannounced vessel, Isabella walks brusquely to the lens view to observe it from closer proximity. It seems to be a small cargo boat, nothing more than that, but there are no wharf runners at the dock to welcome it.

Isabella moves her view toward the coastline of the Island. As she scans the domain, a glimmer catches her eye. She had witnessed that same glimmer before boarding the ship.

Riddled now with curiosity, she intensifies the lens view and found the exact point of her focus. There amongst the green ivy was a sliver of silver. With further inspection, she concludes it to be a staircase, partially embedded in the face of the cliff, and quite purposefully obscured by vines.

Eleneke stands at Isabella's side, laughing as she realises the severity of thought that had taken the Chosen's attention. "How quickly you release your tranquillity, we will work on that young friend." The Eirtherol takes one of her fingers and spins it around in little circles, causing the atmosphere in the In-Between Places to whirl and turn in the same fashion.

The effect of it touches the Tactile Realm, calling for all nearby Eirtherol that reside outside of the sights of Eleneke. In less than one moment, an unknown male Eirtherol approaches, they move their air filled mouths and blow their voiceless words toward each other in an introduction, then Eleneke pours forward her explanation and request, followed by her thanks.

The new Eirtherol, placing his hands on the belly of his own Chosen, a member of the ship's crew, stirs up a message into his being. The man walks directly toward Isabella and speaks in a pleasantly deep voice. "You look concerned; may I offer you my assistance in any way?" Isabella thinks for a moment and then replies, "Actually, I was noticing that small ship going towards the port of the Volcano Island. I am puzzled by this, as ships come and go so infrequently, and if you look, there seems to be no one aware of its attendance."

The man grins at the concerned passenger, "Oh, there is no need for your worry. See that is a delivery ship. If you look to the side of the port, you will notice a small dock on the beach. Look, there is a staircase carved into the side of the cliff, see the silver handrail, there." He points, "The small vessels can deliver their goods easily from that point, with lot less kerfuffle than drawing its content up the winch way. Most are unaware of its presence, except, of course, for those who need it."

Relieved, Isabella thanks the crewmember and places her attention back upon the small boat. An unexpected idea jumps up from her belly and into her mind. *Perhaps that was my intended path; perhaps I was to board the small boat instead, but why?* After more reflection, she decides to pursue this line of thinking once she leaves the ship, but for now, she would embrace the giddying wellbeing that added to her the night before and relish in the remainder of the ride.

★

Aaron stood at the port for quite a while. Having completed the last trip for the season at his return from the Volcano Isle, he was free. With duty finished and crew departed, he leisurely watched the waters splash upon the seashore, listening to its loosely rhythmic crooning against the open shoreline. *There is something about water; I love it.* Aaron understands that it will be some time before he witnesses the coast's compelling beauty again.

In the distance, he sees a large passenger vessel, slowly making its way to the Port. The bulky ship is clumsy and slow, unlike Aarons light vessel. *I can make it there and back and back again before you even skim the shore*, he thought, *still, do not try to remedy this, for it is to my favour.*

For, the researchers of the Volcano Island, being hungry for progress, preferred Aaron. His vessel was faster than the mainstream boats and small enough to utilize the obscured port. Also, he and his crew were prepared to travel the entire Sphere to acquire desired goods. Aaron was highly esteemed by those who knew him and payed handsomely for his efforts.

Aaron, now completely relaxed, makes his next decision. He would take a room in one of the better quality taverns and rest awhile before finalising details for the season ahead. Aaron always kept his calendar clear through the three cycles of Acar of any working responsibilities.

However, through the times of Numa and Ento, Aaron gave himself little rest. During those seasons, he agreed to undertakings that were difficult in nature, undertakings that few honest men would consider. Yet, Aaron pursued them with great integrity, and, in turn, he received an enormous financial reward. In this way, Aaron prepared well for his times of liberation.

The first evening for Aaron was quite usual. After a meal from the street traders outside in the commons, he ventured back to his room and wrote a long and descriptive letter to his Uncle Mauriae, the man who raised him as a child. His uncle, over Aaron's lifespan, had spent considerable time informing him of all the captivating placed that he had visited and many other noteworthy exploits that had occurred. Aaron, by way of letter, reciprocated.

He then went directly to bed and fell into a deep sleep. His peaceful dreams that night were a mixture of things he had seen, and other things that he wished to see. When he awoke at the dawning of the light, he was eager to spend some of his earnings on things luxurious.

It did not take him long to decide on exactly how he would spend his time, and his earnings on this day of his freedom. First on his list, he planned a trip to meet with the ports artisans of fine fabric. They would measure and sew, working quickly on his new clothing. Then, newly outfitted, he would find a place to dispose of all his sea-riddled clothing, shoes and satchels, a ritual he happily observed after a long voyage.

Afterward he would travel to the old stone rooms of spring. The original architects had taken elements of the natural springs nearby and developed upon them to create something quite sophisticated. These rooms were the epitome of extravagance. They were communal, yet remained almost silent aside from the regular stirring of the waters. At any time, a hundred or more Cambrasian's could be in the waters, but with the presence of the hot mists hovering above the pools, one could remain completely oblivious.

After soaking til his receptive body was contented, Aaron would enter the outer rooms to be groomed by a company of Cambrasian's that had dedicated their lives to this practice. Their standard was considered the benchmark of performance by most of the Sphere.

Following that, he would enjoy a meal in the common court once again and taste from a banquet of rare delicacies displayed in copious amounts. Then, finally, after collecting up his new possessions, he would acquire transport to the next town and sojourn with one of his friends for a few cycles of the Greater Lights, as was his custom after a working season.

Aaron always looked forward to times of re-acquaintance with his stayed kin, but, as he considered his plans further, an unsettling sensation began to develop. Being familiar with living by his wits, Aaron paid immediate attention to the mild disharmony. He poured out a mug of the sweet and spicy brewed water that boiled at his bedside, sat down upon the divan and closed his eyes. Aaron gave all his concentration over to what his instincts were attempting to communicate.

As Aaron closed his eyes, something previously hidden comes into clear view. For, standing just steps away from him stands a figure of tremendous stature, and though the Chosen does feel its presence, he was not perturbed, nor did he open his eyes, for Aaron, already acclimatised to the presence of the being in attendance, feels no threat.

The figure turns its full attention to Aaron and after some moments places his strong hands upon the Chosen's shoulder. Even though Aaron is both tall and strong, the forms sizable hand makes his liberal frame appear tiny.

Aaron, remaining undistracted from his mediation, recognises something from outside of himself, pushing in upon his own, very personal and internal world. Aaron wisely allows this inspired notion to flow through, and enter into his being. Reflecting upon the foreign notion further, he gives it the permission to grow, and mingle, and join, with every other imagination that presents itself for evaluation.

Aaron keeps his eyes closed, continuing to bathe his mind in the contemplations. He knows well enough to let this process run its full course, regardless of how long it may take. Holding the introduced thoughts in high regard, he notices which of his own ideas could contain the inspiration, and which ones could not bear them. In this way, he filtered through each idea until they all, were exhausted.

The tall figure from the In-Between realms releases a final and intense rush of sensation into the body of Aaron and then relinquishes his grip. The Eirtherol is now completely satisfied with the work of his hands, and, moves again, off into the unseen places.

Aaron opens his eyes. His mind, now clear as to why a caution had echoes into his heart, felt peaceful again. He now understood, at this time, it would not be profitable for him to visit his friends in the nearby township. A greater benefit would be his if he were to stay in the port town for a few more cycles of the Daystars. However, there was one detail not understood; would ill fortune fall should he visit his friend's village or unexpected good occur when he stays in the seaside town for longer.

Thank you for your input; input I will regard, though it, he reasoned to himself, *does not need to change my immediate plans.* Aaron continues with intent to enjoy thoroughly his time at the artisan port as originally intended, though now, he will keep an open mind to any spontaneous happenings that present around him. With high expectation, he leaves the tavern to immerse himself in the striking and unfamiliar culture.

Though the day was most refreshing, nothing that was unexpected crossed Aaron's path. As the Greater Lights bow out of sight, he suspects that the mysteries he looks for would not reveal to him that day. Settling upon the idea of being idle in the comfortable bed that lay in wait for him, he takes swift steps toward the tavern when a fresh notion captures his mind.

Aaron remembers his uncle, his adoption father, and entertains some of the many stories shared about this little portside town. It was one of Mauriae's favourite places; a place he often visited when he too, could travel.

Aaron recalled Mauriae speaking of an open-air bazaar, held in the times of Acar underneath the hazy glow of the Lesser Lights. Often, he would describe the sweet smell of the Esbon blooms. This precious flower releases an undeniable scent only as the Lesser Lights display their shine upon the darkened, moody skies. He spoke of the incomparable ambience of the many small fires tended by the fairs men, and how they emit a warm yellow/orange light; changing, even the appearance of the landscape by their casting shadow. It was a place of intrigue indeed.

Aaron had ventured to the port town before, yet he had never attended in the season of Acar. Freshly enthusiastic, he quickens his pace, and passes straight by the tavern and instead, chooses to enter the bazaar in the centre of the village and squander his time, searching for peculiar treasures and obscure fare while enjoying the richness of the town's people.

It takes only a short while until he spies the lights that will lead him directly to the event; their luminous glow, along with the fragrances from the bazaar, reaches his senses quite some time before he reached the destination. Even so, it does not take long for Aaron to sight the fare, which is brimming over with local life. Textiles, works of art, clothing and produce dominate the merchant tables. Manned by the towns' people, their merchant songs flow to an animated audience comprised of both native, and visitors.

The natives are quite distinctive in their colourful silken outfits, entirely appropriate for their busy agenda. The generous fabric, motioning in the breeze, had the appearance of flags and ribbons that flowed freely. The colourings and style indicate their ancestral family lines, of which, only four reside in that port.

People not native to the port town are equally distinctive. They are dressed in the beautiful clothing designed by the artisans in the nearby spa houses. These clothes, are elegantly tailored, subtle in colour, and beautifully designed, yet, they are not practical, and, in the long run, quite unsuitable for this port town's ever-changing climate.

Aaron quickly internalising his focus, begins to inwardly chuckle. For, as an experienced traveller, it was his intention to appear as a local, and in doing so, avoid the unseemly kind who would try to profit from his ignorance. Yet, this time, his own rule had been apparently forgotten, and his foreign position very evident.

Interrupting his amusement, a face in Aaron's eye line catches him off guard. A young woman, with pretty features and dark blond locks, is standing at a produce stall, paying for her purchase. She appears guarded and uncertain. He studied her face for some moments, attempting to discern her heritage. She wore neither the uniform of the tourist nor the covering of the local. His curiosity had been ignited.

Aaron walked immediately toward the young woman and tapped her on the forearm to reveal intention to converse. Once she faced him, he began to talk to her in his clearest voice. "I noticed that you are unfamiliar with this land. I would very much like to accompany you for a while until you feel more at ease in your surroundings. I am named Aaron."

Isabella, suspicious of intruding characters, gives no indication of friendliness. Aaron, already prepared for this most predictable reaction, was not off put, for he understood well, the need for self-protection. Aaron continues in his warming manner, "I am not from this town either, as you can clearly see." He gestured to his clothing, chuckled to himself, and unsure if she understands the joke, continues, "I reside further in the Greater Lands, that is, when I am not working, or traveling for my own pleasure."

Isabella still does not respond, though neither does she regress. Aaron, utterly incapable of recognising personal rejection, speaks again, "You are quite odd and unfamiliar, so." But before he had the chance to finish his sentence and deem his statement inoffensive, Isabella, held her head high, looked directly into his eyes and prepared to rebuff. As she did, she was too taken aback to open her mouth.

For, deep in one of his eyes is a pattern, a shape that sits behind his pupil and underneath his iris. The usual grading of the eye is there.

Line upon line of different hues, both blue and grey sitting above, but underneath that, and more condensed in a shade, there lies a definite shape of a teardrop.

Isabella quickly recollects the night vision that propelled her on to the unconventional path she now, so bravely treads. Quick flashes of memory storm her brain, sorting, and then revealing things pertinent to the situation. She remembers the figure that rocketed into the atmosphere aside her, leaving a trail in his wake. She remembered the face of this one, and though it was not the same as this stranger, this Aaron, the quality of his eye is undeniably reminiscent of it. Could this be the man that came alongside her, one that has something of value to contribute to her journey? Still unsure, she allows her defensiveness to drop just enough to invest deeper into this conversation with the stranger.

Aaron keeps talking while Isabella continues to listen, half to Aaron, and a half to her own ponderings. "I have just returned from the Volcano Islands. I had an agreement to deliver some unusual vegetation that I acquired from another, distant and more," he searched for his words, "more treacherous place." Hoping to impress, he continued, "I have left my boat at the dock where it will be kept in a private holding until I find need to return. Having finished my duty, I take a prolonged rest until I continue upon adventures of my own volition."

The young woman animates as another idea presents inside her. She speaks, "I am Isabella, and I was born in the Volcano Islands. This, this is my first attendance of the Greater Lands." She paused long enough to remember the encouragement received in the previous night, the encouragement to see what she could not see before she left the Island. "On my way, I witnessed a small boat crossing where I did not expect to see one. My attention was drawn to it, and I surveyed it from the ship's deck. Indeed, I believe I that I saw your boat."

She pauses to re-evaluate her situation, and then boldly reveals her deeper thoughts "Do not think me odd for saying this, but perhaps I was supposed to meet you before. Maybe I was meant to attend the Greater Lands via your vessel instead of the one that I did travel on. I have my reasons to believe this though I shall not tell them to you now."

Aaron, knowing now for certain, that Isabella, or at least, something about her, was the reason he had been detained in the small port town, and, Isabella feeling assured that whatever she had missed at the dock of the Volcano Island will be disclosed to her in the meeting with Aaron. Therefore, with a renewed sense of providence in their meeting, both Chosen quietly knew that their intense curiosity would be satiated.

The silent companions are equally pleased. For though the beginning of the journey did not follow its intended path, Isabella and Aaron's current choices now guaranteed the same results. The Eirtherol grasp hands and look deeply into each other's being. Where they were strong as one, as two, they are more than double in their effectiveness.

Isabella and Aaron, becoming quickly at ease in each other's company, spend every hour of their waking together. Sometimes divulging mysteries deeply stored away within their hearts, while, at another time, they played and bantered and just relish in the others being. Though only having known each other for a short while, they develop a profound confidence in each other.

The ever-surrounding Eirtherol, enthusiastic about the recent turn of events, amplify the mutual adoration levels by weaving the colourful substance of favour over and between the gushing beings. For further fortification, Eleneke and Asher, directing and moulding concentrations of light through the greatest virtues of Isabella and Aaron until those qualities hold in the forefront of their companion's mind, and in so doing, the bonding of Isabella and Aaron concreted.

★

Eleneke and Asher, basking in the union of Isabella and Aaron, experience a sudden jarring, as a dark shadow crosses their hearts, interrupting their celebratory mood. Threats of movement, whispers of intention and cunning resolve press into their minds. Asher, grasping for understanding gives voice to his developing perception, "Isabella and Aaron no longer walk in the safety of anonymity for they are now recognised. Throughout the In–Between Places and beyond it is most evident; with their new connection, they carry a conceivably important destination."

Eleneke and Asher, understanding the gravity of the situation, search around for confirmation. They note the squirming discomfort felt in the In–Between Places. For now, it bore a load that it was never supposed to carry, a burden best contained in the formless places outside of the original dimensions. For now, the In–Between Places held Mockery.

Mockery, a powerful Lesser Prince, did not travel alone. Maintaining a deep understanding of the hurtfulness of shame, and, most cruelly, he is willing to explore it to its utmost depths. Easily recognisable, this Prince, with his bulbous nose and massive grin, resembles a ghastly wooden puppet. His eyes, full of laughter at the misfortune of others, had held to a tightly squinted position for all of the ages, and consequently, could no longer open them enough to see. Unperturbed, Mockery took into his service a kindred Lesser Prince, one most complimentary to his own nature, one who could interpret what she saw for him. This was the employment of Flattery, who enjoys her place of influence upon one so commanding.

Mockery's legs also inhibited him, severely weakened by attacks that he had sustained in the In–Between Places in times gone by. Near useless, his legs can no longer carry him, so, another Lesser Prince was required for the task, and Ridicule was Mockery's choice.

Ridicule pushes Mockery around in a large wheelbarrow, enjoying the exhibition of his own power of strength as his reward.

The collaboration of the three was cleverly strategic. As Flattery and Ridicule whispered their vile insincerities toward a target's heart, Mockery's mighty laughter would boom forward, and cause the atmosphere to compress tightly around the victim, holding firmly to it, any experience of humiliation. While Mockery's skill extended the time of opportunity, Flattery and Ridicule would work furiously to weave the substance into the actual fabric of the victim and thereby corrupting them for all time.

The Eirtherol, considering it of great importance, continue to take particular note of this information yet, there is another voice calling to them, capturing the larger share of their attention. Bubbling up from within, this voice is pure, still, and unmoved by the circumstances. It stands, as always, their true compass and most recognisable guide.

This voices gentle and sure tone quickly reminds the Eirtherol that these physical injuries of their enemy are just illusions. For eyes are not needed to see the unseen worlds, and legs are not required to move; but none the less, they are important to take heed of, for these false wounds indicate where Mockery is now bound, areas that he once used freely.

The voice also reminded them that though Isabella and Aaron may have to face these tyrannical forces at one time, they are also not to be lightly reckoned with, especially now. For the Chosen would not ponder on, or conceal within their hearts, anything that would threaten them with separation, for their coupling is strong. Instead, they would address any insanity presented by Flattery and Ridicule, therefore exposing and extinguishing them, rendering Mockery without employment of his own.

The Eirtherol, weighing up the matter, placed it in its proper perspective. As soon as they had finished, they perceive a call, a request to enter into the In-Between Places. As soon as the ones from the In-Between sent the call, Eleneke and Asher had already arrived in the dazzling company that had summoned them.

★

By the time Eleneke and Asher returned to the Cambrae Sphere, Isabella and Aaron had made some significant discoveries of their own. Feeling secure in each other's presence, they divulged many of the secrets locked away, deep within their hearts.

Isabella revealed the night vision to Aaron, carefully describing each relevant detail. She talked about her unexpected journey, divulging the strange twists and turns throughout.

She explained about the glimmer of light at the dock of the Volcano Isle, and how she silently feared that a wrong turn taken had concealed her way. She also freely poured out her memories of the contemptuous and bitter man whose uncanny insights had hounded and confused her.

Aaron had also shared, quite candidly, of his unplanned and lengthy stay at the Artisan Port Town. He explained that it was quite usual for him to follow his instincts and, realising his new friends hunger for the topic, talked openly and at length, of how he had cultivated this ability.

Isabella, filled with intrigue, responded by exploring this type of inner vision on her own and, with Aaron's guidance, came to the realisation that, in this very same way, she had embarked on her travels in the first place.

As the time went on, the newly acquainted couple pondered heavily upon the dream. Making sure to pay attention to the directional pull of their hearts, they followed its leading until a significant conclusion was drawn. Aaron was indeed the man in the vision, the man that held the compass with the tear in his eye, the one that blazed a trail behind him, and though they could not be sure of details, another conclusion was quickly drawn. For, it seemed quite clear that something of much importance was waiting for their exploration.

Upon this understanding, they thought through and developed many possibilities, though none took particular precedence, excepting that, to unravel the conundrum further, they would have to travel. After much more consideration, they reached a mutual decision; their next destination was to be Malcarve - The Ruined City. The pair purchased everything needed for the ambitious trip as the day stars continued to shine, then, enjoying one last meal in the comfort of their surroundings, they separated to their private rooms to spend the last night in solitude, for, at the early light, they would begin journeying.

By the time Eleneke and Asher re-entered the Tactile Measure of time, Isabella and Aaron were ready to begin their journey together. The Eirtherol looked upon the Chosen with happy hearts. Things were in good standing.

As the Chosen stood in peace and agreement, and the Eirtherol beam with joy from the hidden places, a sudden and unfavourable change fell upon them. Each of the four companions turned to their left at precisely the same time, seeking an answer to this undue disruption.

Standing tall and holding no expression upon their faces, two other beings marked out a place and staked the ground. The Eirtherol stood silently, curious to see how the Chosen would react, for, though these characters remained invisible to Isabella and Aaron, all could feel the chilling impression they omitted.

Aaron, quick to recognise the discomfort of his companion, brushed her hand and spoke words of courage into Isabella's troubled heart. "There will always be obstacles, should you choose to stand apart, so it is best to just face your convictions, and not your fears, for, through those convictions, the answers will come. Look forward and you will not part from your intended course. Besides Isabella, we now stand together." Isabella, breathing in his wise words, braces herself with its truth, and smiles.

Eleneke, ignoring the presence of the Lesser Princes, smiles toward Asher, "There is that truth talk that Aaron speaks so well. Isabella will benefit greatly from this maturing quality of Aarons." "Yes, she will," Asher replied, "and, Aaron is sure to profit from the passions and motivations that Isabella carries."

The Lesser Princes, still expressionless, did nothing, and said nothing. They only waited.

★

The Chosen were numerous cycles of the Daystar into their journey and though the company was pleasant, the landscape was not. For, the majority of the space between the Port Towns and the Ruined City was a wasteland, mostly uninhabitable. Its previous occupants had used all the resources of the earth, and, lacking in vision, took without giving, until the last from the perishing land was removed. Soon afterwards, they fled.

Isabella views the land and states what is not visible to the untrained eye, "This land, it is not spent entirely, it needs to be tended, replenished, fed, just like any other living thing, then it will heal and it will live again. It is not hopeless. If you look, Aaron, there are signs all around us, signs of regeneration, recovery without our aid. An even greater improvement will come if someone with the knowledge gives to the task. Perhaps, one day, I will return here, for I am well trained in these matters."

The Chosen ride upon an open-air sledge that harnesses its power from the wind. The force of the air sweeps over their invigorated faces, adding to the excitement of their adventure. Intoxicated by experience, their senses override the presence of the four otherworldly beings travelling alongside. The Eirtherol, equally lively, play together, childlike and contented while the Lesser Princes lack any animation at all.

The Greater Lights begin to glow their deepest hue just before their colours dissolve behind the still pale light of their gentler cousin. Isabella and Aaron discontinuing their journey, take some time to rest.

While Isabella and Aaron prepare a meal, the residing Lesser Princes, Avril and Harshaw, recognise an opportunity for sabotage. Heavily steeped in the nature of Cambrasian's, the Princes are aware of certain weaknesses that they possess. Tired, hungry Grovels are much less likely to question the validity of thought that enters their minds, making this a perfect time to begin another onslaught of barren-slick.

Avril to Isabella and Harshaw to Aaron, the Lesser Princes simultaneously open up their rancorous mouths. Out of them gushes a monotonous barrage of words, words doused in the sticky substance of uncertainty. The Lesser Princes also understand that volume is necessary, for the more words that are accepted, the heavier the element became.

"What are you doing? Where are you going, you stupid and selfish child? You shouldn't be out here with this man you barely know, it's pathetic." Avril gagged at the closeness of the woman and, further angered, continues, "You will return to your people, should they accept you back. You have separated yourself from the reputation that you once proudly built and for a what? A little playing outside of your pen? At the very best, this time is a small reprieve from your lifetime of work, work you are supposed to do, Isabella, you are born to do it.

It is for the better of your people, the Volcano people if you go back. They need you, need you. Do you want to hurt your people Isabella, damage them? What did they ever do to you? Your father and mother will be shrouded in shame for the rest of their lonely and child forsaken lives. They will probably live shorter because of you, your actions, and your self-interest.

On the other hand, perhaps you think to stay in such a place as this. I suppose, if you cannot face the embarrassment of returning to the Island, you could stay here. You would be all alone; still you could compensate for your foolish choices; reinstate your reputation. Look around; you notice that this land needs tending, are you the one to do it? Well, stay here, do something productive, just do not continue with this, this, albeit good looking, opportunist and waste everything invested within you."

Avril continues on, softening her voice, "This dream, this vision you follow is no more than the usual result prompted by the heavy meal you ingested before sleep, no doubt about it. Do not pull it apart, trying to dig out meaning where there is none. Stop revealing your ignorance so freely by listening to it; exposing yourself to those seeking to use you for their own power.

See, nothing good can come from this. You certainly have more intelligence than you require of yourself right now. Where did your lapse in judgement come from? You have become arrogant, thinking that that placed before you is too small for you. You are an embarrassment to yourself, little and unimportant one."

As Avril spills her venom upon Isabella, Harshaw floods the heart of Aaron with colourless whispers. "Your life is your own, and always has been. You have made choices for yourself that may not be safe for another, for you are strong, with many provisions, material and otherwise. Look at this girl, she is young, she has not seen the Sphere as you have, and she is placing a terrible amount of trust in you, you with your very many flaws.

She knows not of your own battles, and you have revealed to her nothing of your weaknesses, yet, but they will seep out and show themselves. You know the ones, many, many, many ones." He sniggered.

"This ridiculous idea of yours, the idea that you listen to your own instincts, your own heart, who indeed, are you that one would entrust you with, what is your delusion called, yes, truth. Why would you think that anything of value could come through you? Ever wondered why you are mostly alone?

You must not develop this insanity in someone so naïve. Isabella should be sent home; she deserves to be in much better company than your own, you know it. You are playing a game with yourself, for she could not survive if she lived within your mind, and you seem intent on giving her full access, well, almost. There is nothing ahead of you; it is but an empty-headed imagination, fuelled by an unsatisfying existence that you already lead. You are on an elusive journey, and you will find nothing, for there is nothing to find."

At the conclusion of this tirade, the Lesser Princes toss a mottled grey and purple cloak around their victims. These cloaks were evidence of unusually strong and intentionally crafted mischief. This action from the Lesser Princes generally provoked any Eirtherol to fight full force, stopping them from lying upon their Chosen. However, this time, no resistance is given. The Lesser Princes, indulging themselves, stand back to observe as the weeds of their work come to life.

Aaron, looking toward Isabella, sees her lovely, innocent face expressing deep concentration. Eyes held downward, crinkling at the corners, brows drew closer together and lips pursed, she is clearly worried. The cloak of hopelessness, inflaming her concerns, presses heavily all around her though she remains unaware of its presence.

Feeling the effects of the cloak wrapped around his body also, Aaron stands tall and expands his ribcage, fighting the restriction of movement he feels. The cloak, compressing even his freedom of breath, holds tighter. "We must be higher in altitude Isabella," says Aaron, attempting to explain the situation.

The Lesser Princes watch with twisted excitement as the garments continue adhering to the Chosen's fragile forms. They took great pleasure in watching the desires of these small beings suffocate under their skins. Believing Aaron to be the initiator of the duo, the Princes turn their full attention toward him first.

The cloak continuously squeezed around Aaron's abdomen, until each breath was laborious. Usually, as he drew air into his lungs, a substance of peace flowed with it, and the two elements entered, side by side. Now, the restriction around him, causing his airways to narrow made no allowance for the peace. Tired and hungry with elevated heart rate and lower quality of breath, Aaron's troubled state started believing that Harshaw's words were his own.

Avril, turning away from the bewildered Aaron, lifted herself toward the Eirtherol and sneered. She could not contain her usual composure for her hatred toward them, at that moment, grew too intense. "Pathetic, futile and useless are the two of you. Your power will serve ours." Eleneke and Asher paid her no attention. They did not even flinch at her violent intent toward them, nor did they pursue their own defence. In fact, there was another type of animation growing in their countenance again.

Avril's sour turning mouth began to burn as she realised what was transpiring around her. The Chosen, without help from the Eirtherol, had started soothing each other with their kindness; interrupting the pace of the barren-slick, their breathing deepened. With words of comfort, they attract the substance of peace from the Invisible Places. The order, joining again to their breath, floods their being while the cloaks of hopelessness start to loosen. With fresh expectations of a bright future increasing, Isabella and Aaron throw off the cloaks and expel the venom of barren-slick.

Avril could not hide her disgust as she looked back upon the radiant Eirtherol. Eleneke smiled at her, "The truth had already been placed inside of them before you even knew what their faces looked like." With that, Avril could take no more. "Do not antagonise me further." With that, she jumped off the Cambrasian Sphere and slipped into the In-Between, followed moments later by Harshaw.

★

Avril and Harshaw met again in the In-Between Place outside of the Tactile Measure of Time. Both creatures stood near the lair that they and Calamity had prepared as a place of their temporary dwelling. However, as often happens, in their absence it had become exposed, and, for the most part, pulled down. Bereft of shelter, the two Lesser Princes dragged out their own cloaks of hopelessness and threw them overhead, attempting to bring some relief from the brightness and fragrance of the Invisible Realm.

Harshaw, looking to understand the situation, spoke with caution, "I would not have believed that those two Grovels could shed the laborious garments so quickly, yet, that is what I have witnessed. We took every precaution as we carefully constructed those cloaks; tailored precisely for those two beings. We made sure that they landed within the right boundary of circumstance. The span of time, indeed accurately calculated as being the best time to deflate their ridiculous notions. We cannot allow this, this dream, taking on a more mature form. I cannot understand. What was not adhered to? What was missed?" Harshaw, perceiving that the trouble was his failure, trembled internally at the thought of Avril's spiteful wrath toward him, though, externally, he held to a controlled composure.

Avril addressed her own thoughts before responding. Her whispered sounds corresponded with the bewilderment she felt, "I have heard rumours, no, it couldn't be yet, Acceleration, no, not yet, and after all, they are in no place for it. Nowhere near, not yet, not any of them." Once she had challenged her own distress, she turned to Harshaw, who was trying to make sense of her garbled murmur.

Gathering composure, she hissed, "They must have been given substance that we know not of. We have been warned of this age, and the many secrets that it holds from us." She felt deep humiliation in admitting her ignorance in front of Harshaw, yet she did not reveal it

"Though we have not yet joined with Calamity and her Grovels, and all that they bring, I had yearned to maim Aaron and Isabella, terribly, before they should even meet. I wanted them to be such a disappointment for those they are to meet. Why shouldn't they be destroyed now? They have upset my mouth with such an active burning, and I do not desire to entertain this for much longer."

Avril and Harshaw sat among the rubble of their meeting place and began to draw up the adjustments to their plans.

★

Isabella's travel weary eyes surveyed the generous proportions of white stone road that directed them on toward the city of Malcarve, The Ruined City.

On both sides of the single road into The Ruined City were many trees, planted in impeccably straight lines. Each perfectly formed tree enjoyed a considerably long life. With lengthy, slender limbs and crimson leaves, their lofty stature afforded a well-received favour to the cold colourings of the road. For, the bows of the trees directed the glow from the Greater Lights downward, causing a dance of mottled pattern upon the white stone path. Ample sized fruit clung to their branches, occasionally spilling onto the road where they relinquished their plentiful juices.

Isabella's wide eyes struggle to take in this sight of the dreamlike city that stretched on and on before her. "It is as bizarre as it is beautiful; I cannot make sense of what it is I am seeing." Aaron allowed the moments of awe to be uninterrupted as he remembered his own first viewing. Once Isabella regained herself, he began speaking.

"The entire city is made out of gigantic slabs of sandstone, including this road. Its water is phenomenally rich in minerals; it has no comparison, not anywhere on the Cambrasian Sphere." He pauses to point out the fruit trees that are now above their heads. "Everything that grew within those walls was told to be oversized and brilliant, all manner of vegetation benefited from the soil that lay underneath the stone. Its quality is also far superior to anything else on the Sphere, even more than the Volcano Islands. The Cambrasian's that are bred here live higher than most of us, reaping vast physical benefit from the land, they are told to be ancestors of Talinet and his men."

"Talinet, I have not heard of Talinet?" Isabella inquired. With eyes wider still, Isabella listens as Aaron recounts the story.

"It was told to me that the people who once resided here were Colossi and bloodthirsty ones at that. Before their extinction they were intent on finishing the line of Cambrasian's, and would execute them with perfection. Talinet and his men, understanding the colossi ambition, diminished the number of them by a skilful assault. They had this way of sneaking up on their enemy and taking them by surprise. With only a few colossi still in existence, Talinet ordered them to encase the city with the same stone as a way to make a monument of their triumph, then, the last of the giants put to their deaths.

Nevertheless, sandstone, as its name suggests, can easily crumble over time, and that is what has happened both within the walls and without. When we enter the gates, you will see. The soil pushes vegetation through the cracks, increase their size. Its result is breathtaking, yet unnerving. You will see."

Coming toward the gate and into the unknown, the pair of awestruck travellers quietly brace themselves, and press forward.

★

Wry and Cara had been looking forward of this time of light for a long while now. At the turning of Numa, the second cycle of the Greater Lights, Cara had set herself down to focus on the Unseen. As she did this, a riddle had been presented for her to search out. So throughout Numa, and then through all three cycles of Ento, she and Wry made a commitment to finding an answer.

Both Cambrasian's had spent time in study to search out the meaning of this riddle, but, though some new light was shed upon it, the answer remained hidden until all their focus was placed upon the unseen.

At first, the couple playfully experimented in this new venture, just enjoying the experience, and each other. Yet, as time passed, they noticed the riddle unravelling in ways they could not have otherwise grasped, so their exploration took upon new weight. As it did, a great hope in its reality grew, until suddenly, hope gave way to expectation. Today was the day of proving.

"It is time." Spoke Cara. Her beautiful face radiated with the excitement that she contained. She and Wry began their eagerly anticipated passage and walked briskly toward the city gates. Both Greater and Lesser Lights shone out from the electrifying sky, though now, the Lesser Lights had begun to dominate.

As the couple neared the gates, they realised that all was not as it should be. For, the people of Malcarve, who tended to be reclined in their luxurious abodes by now, clearly, were not. A flurry had been triggered by an unusual event. The cause was unveiled quickly enough to the bemused couple, as the sounds of surrounding voices gave the narrative.

Some unknown's had entered the gates without giving Address, a long held and respected tradition among the Malcarvians. So, not knowing what to do in situations like these, the young court guard had alerted the Consortia in their grand buildings, and in doing so, aroused the curiosity of the hundreds of attendants in their waiting. The bothered horde then joined the unfriendly greeting parade at the City Gates.

Wry and Cara, delighted by the sounds, knew full well, that this was what they had been waiting for. So, with quickened pace, the couple reached their destination.

Once they had arrived, the Consortia, eventually persuaded by the intruder's explanation and apology, deemed them safe, and encouraged the people to return to their buildings. The Consortia left quickly, yet, the attendants of the Consortia stayed on and milled around, hoping to be entertained.

With chest's still pounding from their sizeable sprint, Wry and Cara stood still to recover for a moment. Cara arranges her dark, long hair away from her face and then closes her heavily made up eyes, intending to enjoy this deep satisfaction rising in her heart. It felt as though a powerful white light took root at her very core, and then shot out shards of its glow through her body until she was completely filled with it.

"There, there they are," she said, pointing toward them. "We are to grab their hands. They will come." The couple presses through the crowd, spots the strangers, and takes hold of their hands, Wry to Isabella, and Cara to Aaron. As their hands are connected, something imperceptibly extraordinary happened. The internal sense of light that flooded through the being of Cara only a short time before now began swelling up and bursting about the inside of the other three, connecting them in an unorthodox way. There is, quite undeniably, destiny in their meeting.

Cara and Wry led the thankful pair out from the jostling crowd, telling anyone who resisted that the strangers were guests to their own dwellings. With each step, the distance between the Chosen and the dwindling swarm increases, and the pace of the newly acquainted decreases.

Still holding onto Aaron, Cara also grabbed Isabella's hand and then sighed out a smile. "We have been waiting such a long time for your arrival. It is so good to finally see how you appear," her voice bouncing with laughter.

Cara pauses and takes the time to search the faces of her new friends. Perceiving no wariness from their part, she continues. "I can see that you are in need of a quiet place of rest. We have prepared you a portion of our building, making it a private place for you. There, you can bathe, have your fill of fare, and take in some sleep. Afterwards, when the Daystar shines bright again, we will meet with you and talk in more length."

Satisfied with the proposal, Aaron and Isabella follow on.

★

One by one, the Chosen awoke. Fuelled by a searching curiosity, each one dress, leave their bedchambers, and makes their way into an elegant common room pointed out the previous evening. There the Chosen neglect the inviting daybed, preferring instead to sit on the oversized silken pillows generously strewn about the room.

A glow from the celestial bodies hanging in the still darkened skies filtered through the high ceiling windows and dances patterns over the white stone floor. A large fireplace taking residence in the centre of the room glows with warmth, and all four Chosen sip upon fine-spiced wine served up in silver goblets by an eager to please house attendant.

Unbeknownst to the new friends, there, standing with them, are four other beings. The great ones, reaching into pockets that lined their garments, retrieve dainty packages, and release their liquid contents liberally into the atmosphere. They, having no fear of discovery, were laughing and singing vigorous songs that brought with them joy and life, and they continued to do so until every possible space in the atmosphere about them filled up with this life-enhancing delivery. They watched on as the sound and the mists of affection stopped and rested upon the Cambrasian's bodies.

Once settled, the vapour formations combined with the harmonious sounds and sunk into the skin of the blind recipients. The divine concoction brought out memories hidden within the Chosen at the time of their making.

For, in fact, they had already met, pre-existing in the Invisible Realm, and although they could not remember, the truth of it, printed upon their bodies, held to their very DNA. So Isabella, Aaron, Cara and Wry basked in an unexplained knowing of one another, an affectionate favour for each other, and peace that is usually only felt in the closest of families.

The Eirtherol, caught unaware with the ease in which the little ones received these truths, felt a rush of excitement within. For, unlike the Cambrasian's, the Eirtherol already knew the most favourable destinations for them, and could see new possibilities unfolding into the lives and minds. In fact, many things that could not have been before their meeting were now most likely.

Eleneke, Asher, Darién and Althai walked toward the fire in the middle of the room intent upon greeting one another with kind words of introduction. With arms extended forward, the beings hold their open palms to the ceiling, and then grasp each other's hands. Once their hands were touched, powerful words of greeting flowed from their mouths and the atmosphere all about them rushed with intense wellbeing.

The effect upon the Cambrae Sphere was particularly strong this time. It caused the surface matter of the visible to melt into a supple and thin veneer that readily receives the intensities from Invisible Realm. For, in this meeting, something of a different ilk was yet to be revealed, something that the Eirtherol could not have anticipated.

The Chosen immediately respond to the changed circumstances and, within a few short moments, fell into a profound and silent amazement. For, though Eleneke, Asher and Darién had frequently shared close proximity on many planes, not one of them had ever met Althai before. Althai was of a different sort.

He, and many like him, stood shrouded within the Invisible Realm from the time of their conception, and through every age, positioned to soak up the greatness, beauty and power that surrounded them. Eleneke, Asher and Darién had heard of these magnificent beings for their reputations were legendary, but not they, or any Tactile or In-Between dwelling Eirtherol or any Cambrasian from the Tactile Plain had ever witnessed one, that is, up until now.

Althai released all concealment to fully disclose his powerful form. Eleneke, Asher and Darién, flooding with excitement and privilege, quickly fall as profoundly silent as the dumbstruck Chosen.

As the Eirtherol took in Althai's commanding presence, they grew enthralled by his appearance. For, in his person, he embodied many chambers, and pipes, and valves. He both carried, and was, a weapon of sorts, an instrument, a sound.

Althai started to play. It began as an orchestra of horns, all warming up, with their dissonant and unexpected noises testing their own capacities, but then, the sound started to change as the clattering found its rightful place and modified into the sound of a single commanding siren.

The siren had the authority to slice between the Invisible and Tactile Realms in an instant. There was no need for Althai to trifle with the profane. He did not have to suffer at all with the In Between Places should he choose not. For, when the time was right, Althai could just release the sound from his shape, and crack the micro planes wide open, then place in, or take out, that which he desires.

The Chosen lay themselves down on the floor, not knowing how to deal with the enormity of the goodness that they now experienced. "Will we die now, in this perfection of being?" asked Cara. Althai laughed at the exhibition before him, Eirtherol with mouths held open in astonishment, and Chosen, curled up on the floor, eyes beaming, empty of all concern, though grasping for words but not finding any. He wound down his sound until it became a quiet whistle, and then, diminished altogether.

Althai spoke with his siren-like voice, "I have been looking forward to this appointment for quite some time. The others like me are also in the same situation, for time has ripened enough to contain us. We bring with us acceleration, as something great is about to happen in Cambrae Sphere. Also the In-Between Places for that matter." Pausing for a moment, with the desire to be more personal, Althai continues, "Though you have not met me before, I have had the honour of meeting you, and I have established you all in my own heart for an entire era." He pauses again, "now, I am greatly pleased to be joined with your good company."

Silenced by the authority dripping from his mouth, the unacquainted Eirtherol did not know what to do. Eventually, Eleneke broke the silence, "My mouth is in lack, for you are an extraordinary sight. I do not know what I should say for I am completely overcome." With that said, she reached forward to embrace him, and as she did, Asher and Darién came to join her.

The majesty of Althai was tremendous, yet, that was not the only reason his presence overthrew them. For, with his presence, an insightful understanding took residence in their reasoning. Something new was about to happen, something never witnessed before. For now, it is certain that a new era had been born.

Each Eirtherol gasps as the enormity of the situation overtake them. "To be here! To be here!" whispered Darién in ecstatic bewilderment. "It has been a great while since I walked in unfamiliar places." "Darién, your sentiment, is not just your own" sparked Asher, and the four beings felt a pronounced connectedness.

Groove like ripples began to form in the serene atmosphere around them. Eleneke advises, "The call to the In-Between Places has come again. Let us meet with those who dwell there and we will prepare for the needs of the Chosen together." Hastily, they depart.

★

Upon the Tactile Plain, a lengthy conversation had begun. The exchange inspired by the otherworldly atmosphere that remained from the meeting of Eirtherol. With any caution to divulge their most private of opinions wiped away, Isabella, Aaron, Wry and Cara openly shared of the events that had transpired in recent times, along with any conclusion that were drawn from them.

The discussions continued to flow as the splendour of the Greater Lights recaptured the unclouded skies; and, though they showed great interest toward the most unusual and unnatural, it was not anything of tangible quality that held the most intrigue.

"We could all explore the unseen things together. Let's wait and listen, and see what results." Spoke Isabella, both pleased, and relieved, to be sharing this part of the journey with them. "Well, I see no reason why we should not start here and now, do you?" Cara poured, looking around for objections. Seeing none, the exploration begins.

In anticipation, the new friends embark upon their secret quest, hoping to gain greater clarity. For most certainly, where one was strong, and two were stronger, four should yield a much larger return. However, to their disappointment, the outcome offered little.

Despite the sacrifice of two meals, nothing new came to them, even though the power felt earlier remained with them. Still, thoughts of the compass from Isabella's dream seemed a reoccurring theme, and a vague inner knowing that they had taken the right paths came, but nothing more. Disheartened, the new friends decide to let go and try again another time.

Isabella and Aaron thanking their hosts excuse themselves and head toward the private quarters allocated to them to enter personal discussions. Though they had decided that Malcarve -The Ruined City was not their final destination, they were unsure of the part that Wry and Cara are to play. Were they constant companions or were they hospitable strangers along the way.

As Isabella and Aaron discussed the different possibilities of the future, and whether that would include Cara and Wry, they failed to notice an unfavourable flavour that lay in the air about them. For, in a quiet corner of the room, stood Avril and Harshaw, wielding plans of their own. They, along with Calamity, had been watching from the In-Between Places for another convenient time of opportunity, and this, disappointment mixed in with the possibility of separation, was one of those times.

Still feeling the effects of the sour taste clinging to her throat at the thought of Althai now being involved, Avril suffered from the clawing of anxiousness scraping at her very being, but again, she did not show it. "Keep your wits about you Harshaw; we are soon to grind down these little Grovels into the dust from which they came." Without moving his head, Harshaw directed his eyes toward Avril and grins. With cheeks lifting high, his face pulls up to resemble who he once was. Reminded of his loss, he quickly releases the smile and viciously proclaims, "We shall incite riots."

By this time, Isabella and Aaron had made their way to the balcony, and looking over the edge, Isabella remembers the beach from the Volcano Island. Underneath the Lesser Lights, the wind swept the freshness of the sea into her lungs, sweeping through her body and bringing its invigoration. Outside the confines of Wry and Cara's property, Isabella felt the same. As quietness takes residence in her mind, she readily discerns a bubbling up from within. Not being the origin of the inspiration, Isabella does not fully understand, yet it is clear, she must share.

Taking deep breaths, Isabella begins, "Do not let go of your hope, for I fear something will surely test us to abandon it by calling dismay good reason. This will be a place that much courage is needed to continue, but, we must persist, for all of our sakes. There is a feeling rising up within me, that what we are walking toward is of much more consequence than we would ever expect."

As soon as Isabella's words took their form into the heart of Aaron, the mood around them grew dark. Within moments, Avril and Harshaw crept up toward the unsuspecting pair and hoisted the cloaks of hopelessness around them again. These cloaks, re-tailored with newly gained knowledge, and increased in length, were sure to cover the Chosen, leaving nothing visible in the In-Between Places.

With cloaks tightly secured, the Lesser Princes jumped upon and clung to, the backs of Isabella and Aaron, making sure they applied extra pressure to their throats. Once in place, the Lesser Princes whispered into the captives ears.

The foul melody rang forth like a mournful and sombre song, void of hope, void of happiness. Their words filled with incessant intimidations, mixed with twisted truth, and drawn from any known paranoia or insecurity. They Princes did not pause; nor did they slow their pace.

Though Aaron and Isabella could not see what was happening to them, they could feel the heaviness of the pressure applied. The severe stress of unrest bought strain to their hearts as the viperous whispers suspended around, adding to the pressure. Isabella began to feel sick while Aaron suffers a tiredness that would endure for quite some time.

Harshaw, enjoying the Grovels lowly state, pushes his caustic weaponry harder. "See this Avril; I will make the fool give his assistance to us." Stepping into the In-Between Places while continuing to sing a song over Aaron, Harshaw takes words of Aaron, and some from Isabella, adds his own to the lyric, then placed them to form a pattern.

This pattern of words connected to each other in the shape of a child's song, or chorus, that spun the end into the beginning once again, until the lyric became one continuous circle of malice. Harshaw, pleased with what he had made, began to establish a trancelike rhythm, connecting it to the pattern of words playing out.

The rhythm caught on, and Aaron aided Harshaw well. So focused on the pivoting design, Aaron considered it a form of truth and did not think to look outside of it for further reasoning. He instead searches for its ending, and finding none, causes the pattern to spin faster and faster, creating grooves and fractures to his very soul.

"The fool has contributed greatly to his own demise. Not that we needed your help Grovel, but thank you anyway." Harshaw congratulates himself regarding his greatness as his villainous companion, laughs freely, fully appreciating his swagger.

Isabella, though harassed from the outside, retained a steadiness within. From this internal repose, she felt the bubbling of Invisible things rising up again, providing her with wisdom. From deep within, teachings she had received from the Invisible Realm before her birth rose up and spoke. They alerted her to listen to only their call. Then, shaking off the attempted infestation, she grips the hand of Aaron and directs him to the common room. "We must find Wry and Cara."

By the time Isabella and Aaron found Cara and Wry, they too were suffering. Standing aside her Grovels, Calamity was present with companion forces in attendance. Within her hands, she tightly held a leash make up from a densely woven chain. This restraint had previously secured two insidious creatures that held only to Calamity in submission.

These impish creatures are small but effective at causing pain, both physical and otherwise. They crawl about the Chosen's bodies, undetectable in the visible realms, wantonly in the In-Between Places, simultaneously putting pressure on whatever attracts their menace.

"There you are," Isabella called out from the passage that lead to the common room. "Your estate is so large; we thought we would never find you." She laughs, attempting to bring some lightness to the mood, but without success. Still holding firm on Aaron's hand, she guides him into the room. Isabella notices instantly that Wry and Cara do not seem to possess the same magnetism that had made them so attractive at the first meeting for now they seem quite dull.

Quickly, more bubbles released through Isabella, imploring her to recognise this as a temporary and false appearance. Upon that realisation, Isabella smiled softly, clutching to the small hope. "Strange things abound in our midst, but even so, place your trust in me for what I am about to say. Let us just stay together, in the company of each other right now, regardless of what is standing against us. I can feel it pressing upon me, as I know you can, and I am tempted to walk away from this, the recent notion that I have listened to, this place, and you, my friends. But, at the same time, I am constantly reminded, all that is seen and felt is not necessarily true, nor can any perception we hold to be fully trusted, especially now."

With her hands, Isabella motions for them to leave, but Aaron, Cara and Wry remain. Reassured, Isabella continues, "We must remind ourselves of what we have been holding to. I listened to a dream, one that has affected me profoundly, challenging my course of existence, and leading me to places unknown. Aaron, you know well about looking with your heart, very well, and you have taught me. You knew to wait for me though you did not know me."

Isabella stops, looks toward Cara and Wry, and continues. "You two; both of you have been waiting for the day of our arrival in hopes, and we did come, on the very same day that you expected, at the same time no less. These are not playful imaginings that we experience; something brought us together. We must not lose sight of these things now, even though they remain unclear. I am sure that this, this discomfort that is happening to us, I am confident it will pass."

Each tortured chosen knew that Isabella's words were true, for when she spoke an effervescence of knowing rose up within their beings and ministered confirmation. Yet, with most strength drained from their weary bodies, they were unable to express agreement. Instead, Aaron, Wry and Cara, drawing from the little vigour they had left, stay together, silently vowing in their hearts not to leave.

★

Eleneke, Asher, Darién and Althai stand in the In-Between Places along with other Eirtherol and Returned Kings with destinies attached to the Chosen, along with some Cambrasian's who had experience in similar matters.

The diverse group, joined for a purpose, carry a fresh commissioning. They were to pull through spoken, yet undeveloped impressions from the Invisible Realms and place them onto the surface of the In-Between Places. Once successful in this endeavour, they were to prepare for the final transition over to the Tactile Plains.

The assembly laboured conscientiously, employing many capable hands, yet, it had not been an easy task. For, in the deeper layers between the Invisible and In-Between Places, a band of Lesser Princes had gone unnoticed and filled the pirated address with many of their own oddments. The unsolicited additions, left sitting for so long, had become entrenched into the hybrid meshing that separated the Realms. Removing them was a complex task, requiring the separation of thread out from the tightly woven fabric to release the foreign substances, piece by piece.

Althai felt the thrill of it all as he surveyed his surroundings. There were parchments rolled up and sealed, with the names of Cambrasian's inked onto ribbons that encircled them. Small liquid beads, contained in larger beads, were moving about in circular motions, ambitious to reveal discoveries and concepts that previously unknown. There was also the form of physical items and situations yet to be owned.

Clinging to space above Althai's head were Cambrasian's and Eirtherol, re-lacing the deeper layers of meshing. Their task was almost complete. Althai looked on at his fellow colleagues and observed their merriment. Their play was of equal importance to their work, and they indulged in both with the same amount of enthusiasm. Althai, finding great amusement in his sight, began laughing unashamedly at the happiness of his friends, and, as he did, the sound of his siren rang out. Each time the sound exploded from his body, a handful of the collected objects immediately slip from the In–Between and into the Tactile Plains.

Every being working within the company of Althai stopped what they were doing to witness the delightful display. Unsuspecting Cambrasian's upon the Tactile Plains began receiving their complimentary deliveries, and, as they did, their eyes grew wide with wonder at the newfound knowing's that the distributions had presented.

The company laughs heartily as the wonder upon the Tactile Plains increases. The group, simultaneously recalling a knowing, turn silent. Each time a Cambrasian dwelling upon the Tactile Plain successfully receives a deposit from the Invisible Realm, it weakens barren-slick, and the recipients are a step closer to remembering who they really were. They laugh some more.

The group turned their gaze to a slightly bewildered Althai. "I had not intended to release my sound, it just slipped out along with the laughter," he explains. With his body still shimmering from the liberation of his siren, he sheepishly grins at his captivated audience.

Eleneke, noticing Althai's awkwardness in the situation, speaks to him with great tenderness. "You must understand Althai that it takes so much effort, along with extensive preparation before any parchments will fall into its intended place for us, but with you, your sound, there seem to be little need to engage ourselves at all. You do a beautiful thing, quite unintentionally; we have not seen this before."

Althai's face lit up with understanding, "I take comfort in your words and now understand your attentions towards me. Please know this; I am just as you are, no different though my being reflects the intensity of greatness that had surrounded me forever. Remember, it is not my own greatness at all; it belongs to another though he is most happy to share. If you had stood in my position from your very beginning, and onward, then it would be I that marvel at you."

Eleneke, Asher, Darién and Althai eventually remove themselves from the jubilant crowd. With the primary task complete, it is time for the four beings to search out the location of their Chosen and re-join them upon the Tactile Plains. Most often, the positioning of the Chosen is easy to find, but this was not one of those times.

After the initial surprise, the Eirtherol look out toward each place that holds favourable destinies toward the four little ones. After all, the Chosen, being somewhat unpredictable, could have advanced their position before the due time. However, this also is not the case.

Eleneke speaks her mind, "I do not feel them, and I do not feel any connection between them and the In-Between Places either." Darién and Asher nod their agreement and the three look toward Althai. With widening eyes, Althai's powerful voice rings out with understanding. "Covered, they are covered with the Cloaks of Hopelessness. The Lesser Princes are desperate to separate them." Even as his voice chimed, the atmosphere split and the Eirtherol returned into the Cambrae Sphere.

★

"**T**hey are coming back for the Grovels," yelps Calamity. "It would be best for us to leave now." With panic overtaking her, she quickly directs her pets away from Cara and Wry, and, grasping the imps by their throats, re-leashes them. Avril, disguising her irritation, slips backward into the In-Between Places, followed immediately by Harshaw and Calamity.

The Eirtherol, seeing the state of the tactile inhabitants, experience deep tenderness toward them. Quick to relieve, they pull the cumbersome Cloaks of Hopelessness from the small and burdened bodies of the Chosen, then release comfort upon them.

"You have fought hard Isabella," Eleneke whispers as she places one hand upon the small of Isabella's back and the other behind her head. She directs her whispers toward Isabella's ear and sings melodies that release internal bubbles from the Invisible Realms, causing them to rise more quickly inside of the Chosen's body. As the bubbles rise up, they explode, and by their content, expel the remainder of barren-slick.

As the malicious elements leave the rest of the Chosen, Asher and Darién release their own sounds. Their melodies, soothing as a salve to the areas that barren-slick had penetrated. The weakened places are quickly fortified and provided protection, allowing time for the healing of each inconsistency.

Althai moves around to each of the Chosen. He does not make his sound. Instead, he slips through to the Invisible Realm, and then back again, many times in each moment, carrying back the atmosphere from the Invisible Place, then breathing it over, and into each one.

As the activity of the Eirtherol continues, one of the Chosen's appearances begins to change. Moments before, Cara had been dulled, almost grey, but now, she was flushed with colour and brilliance. Feeling the great sense of relief, she relishes the lightness experienced, and laughs.

It was at this point that a most divine union took place. The Invisible and the Tactile collided together as the substance of Cara's laughter intermingles with the whispering melody from Eleneke. At their joining, their totality becomes much more than Eleneke's whispers plus Cara's contributions. What became was an entirely new and powerful force.

This new energy erupts into the air, causing the boundary between the seen and unseen to lessen. Each Chosen begins to perceive the activity that surrounds them with their eyes, though only as a faint silhouette. Then, each Eirtherol stoops down until directly looking into the eyes of their Chosen, and once in position, Althai releases his siren. The outlines become precise figures as the boundaries of time and space temporarily collapsed. Each Chosen examines the visible face of their Eirtherol.

Drawing no breath, the chosen experience a mixture of both excitement and terror. The Eirtherol quickly assure each one that no harm would befall them. Knowing what they heard was the truth, Isabella, Aaron, Cara and Wry began to breathe again, though very shallowly at first, as they attempt to contain themselves. After a few more moments, the boundaries once again, re-established themselves, though not entirely. For now, the Chosen are able to witness a little more of the Invisible than they had been able to capture before.

Isabella was the first to speak. Her words directed toward Eleneke, "I find security as I look on your face, for now, I have seen it more than once. My very survival was guaranteed at your hand. It was you that kept me from entering my death upon the boat." Eleneke did not reply.

A heartfelt and mutual understanding resonated within both beings, formed at that moment between them. Isabella now knew what Eleneke had known all along. Although they are separate, their destinies are, and always had been, deeply connected. Isabella rests on a profound sense of security that she dared not feel before, and Eleneke relished her recognition.

Suddenly, a loud voice interrupts the appreciative party. "We should do it now, now, this very moment," shrieks Cara. Unable to restrain her own sense of excitement any longer, she continues. "Let us listen to what we cannot see, well I mean, to what we could not see.

Perhaps we can hear better now, that our eyes have become a little more, opened."

Isabella, Aaron and Wry did not use their voices; they just placed their awestruck bodies down upon the surface of the ground in agreement. Cara quickly sat down too.

The air in the room was still highly charged, and in this environment, the Chosen heard many hope-filled things. They became aware of effective plans awaiting their acceptance, along with upgraded knowledge meant to dispel places of myth and disillusionment in their own personal thinking. Also, they were acquainted with unknown talents and shown how these gifts strengthened, balanced and complimented each other.

Isabella, Aaron, Cara, and Wry succumb to bouts of uncontrollable laughter, as they are suddenly aware of the company they belong to in the In-Between Places, realising they never have, or never will be, alone. This jubilance significantly increases when they perceive their victory, though not yet obtained. Along with the extreme emotion, or perhaps because of it, a sudden apprehension grew. Not sure that their bodies could take this intensity of joy, the Chosen began to withdraw themselves.

As they withdraw, the atmosphere returns to its normal state, almost. For now, a residue was to follow them, always. The four, elated by the experience, chatter and laugh, amazed to be included in something so unique. Isabella falls quiet, collating her thoughts into shareable form. "It is clear to me, we are to pack and be on our way, for if we stay here we could stagnate and forget the urgency of our vision altogether. Has anyone come know where we need to go next, for it is not printed in my heart?"

Aaron replies, "I did not hear where our destination is either, but I did hear this, time will not wait for an appointment has been set, and it will not be changed again, so you and I agree on this Isabella, there is much urgency in our leaving."

Then, quite unexpectedly, the answer that they were searching for came. Cara and Wry, having both heard the same answer, spoke it out simultaneously, "Emphara." Wry continues on, "I asked in my heart, and I heard, Emphara, we are to go to Emphara." There is silence for a moment as Isabella and Aaron began to digest this distasteful suggestion. "The land of the slaves?" questioned Aaron. Wry continued, "I feel it is the way we should go though I doubt strongly that it is where we will settle. It is there, in the land of the slaves, where we will be handed the compass needed for us to continue our track, the compass from Isabella's night vision." Wry's face, overtaken by a frown, appears a little less confident, as he continues, "For it is the compass that holds the key?" Pausing, he attempts to decipher his words, and then continued, "I do not think we will find our destination until we take this next step."

Each Chosen instantly receives a conviction that the words of Wry were correct. Therefore, with all in agreement, they would depart from Malcarve- the Ruined City, as soon as was possible, and make their way toward the frightful land.

★

"**I** have seen something that will exhaust your capacity to ever overestimate these Grovels again," snapped Avril. "Do you see it; there is something that is piercing the light of that one over there? It is small, yet it exists." Avril extends her hand, indicating to the form of a Chosen as he appears in the In-Between Places.

The Cambrasian had grown considerably in this realm and was now standing just a little smaller than a giant does. His considerable stature had also increased in density, and that extra density provides more space to carry light, the compound light from the Invisible Realm, the same light that repels the Princes. "Look now!" screeches Avril.

Harshaw and Calamity hesitate because of the discomfort it would cause them, yet, they knew to obey Avril. The pair shielded their eyes the best they could and searched out the form pointed out to them.

What they saw, they did not expect. "This is not the Grovel that I thought would lend itself to our workings. There is a full opening for a deposit. In fact, that dark shard that pierces its light lends itself to something specific," replies Harshaw. Calamity, rolling forward onto her toes, jeers, "That one has held to a fear, it thinks it be part of him. So, let it be part of him."

Knowing what they must now do, the Lesser Princes leapt into a small and generally vacant space that existed just outside of the familiar realms. It was an eerie space, one without walls, doors, windows or floors. Having no bottom, top or sides, it contains no direction or movement at all. There was only darkness, blackness, emptiness and a very pronounced silence.

Upon arrival, the Lesser Princes found the need to acclimatise, for, even the reality of their own thoughts are challenged by the dark nothingness surrounding them. In fact, the only proof the Princes have of their continued existence is a constrictive pressure that surrounds their forms in tight confinement. Avril, Harshaw and Calamity each take a moment to bask in the unparalleled level of discomfort, and then rapidly return to the pressing task set before them.

With just perception to guide them, the Princes search thoroughly and continually until they sense a presence of a small figure in the nothingness. The closer the Princes get, the more anxious the little creature became, and the more anxious it became, the more it gives away its own position.

With arms and legs no longer content in the safety of containment, the creature begins to flail about, thrashing in the distress of being located. As its terror increases, so does its sound, and in hopes of deterring those that intrude upon it, it lets out a shrill whistle-like scream. The scream it releases is to no avail, for the sound disappears, instantly swallowed by the alarming compression holding everything together throughout the forsaken place.

Avril violently yanks Harshaw and Calamity in close to her side. Pulling their heads toward her mouth, she speaks. "That creature is not aware that it has a name; in fact, it remains completely ignorant of anything else other than what it feels. Beyond mad, this place, this void of a location outside of the familiar realms, is the safest position that this creature believes there to be, where the emptiness and compression contain it, and the darkness shields its eyes."

"What a fool," Mocks Calamity, pulling away from Avril, "For it has bound itself to this small chamber." Without mercy, the Lesser Princes wrench it up from its place of hiding and smother it with heavy cloth, then, secure the material with sturdy rope. Avril kicks the covered creature until it gave up all resistance, then, in silence, the Princes return to the In-Between Places, captive in tow, waiting for an opportune time.

★

Having prepared themselves throughout the Lesser Lights glow, the Chosen began their dubious journey wearied, and, though only half way through the Daystar's passage, they were in need of rest. The tiredness that each one experienced was more than just an unrested body, for, as their bodies were, so was their minds.

It was not long ago that they walked through, and feebly escaped, an ordeal with the unseen. Though generally recovered from the physical symptoms, the blow to their morale was still very real. The questions that the occurrence posed were indeed pertinent, and each Chosen needed to deal with the imposing thoughts that had presented.

Within the privacy of their own minds, Isabella, Aaron, Wry and Cara start to comprehend the strong opposition working against them. *I am too weak of myself to win against such brutal force, at least presently. Yet, if I stand in the thickness of Invisible, I am convinced that no such weaknesses matter, not at all. Nevertheless, I feel the power of my frailty the moment I no longer feel the Invisible.* Isabella's thoughts reflect those of her friends, as they grapple with the great discouragement of knowing themselves.

Fighting hard against this self-doubt clamouring for position in their heads, they use understanding revealed to them by the Invisible, refuting its claim. Still they are unsuccessful, beaten by a single notion; their own strength had failed; it was something else that spared them.

Clearly, they are at the mercy of something or someone they knew little of, and though the Invisible remains a great comfort to them, it presents humbling uncertainty. Cara speaks, "Something is holding esteem for us, attributing high value for our worth. It gives direction, aid, and this is wonderful, beyond words. Though I cannot help but think about what would happen should it choose not to, should we displease it, most especially in a place like Emphara. I know it is the right thing to do, to go there, yet, I would not have even imagined going that way of my own volition. That place holds much danger."

Wry, looking carefully at the most precious of his friends, moved with sorrow seeing her suffer in that way. Motivated to help her, he offers his opinion to his companions. "I strongly suggest that we stop here for a while. The journey ahead is fraught with complications, and we will need to be in top condition to navigate it. Let us wait until first light, take advantage of the safety in the land we remain upon, for we are all but spent." To his proposal, there is no objection.

Aaron and Wry, experiencing the need for solitude, say their goodbyes and seek out a place to be alone. Isabella and Cara cleave together in conversation. "Cara," spoke Isabella tenderly, "Will you join me as I practice listening to the unseen again. It seems, to me at least, easier when we are together. I think that we may need some help." Cara contains a muffled giggle at the idea of their many weaknesses, and then quickly agrees. "Of course I will".

The pair, spying an attractive grassy area, walks directly to it. Sitting down, they close their eyes tightly, intent on banishing anything that would steal away their concentration. The moment their eyelids touched, a gathering of blue wrens joins them in an adjacent tree and begins to chirp out their chattering melodies. As this birdsong fills the air, it draws the women, out from the confines of their own minds, and into the song. They relax further. "It's like those birds want to help us," whispered Cara. The sounds, impressing upon them further, remove the consciousness of all other distraction.

Out from languid peace, the women quickly move into attentiveness as they witness a picture growing in their hearts, one that they did not expect to see. This vision begins agreeably enough. Between them, they see a being of great beauty. Entirely constructed with golden light, he stands tall. There is ease about him, a peacefulness that brings Isabella and Cara great reassurance.

Next, a shadowy figure stood near, but undetected. It began to make for itself a shade from the light that emanated from the being, then, when it had completed its task, it approached the being of light in secret. The figure hid behind anything that would shelter it until it was close enough to touch the golden being.

Remaining hidden, the menacing figure cast a spear through the being of light, and though the spear is quickly withdrawn, a shard of darkness and void remained. The being of light placed his hand into the hole that the spear had made and began tugging at it in discomfort, and, in doing so; he caused the void to grow larger.

Then, most quickly, two more shadowy figures joined the first one, though they did not bother to hide, for the being of light, too occupied with the dark shard, and did not notice them. Between the two new figures, they carried a dark grey sack that moaned and turned and shook. Acting quickly, the first shadowy figure wrenched open the beings mouth and then, the other two figures cast the contents of the sack into it.

A small thrashing creature rolled its way down the mouth, and then through the body of the light one until it joined up with the wound from the spear. Once in place, it changed shape to adhere to every gap made available to it.

Suddenly, the shapeless face of the thrashing creature was looking eye to eye with Isabella and Cara. Its form began to change and take on features that were not its own. Slowly, the shape resembled a Cambrasian; a distorted image of one they knew and loved. "He looks somewhat familiar," Cara yelled with fright. "No, please no," realises Isabella, "not him."

Neither Isabella nor Cara witnessed the entire scenario; they saw only pieces of the shocking scene, yet both women were convinced of one notion. As uncomfortable as the situation was, the vision was given for their benefit, for this was, quite clearly, a forewarning. A feeling of unrest fell upon Isabella and Cara as, having never experienced such a thing before; they did not know what to do.

Eleneke and Althai were watching Isabella and Cara from where the blue wrens had settled at the beginning of their meeting. They had been standing underneath the trees, cloaked in the Invisible; yet, the birds knew where they were and flocked toward them.

"Let us go over to them, they look bewildered," chimed Althai. So, both Eirtherol walked toward the Chosen to bring about reassurance. As the Eirtherol drew closer, the atmosphere around the women lightened, and this time, the presence of the invisible beings were immediately recognised. "Thank you for coming to us, we are in need of you," Isabella's words poured straight from her vulnerable heart.

Both Eirtherol embraced the warmth of their recognition by the ones that they love and took action. They called upon the atmosphere of the Invisible Realm and placed it over and around the chosen until they were entirely contained within its safety.

The inviting atmosphere of the Invisible Realm drew toward itself entities from the same origin. Responding to this magnetism, the women's bodies release the Invisible embedded within their own beings. Tiny incandescent bulbs pop open inside of them, changing form to become instantly recognisable in the tactile places. Words, feelings and impressions tumble upward into hearts and minds, revealing the entirety of depth that the bulbs contain.

Once the otherworldly exchange is complete, Althai, gesturing with his hands, loosens the atmosphere of the Invisible Realm from around the Chosen and receives it back into his own body. The Eirtherol stay for a little longer, making sure that the Chosen have received the courage they needed, and then left the pair to mull over their own impressions.

Isabella and Cara, sensing the change of atmosphere, recognise that they were now alone. "I am filled with fresh courage though I do not know what should be done about the forewarning," Cara replies, "I have no particular reassurance for what lies ahead either."

"But I do know this," Cara takes the hand of her shaken friend, "That I will lend you my strength in times of need, and you will give me yours. We will stand together, and we will stand strong." Having taken comfort in the assurance of their connected hearts, they walked back toward the encampment.

★

Aaron and Wry make their way up the small, well-trodden path toward the makeshift campsite where they would soon spend the night. Wry's pace quickens as he sees Cara waiting for him and soon, he takes a seat at her side. Isabella rushes to meet Aaron on the path, and, taking his hand, she guides him backward to seek their solitude.

The two, rapidly growing in deep affection for each other, display a mutual tenderness. Yet it is evident to both, that neither is prepared to explore the possibility any further, at least not until they had found the elusive destination that offered more privacy.

After walking a little further away, the two sit down underneath a tall tree near a small and rocky stream. As the birds sang, and the water trickled, Isabella reclined into the arms of Aaron. Listening to the beat of his heart, she drew in quiet, but full breaths, gathering her courage to speak.

Sitting up, Isabella looks directly into the eyes of the one she loves, "Aaron, you are like no other that I have ever known. Your friendship with me runs so deep that I care not to imagine this existence without having known it. I am continually intrigued by your carefree strength, unencumbered by the opinions and enticements of others.

But, there is something I must say to you although I do fear that your strength could now become your weakness as I need to tell you something that may feel, on your part, as an intrusion."

Aaron looked confused, as though he was expecting another conversation altogether. "Continue on, I am listening." Evidence of tenderness returned to his face.

Isabella presses herself to continue, "I have seen something that has set itself against you. It has found within you a position to hide and is seeking out for comfort. When we were in Malcarve – The Ruined City, we all succumbed to something that we could not see. Thoughts began to fight for position in our minds, thoughts with intent to take us over, to separate us, to cause us great fear." Aaron nods. Isabella content with his response continues. "Yet we, with the aid of things unknown, could separate from the internal terror, and we have become stronger and wiser." She blows out her breath and inhales, long and slow, through her nose, then closing her eyes, she continues, "Aaron," she spoke cautiously, "Aaron, I think that there is a matter that was left unsettled within your own heart. One that has enticed you into accepting its validity and it is in that very fear that an enemy will try to become your undoing. The matter can be easily settled, though unpleasant for a moment. You must search out what it is that you have held on to, and then expel it with the truth. You will, by this action, take footing from one that attempts to make a claim upon you."

Aaron was feeling disappointed. He had expected an entirely different and more pleasant conversation, but now, indignation rose up inside against his closest of friends. Her words to him were like sharp needles, prickling into his wide-open heart. Not trusting her intention, he quickly changes the depiction that he held of Isabella within his heart, creating an invisible barrier that Isabella would not be able to cross.

Isabella looks into the face of Aaron again, hoping that he had received her well. His reserve was so subtle that outwardly, it was undetectable, and appearances told her that he had accepted her words and the manner in which she intended them. Yet, at the same time, doubt rang out in her heart. *Perhaps it was not a good idea to speak that way to him, perhaps there was another way to do it.* Quickly, she silenced that thought and reasons with herself, *I worry needlessly, for he knows me well and trusts my heart toward him.* Aaron smiles, his handsome face covering the pain, and Isabella is satisfied.

Chapter 4

A stream of light pours out from the Invisible Realm and into Eleneke's being. She ponders.

Numa, now dominating the skies, throws down her harsh red beams. Accompanied by the blistering heat and searing winds, her demeanour promotes an atmosphere of violent extremes.

Undoubtedly, this star also reflects the path forward for the Chosen. In one moment, they will witness many marvellous things, and then in the next, they will fall to their knees in despair. I must bring them strength to bear it.

It was the beginning of a new season. The hue of colour in the sky begins to deepen as Numa, the red Daystar, takes her turn in the place of prominence. The Chosen, surrounded by a throng of Eirtherol, enter the borders of Emphara.

Emphara has no walls. Its outskirts are defined by ill maintained and shabby wire fences that are disconnected and falling down. At the periphery of the province stands the occasional guarding station, but the residing rulers rely mostly upon its reputation as a deterrent to any intruders.

The Chosen, guided by Eirtherol, began sensing their surroundings. A peculiar odour hangs in the air, smelling like a mixture of sweat and blood. "That sickening stench reminds me of the sadness that this land is built upon. The Kings, they were cruel. They procured, and upheld this land, paying a high price, though not from their own pockets.

In premeditated fashion, these rulers, using currency as the vehicle, oppressed the people of these lands, slowly at first, and then increasingly, until, brimming over with the worries of poverty, they no longer remembered their desires, and forgot how to exercise their own wills.

With freedom forgotten, they quickly accepted any crumb thrown at them, and spent their lives, ultimately, for the wealth of others. The Kings of this land, believing they had found the methodology for success, still operate in the same way." Aaron spoke with both sorrow and anger.

Cara began to weep silently for the land and its inhabitants. As the tears well up in her eyes, she expertly brushes them away in a manner that would not be recognised by others. Althai however, paying her particular attention, drew quickly near.

Looking deeply into her dampened eyes, he read the stories that played out in each tear. For in her tears, memorials were released, memorials that acknowledged the lives of those that had gone unnoticed, despite their significant value. Althai filled with compassion and wonder toward the young woman, for she had retained the extraordinarily soft heart that she wields. He whispers, "This is a great gift you bring Cara, you are of rare beauty."

The Voyagers continue their journey even though their particular destination within the land remains hidden. "I say we follow our peace, and move slowly around the outer boundaries until we are all sure of heart." Wry's suggestion goes uncontested and in this careful manner, they continue.

Isabella observes in silence as the sledge pulls upon external forces to fulfil its needs. She looks downward, and back, at the lines drawn in the dust by the blades as it slowly passes post after post after post, and then watches as the lines, quickly covered over by the winds.

Remaining quiet, she closes her eyes to take a glimpse of what she could not see. Now that her physical sights no longer dominate her senses, she soon recognised the arcane sadness that had settled in the air. It flittered across her face as the sledge forged forward and with it, told wordless tales of woe.

This same sadness is embedded in the grainy flecks of soil that flew up from the ground and settled on the floor of the sledge. Isabella reached down to the floor of the sledge and picked a pinch of the substance. Again, closing her eyes, she senses the unseen. *This spirit has settled for such a long time upon this land that it believes itself to be a part of the terrain.*

Isabella wonders about the people from Emphara, living upon the terrain. *Each time you take a breath of air into your lungs, do you ingest this foul substance; are you coated on the inside with hopelessness and sadness?*

When you eat of the earth and its fruits, swallowing more, does it confirm to you, inwardly, that all is lost?

Isabella, continuing to ponder, senses another notion vying for attention. Alerted, she opens her eyes and looks around at the pitiful landscape. As she does, an inconsistency presents to her. Placing a hand on her middle, she acknowledges the fluttering of the tiny bubbles of knowing breaking up and through. Isabella gratefully receives the outlandish viewpoint into her thoughts.

Impressions, both new and old, mix and meld until the new account becomes clearer and a completed image, now formed. This picture told a story of immense hope and a future for both the land and the people of Emphara. The perfection of the image grew within, so much so, that her previously shallow and sombre breath, deepened and filled her lungs with such exhilaration that it soon overtook her whole being. Yet, she doubted herself and refused to speak it.

Eleneke, who had been watching the Chosen all along, laughed at Isabella's uncertainly. "Easily remedied," she whispered. Eleneke placed her hand upon Isabella's shoulder and released her own voice to the doubter. "Don't be afraid to speak, for you carry hope for many, a hope specially designed to come from you."

Though Isabella was not aware of the words spoken over her, they were effective nonetheless. She quickly dismissed all uncertainty to accommodate the new picture, allowing it to take up her every thought once again; through this action, exhilaration returned and she could not help but speak.

"Great things will come to this land and its people. Just like a desert after a long and hot season, it is dry, cracked, and scorched, yet, when the rain comes, the land lives again. All manner of life will show itself, flourishing in the freshness of the restored terrain. The people of this area will gather their own strength when they see the hope springing up before them, for, that which they thought had died, was now alive; that which they thought had abandoned them had never actually left in the first place. It was always there, just concealed below a bleakly painted canvas." Her words ceased though she knew there was more to speak. Then, as a fullness of understanding opened up to her she concludes, "Emphara will become what it was made to be; it will be splendid, parading all its desirable and compelling distinctions once again."

As Isabella's mouth released the words, the substance of them flowed over her teeth and across her lips, and then flowed on through to greet the outer tactile sphere. The freed elements of word travel undetectable in the fresh air to a small, yet well-worn groove, that connects the Tactile Plain with the In-Between Places. The groove envelopes the substance gratefully and assists its movement by thrusting the substance forward until its next destination is met.

Along that same groove, follow a small number of tiny lights that resided quietly within Isabella's body. Once released from her body, the little lights locate the substance of word and join to them, marrying the Tactile to the Invisible and increasing its total capacity. The enlarged substance then pulsates and stretches until it forms into a pattern of unfamiliar though intricate beauty.

Eleneke, gratified by what she witnessed, bought further reassurance to Isabella. "Those words of knowing that you have formed with your mouth will grow larger as they attract others to see the same and to speak the same. When the allotted time comes, they will burst open onto this land and cause the very same thing that you have just seen. For your words, and the words of the Invisible, have agreed to something, and that is a powerful thing." Isabella, not hearing Eleneke with her ears, nor seeing her with her eyes, still understood the communication. All of a sudden, deep within her stomach, Isabella just knew, and was again, flooded with joy.

★

After a long time of travelling the outer edges of Emphara, they finally select a place of entry. With skies darkening and the winds retreating, the choosing of it seemed obvious to all.

The stillness was eerie in the near darkness and the level surface of the land attributed to sounds echoing from further than the eye could see. Yet what disturbed the travellers more were the giant shadows that cast themselves around, hiding what may have stood beneath them. Some tall and slim, as though cast from a Cambrasian, while others were broad and seeming depth, looking like small lakes upon the grounds surface.

As the sledge drew nearer to the shadows, their secrets are revealed. Monuments, carved from the minerals that made Emphara a once wealthy land, were erected with intent to intimidate any army that entered. They told stories of victory in battle by immortalising the defeated and displaying their unfortunate demise.

Aaron, being educated about Emphara by his uncle, shared his understanding. "If you look closer, you will notice that these statues no longer reveal the message they were intended for. For now, they show that the lands borders are left mostly unattended. See, the statues were once filled with precious stones, stones that boasted of their wealth, superiority, and a complete, self-sufficient abundance."

Pointing out the missing pieces in the statues, he continues, "Though now, they reveal their lessening riches and lack of allies. See, for the gems, they are missing, most all of them taken, but not only the stones. Parts of the minerals chipped out and sold by natives and sojourners alike. If this land still stood in the power that it once had, the statues would continue to be well maintained. The only power these lands have is fear though that is certainly an efficient taskmaster."

As the sledge pressed slowly on, the other, larger shadows reveal their mysteries. Quarries, large, open quarries, carved out of the rocky ground.

The stillness of the surroundings influences the posture of the Chosen, and they fall into thoughtful silence once again. Isabella follows her mind as it wanders back toward the little Volcano Isle that had been her home. She could not help but reflect on her providence there. Thoughts fell toward her parents and friends, her possessions and her working life, seeking and sorting, then meandered for a while and inevitably, changing their direction.

It could have been me; it could have been my people suffering this appalling existence, spent under the hands of the overbearing slave masters; after all, I did not choose the place of my own birth. Chills run across her body as the unnerving thoughts continue. *Maybe I should have stayed with my own kind in my own land. Perhaps my dissatisfaction is an ignorant greed.*

Immediately, Isabella, shaking herself, decides that this frailty of mind is just a fleeting moment. Drawing the cold air, she takes a long, deep breath, pulls back her shoulders, straightens her fallen posture, and listens to the deeper knowing that continues directing her.

Eleneke watches proudly as Isabella arrested and immobilised the moment of weakness. Then, pouring out the strength of her own quality to undergird it, she whispers, "You left a place of privilege to follow an undefined path. A path dimly lit before your feet, one that poses both risk, and promise. Selfish and greedy, I think not!"

Isabella never considering herself privileged before knew now that it was true. With spirits further lifted, her mind soaring and her courage increased she accepts Eleneke's words as truth, and welcomes them into her own agreeable thoughts.

Asher, Althai, and Darien look toward the passengers in the sledge with great pleasure and again feel the tremendous elation of joining to this company. As the sensation takes over their whole being, it escapes from their form and, surpassing the sombreness of the environment, presses its benefit into each of the four Chosen. Isabella, Aaron, Cara and Wry experience a joyful surge entering their own physicality, lightening their mood and strengthen their resolve.

★

The Greater Light of Numa continues its cycle across the open skies with Acar traveling quietly behind; its dark red glow radiates, and heats up every visible surface. The Chosen, feeling the full force of her rays, encroach deeper into the ominous land. Carefully, they forge their way onward through deserted towns, towns that had once prospered from the now emptied mines.

Traveling further and further in, they approach the centre of the land and happen upon a quarry. At first glance, it appears long abandoned and emptied of anything holding value; promising the offer of much-needed respite. The Chosen inspect further. There, intact, lies a wooden ramp. Slightly left of centre, the ramp had been fashioned to carry heavy machinery safely into its belly, constructed with many layers of sturdy wood is, of course, strong enough to allow for the full weight of sledge and passengers combined.

The next evidence of safety considered regards its sound. The quarry, though cavernous and wide, seemed to prefer to reside in anonymity. Each sound cast into the pit makes its way toward the porous surfaces of the quarry walls. The walls, dampening out the sound, leave an auspicious silence in its wake. Satisfied again of its safety, the Chosen proceed.

Peculiarly, upon the quarry floor stood a sturdy wooden water trough, unbroken and unaffected by age, and even more oddly, fresh water, during the dry term of Numa, fills it. For this reason, the Chosen had ascertained their next place of shelter. The four companions, in need of refreshing, quickly wash, drink and eat before taking the opportunity to sleep.

As the skies turned to brightness, the recharged Chosen arise. In solitude, they go for a brisk walk around on the surface of the quarry, preparing their bodies for action while surveying the land with inner and outer eyes. Then reconnecting, they fix and ingest their morning meal.

The Eirtherol assembled around the encamped Chosen. With mouth opening slightly, and then pursing closed again, it was easy to recognise that Althai was eager to talk. "Hold your tongue no more Althai speak," laughs Asher, feeling entertained. All eyes turn toward the Eirtherol, who is clearly having difficulty containing his excitement.

Althai's eyes glint and his mouth drew up into a closed smile. Throwing his hands in the air, he sends images into the minds of his companions, pictures of things revealed to him at an earlier time. The pictures take some moments to understand, for the Eirtherol know well to release preconception before they receive from anyone.

Althai, becoming more buoyant with anticipation, shuffles out a little dance. Looking at his friends faces, it was unmistakable, "Almost, Almost. You almost have it" he sings.

The images grow clearer and clearer in their minds until Eleneke, Asher and Darién can make no mistake about what they have viewed. Now, holding to the same excitement as Althai, are eager to receive further information.

"As you can clearly see, the Chosen have grown substantially in the In-Between Places. They are ready." Eleneke, Darién and Asher, eyes as large as saucers, hang on to each word proceeding from his mouth. "What are they ready for? Do not play with us now Althai!" bounces out Darién smiling his broadest. Althai, amused, continues on, "Well, we are here, in the place that every Eirtherol hopes to see. That is right; we can lead the Chosen straight past the In-Between Places and right into the invisible Realms, immediately. The Lesser Princes can overhear nothing and certainly cannot add their own interpretations. The Chosen are prepared enough, and ready to come; they will follow you through. Today, they will begin to learn to live their lives out of the Invisible!"

Without wasting a moment, the Eirtherol start calling and cooing and singing out their invitations toward the Chosen. An agreeable sensation enters the Tactile Plain, pressing heavily upon each physical body present. Isabella, Aaron, Cara and Wry respond immediately by accepting the call, and permitting the substance to stay with them. The Eirtherol happily release heavier and more intoxicating songs, and as they do, this activity upon the Tactile Plain increases. The Cambrasian bodies feel the introduced substance and grow heavier than gravity. They lay down.

Peace, hope and happiness increase, their elements fill each nearby place void of good. As this Invisible transfer continues, the free space swells up, becoming much heavier than before. The mounting pressure causes immense warmth upon the bodies of the Chosen and pushes them down to the ground until they can no longer move at all.

"This portion is enough I think," States Eleneke, "Heavy enough to ensure they stay for a while, sufficiently dense to obscure distraction of any kind though not enough to leave them dazed for the complete cycle of Numa." Eleneke laughed out her words, for she felt so much joy for Isabella. Then, turning to Althai, she asks, "Do we go straight through the In-Between Places, or can we start from the Invisible?" Althai smiles his largest, and answers what was already suspected, "Lets bypass the mixed up places altogether." Eleneke squeals with delight and the songs continue.

★

The four bodies still sprawled across the dry Emphara soil after much passing time, perspired in the hot Numa breeze. The Eirtherol, now sitting atop of the Chosen's bodies, stare into the faces of the beings they love, openly laughing at soft smiles, and beaming countenance reflecting the Chosen's total fulfilment. "It is a good thing that no one is near. For our little ones would appear dead to those who do not understand. Most happily dead, obviously, but dead none the less." Darién mused aloud.

For, though the air breathed in upon the Cambrasian ground still nurtures their physical bodies, their inner beings are not contained. Having been broken free of the laws that bind them physically to their bodies, they abide in the place of their conception.

Lacking from corporeal restraint, the four un-expecting tactile beings attempt to make sense of their new environment. However, no comprehension they hold can contain it. Their only option is to retire all previous understanding, and in a childlike manner, receive the new information unquestioning. For, no knowledge that they possess could hold this acute awareness of existence, the intensity of emotion, and ever presenting wellbeing that they experienced. A silent question presented to each one of their hearts, *have I ever known life before?*

Sharp colour and eccentric sound, indistinguishable through tactile lenses, are in abundance, further confounding their intensified states. Colour melts into colour and sound into sound, revealing the outline of form, shapes and beings, though the Chosen, holding no relevant framework, cannot recognise them that way. They see only a wash of multi-coloured light, varying in density and hue, with the whooshing of sounds breaking through its solidity and leaving a less compacted impression.

Isabella, Aaron, Cara and Wry, regarding this condition as a by-product of the unique surroundings, surrender freely to the situation of now knowing. Although powerless in the beauty of their experience, they feel rich and profound peace.

The Eirtherol stay with the Chosen, upon their bodies in the Tactile Plain, and with their beings in the Invisible. Their own excitements rise to such a degree that their bodies expand to contain it. Once filled to capacity, the distended beings release, erupting into a mass of exploding lights, popping, crackling, emitting colour after colour into both Invisible and Tactile.

As the otherworldly light show plays out, they stare, one to another, Eirtherol to Chosen, Chosen to Eirtherol, and Chosen to Chosen. There and then, all barriers to perception, to interpretation, are gone, leaving no room for misdiagnosis due to lack of knowledge and understanding. Now, really looking at each other, they could see perfectly well, perfectly clearly, that their own beauty and that of their companions is immense.

Isabella, thinking back to when she was in her body, realises the vast difference between then and now. She could now connect every thought, every sensation and every function of her body. Things previously considered separate, or gone unnoticed, now intermingle and enhance each other instantaneously. Even sensation originating from her toes drew lines of knowing into all other parts of her body. The information it contains, just as pertinent to her fingers as it is to her mind.

On examining further, she notices that, even information received through the tips of Cara's hair is for her own benefit also, and though she understands the distinction between Cara and herself, the connection is undeniable. "There is such a complicated integration that connects me to you, and you, and you. I can draw sense from you just as I draw sense from myself." Her friends understand Isabella's statement, though not adequately put, as it is their own experience also. After having processed this new idea for a little longer, a conversation began.

Eleneke starts, "Now that you are here, in a way, you will never leave." She smiles a convincing smile and then continues. "That is to say, this is your home, the Invisible, even though you live in the Tactile Plain; you are in both places at the same time, just like now. Isabella, Aaron, Wry and Cara, you all carry the Invisible Realm in you, you always have really, but now, becoming aware of it, you know to access it at any time. You can pull the substance of Invisible right through to the Cambrasian Sphere. Like Midwives from the Invisible Places, learning as you go, to bring the very best into each place, bringing its goodness to both land and inhabitants. You are set to take part in this reformation, this recognition of Original Intent."

Appreciating both the privilege and humility of their situation, the Chosen became silent. *What does it all mean?* They ponder, and, upon that question, the answers were ready to be born.

Surprisingly the level of depth falls out from their minds as playfulness overtakes. Isabella, Aaron, Wry and Cara, drawn to investigate their own creative abilities, relax into their now unhindered imaginations. Remembering things previously hoped for, both large and small, they form tiny worlds situated within little globes residing inside their expanding hearts. The globes, filled with inspiration, grow in detail until eventually; they burst out from the imaginations of the Chosen, and stand in the reality of the Invisible.

The Eirtherol stay quiet, and not wanting to distract the Chosen, take a few steps back. With mouths softly upturned and eyes immersed, their focus gives over completely to the curious little beings. Watching on quietly, they prepare to enjoy being spectators of this experimental play

Cara, the most hospitable of the friends, succeeded first. Many tables, uniform in size, decorated extravagantly with colourful and exotic fabrics, held the finest of foods most exquisitely displayed. Vases spilling over with voluptuous bloom adorned the centre of these luxuriant tables. Names written in elaborate script upon cream coloured invitations, folded neatly, sealed, and tied in with purple ribbon, and placed upon the only smaller sized table, ready for delivery.

Overhead, silken materials dangle and bulge, creating a marquee reminiscent of clouds. Lanterns become evident and torches shine their light, adding a romantic flicker to the environment. Cara smiles confidently, now risking full expression of her ambition. She brings about many more lights, but softens them to allow their light and shadow to define pathways upon the ground, now covered in plush, fawn coloured rugs. Cara pauses to regard her work, and considering pots, statues, and ornaments necessary, she further develops her design.

Cara pulls her dark hair back behind her shoulders. Mouth held open and eyes wide she lifts her chest and pulls back her shoulders, clearly proud of her work. "It is finished," proclaims Cara loudly, motioning with her hands for everyone to feast their eyes. Isabella partakes.

Giggling politely at first, and then more raucously, Isabella sees Aaron pulling gaudy statues from his own imagination, and placing them around Cara's elegant affair. Wry, motivated to do the same joins in, putting in his own silly additions to what was once perfectly splendid.

"Look what they do," reveals Isabella to Cara, who is clearly befuddled. "I will help you, Cara," Isabella laughs. She points toward her target, a large, ridiculous sea creature statue, situated by the entrance. "We cannot have that." Suddenly, the ugly creature is wearing a dress suit. "No one attending something this elegant should come underdressed." Cara, temporarily stunned, draws in a breath. Feigning displeasure, she frowns. Then, to the relief and amusement of all, Cara joins in with the game. In this way, the four played and practised their new talents for quite a while.

Isabella was the first to stop, preferring to observe her playful companions, their faces radiant with happiness as they continue in the game. Suddenly taken aback at the high quality of her friends, she steps back nearer the Eirtherol to immerse into deeper reflection. She had seen them this way before, but not as vividly. Her admiration grew. *I see who you are*; she thought merrily and continued her observation.

As time passed, Isabella turns her attentions solely toward Aaron. His cheerful countenance suddenly darkens as a disconcerted expression takes over. *Clearly, Aaron, you have concern.* As the playfulness winds down, Isabella searches for the space of quietness in which to enter, then walks toward the group, followed by the foreknowing Eirtherol. "What is it, Aaron?" She asks gently. Aaron thinks for a moment and then directs a question toward Asher, "But, what if the imagination turns darker?"

The comment quickly quieted any joviality that had been. "This power that you have access to comes directly from the Invisible Places. Therefore, only that from the Invisible can arise from you, and burst forth from you, and into a Cambrasian reality in any... flourishing way. Those that come from you, they are well meant, but lacking intuition are mostly flawed, not having the insight from the Invisible, they cannot succeed. At least, not in the way intended. Still, do not worry about that, for this too, is sure to be used for your sake, and still progress the vision of the Invisible.

If, however, a globe of imagining that is of darker quality arises from your inside, it is a clear indication to us that you need more truth to enter into your being. So, we will attend to your need, and the globe will not be released with any significant effect."

"But, globes that are formed from darker intent can be released from others, and effectively into the Tactile Plains. These globes can harm you. Nevertheless, even this can be used to your favour. You see the force that drives them, their power, their understanding, is from only two of the three commonly known realms, the lesser two. Their source does not come from the place where being actually originates." Asher continues talking to his wide-eyed audience. "Though, not every globe originating in this way is dark, some are intelligent and kind, administered with every bit of good intention, though without the abundant foresight of the Invisible Realm, they produce, less."

Aaron, not satisfied with this answer, interjects, "Then, why does the Cambrae Sphere seem to be collapsing under ill intent if there is not sufficient power in it? Are we the first to be given this tool from the Invisible?" "Absolutely not," spoke Althai with an amused ringing in his voice. Neither he nor the other Eirtherol is perturbed by the question, in fact, all gladly invited the probing. "There are many, many, many a Cambrasian with this tool. Most are completely unaware of it, and, of the ones that do know, many of these have been intimidated by the perception of their own weakness, but, that is about to change." The Eirtherol begin laughing at what seems to be a private joke.

"Think about this Aaron" spoke Eleneke, "If the power of the beings without the keys from the Invisible Realm seems great to you, and their influence on your Sphere so significant, then how much greater is that which will come to, and then from you, and ones like you. Individuals who were given the gift from the original source, and having paid attention to its voice, have developed and trained under its understanding?" With relieved hearts, the Chosen return to the joy and hope now making its residence within them.

Wave after wave of gratefulness poured over both minds and hearts as the Chosen recognised the extent of gifts given to them. With each new wave came deeper recognition, and with each realisation came a deeper wave. Within this circle of awareness, they rested.

Eleneke looked on at the blissful four resting in great peace. Their faces, drenched with fulfilment, displayed quiet smiles proving their complete delight. "To see you here is to see you as you were meant, free from worry, belonging wholly," she whispers to herself before addressing her companions in a louder voice. "It is with some regret that I tell you this, but, soon you must return to the Tactile Plain."

The Chosen open their eyes and lift themselves up into a seated position, eager for Eleneke's next words. "There is something that you need to grasp before you return. The gifts that have been given to you, the ones you have been practising here remain with you, always. However, once you return, they will not be evident immediately, and certainly not as easily accessed as you are now expecting. Nevertheless, do not let discouragement rob you. These gifts are yours, and there is a reason for the seeming delay. Just trust us." Smiling at the captive bunch, Eleneke continues. "As you give you attentions to the Invisible Places, your direction will be opened up to you. Nevertheless, you must prepare yourselves, for you will not know every step before you take it, and at times, you will feel quite unsure. Each one of you houses a deepening conviction that, the source from which you listen is good and trustworthy and worth your attentions, and at times, this will be your only stability."

"There is a picture in your hearts, a vague outline, a sense, a promise. It is the same picture you share, and it has propelled you all forward to this very place. When your path seems unclear, remember it, let it direct you, let it inspire you. For, what you are walking toward from the start, will be approaching you from the finish, and from before the start, making a way where there was none before. I have told you in words, but when you go back to the Tactile Plain's, your experience will bring you understanding in a more practical way." Eleneke concluded.

Althai walks into the centre of the group, draws tiny pictures in the air, whispers his words into them and sits down. "When you all return to the Tactile Plain, you will see waters. Tell the waters to flow; for it is there that, you will meet with a most authoritative of sources. It is there that you will find shelter and it is there that you will be confirmed in your believing."

"What waters?" Aaron's brows draw closer together, "You are full of puzzles." The Eirtherol looks directly into Aaron's eyes and smiles, "You Aaron will know. Trust, trust." With that, the invisible rolls back, revealing the solidity of the tactile realm once again.

★

The conversation was lively as the Chosen packed up the sledge for the next leg of their journey. Having carefully covering all trace of themselves, they walk to the water trough intent on refreshing their dwindling supplies. The water is cold and refreshing so the four take time in filling up their bottles.

"After all that, not one of us asked where we are to go!" Wry stated in amazement. Silence fell as each one realised they still had no direction. "Well, we know about speaking to the water and telling it to flow, so, there must be a river or stream nearby," Isabella remembered. Wry and Cara shook their heads "No, there is no body of water near here, it's practically a desert. I suspect that the water must be somewhere ahead. For surely it is not right to turn back to where we came from. That would not be safe for us, not in this cycle of lights. The masters of the Land are always looking for new recruits." Wry replied, looking at his beautiful mate, knowing she would be quickly sought after.

Aaron listened to his companions but he could not agree, for something was welling up within him, something undeniable. Having given all focus toward the growing feeling, he did not bother wasting time to explain. Turning his face toward the trough water, Aaron releases his words, "Water, flow." "Water flow," he repeated. Silenced, and somewhat bemused, Isabella, Wry and Cara watch on. A small, shallow ripple twirled upon the water's still surface, then disappears.

"Aaron, it is your breath that caused the ripple," Wry teased. "You are free to think your own thoughts Wry." Aaron, quite undeterred by his companions comment continues, repeatedly trying, but without result. "Look Wry, I know this seems peculiar to you, but I will not be influenced by your opinion. My heart is telling me something to the contrary and I know enough to listen to it. I need some time, I will be over there." He points toward a large boulder, lying alongside the quarry wall. "I will ask myself questions and examine the meaning of what I sense." Aaron, walking away from the group, makes his way toward the boulder.

With Aaron away, Isabella, Wry and Cara continue on filling the remaining water bottles. Before they had finished the chore, sounds ring out across the dusty quarry. Standing to attention, the three listen intently, trying to discern the cause. Clank, rustle, ting, rustle, the sounds come from inside the quarry. Someone is amongst them; someone is rummaging through their sledge.

Isabella, Cara and Wry run as quickly as they can toward their property. Wry and Isabella are swift, forging forward at good speed, whereas Cara, not being as fast, lags behind. Stopping briefly to catch her breath, Cara decides it much wiser to inform Aaron of the situation. So, at a quick walking pace she returns.

By this time, Isabella and Wry had arrived at the sledge and could clearly see, sitting amongst their possessions, a young boy. The boy looks up at them, his dilemma is written all over his small face. Clearly, having little chance of escape, the boy cowers and begs toward the bemused duo looking on.

Isabella, still out of breath, gently reaches out her hand to touch the boy with intent to calm him down, but his fear is so great that he does not recognise the tenderness of her gesture. Instead, fearing the worst, he grabs her extended hand and bites down hard. Shrieking out from the pain, Isabella violently pulls her hand away from the boy and holds it in toward her body. The boy, surprisingly alarmed by her reaction, attempts to push past her, but Wry, now stood behind Isabella, quickly apprehends him.

He kicks, punches, and squeals, but to no avail. He is no match for Wry. "Though you are slight, you have a great deal of fighting in you," spoke Wry. "Be calm. Just let go of what is in your hand, and I will release you," Wry pleaded. The boy quickly opened his hands, letting go of the stolen property, and in turn, Wry let him go.

The boy ran a small distance, just enough to feel safe, and then turned to look at the strangers. It was obvious to Isabella that he is malnourished and not given to much rest. His wiry little body jumped up and down as he spoke out in the language of the land, one that she did not understand.

Taking a large portion of fruit from an opened satchel, Isabella threw it toward the boy. The boy immediately stopped his jumping up and down, picked the fruit up from the ground and ate, demolishing the fruit in no time at all. He then cautiously steps closer to the Chosen. Cupping his hands together, he stretches them toward Isabella, and in his native tongue, asks for more. "Poor boy, his face is gaunt, look how big it makes his eyes appear," whispers Isabella to Wry. "Let us give him something else."

This time, Wry pulled a package of nuts from his satchel, took a few steps forward, and extended his hand. To his disappointment the boy, making it quite clear that he did not trust them, retreated backwards, agitating his body once again. "You are hungry, we have food," Wry called, but the boy kept his distance. Not wanting to increase his anxiety further, Wry gently threw the package of nuts toward the boy's feet. With Wry's target met, the boy hurriedly obtained the package, and quickly devoured its contents.

Wry's eyes filled with tears as he looked at the hungry child. "That is not enough for you," he muttered underneath his breath. "What else can we do?" Hastily, he grabbed a small container filled with water, and placed it on the floor with a quantity of bread, then motioning for Isabella to join him, he walked behind the sledge. The boy waited for Isabella to join Wry, uttered some disjointed sounds, quickly gathered the gifts and ran away.

Isabella and Wry watched as the child disappeared over the top of the quarry. "Poor and forsaken little thing," Isabella's tone was low and mournful, "it seems as though no one has taken care of that child. His face will haunt me through my dreams I am sure."

"There is such a cold brutality over the rule of this place. His family have, in all probability, been destroyed, in fact, the boy is most fortunate to be breathing in the air at all. It is likely that he is enslaved to be a water carrier, which is why he came here I suppose." Wry gestured to where the water trough stood, "Perhaps he is the reason that the water remains fresh and full, and the trough in such good repair."

"Though, curiosity could have driven him when he saw the sledge. Perhaps he holds on to hope." Isabella smiled deeply at the thought. "He has expectancy for good, which amazes me, given his needs and wanting's. The resilience of the downtrodden stirs me deeply."

After briefly checking over the sledge, Isabella and Wry hurry back to the camp where they find Cara and Aaron in conversation near the water trough. "A small local boy wanted something in the sledge. He was so hungry, we gave him some food. After a short time, he ran away. I think I would have liked to take him with us if he had stayed." Isabella was quick to share their findings with the others.

"Do you think he will give us away?" asked Cara rapidly clenching and unclenching her hands. Wry took Cara's hand into his and ran his fingers gently across it. "I should not think so my precious one. It is doubtful that anyone would listen to a wild little boy in these lands. Yet, even if he does, it will not matter, for we are leaving very shortly." Looking toward the quarry top, Cara is satisfied.

Isabella, Wry, and Cara, eager to move out of the quarry and onto the trails, pick up their pace. With canteens in hand, they walk back toward the sledge. Aaron however, being certain that his own instincts are correct, stays behind a little longer. Once his friends are far enough away, he places his head in the trough so that his lips touch the water and he starts to whisper, "Waters, flow, water flow, water flow." As he does this, fresh confidence floods into his heart. With this rise of surety, his voice takes on more authority and his request, though still whispered, became a command. As soon as the order leaves his lips, the water obeys.

Beginning softly at first, the water purses up under his lips like a kiss, brushing against his mouth. Then, it swells a little higher, tickling his cheeks and chin. Climbing higher again, the liquid caresses underneath, and around, Aaron's ears. "Waters, rise, rise," Aarons' voice grows louder. The waters sing in their whooshing and splashy way as they continue to rise up above Aaron's ears, playing and tickling as it passes. Growing larger, the splashes cause droplets to bounce out from the trough and spill out onto the parched turf that sits below it. The waters keep on increasing as Aaron continues to speak, and, in only a short time, Aaron is completely submerged.

Small pockets of air, collected by the water, rise up into his nose and mouth in a continual flow, satisfying the need to breathe. Still repeating his words, Aaron floats, part dazed, part happy while experiencing the waters pressing, tapping and popping around his body. It was as though some of the most skilful masseurs in the lands were handling him.

Aaron continues to perceive the sounds of the waters, but by this time, there was form in the noise. Was it Eirtherol whispering their sweet words to him, or, did the waters have a voice of their own? He did not know. Whatever the origin, the whispered sounds developed into murmured words and became clearer. "There are unseen rewards for those who follow through on what they hear, benefits that will not be readily believed." Aaron knew this was the truth, for both his physical body, and his state of mind, had never felt so energised, at least not in the Tactile Plains. After the words were spoken, Aaron, entirely submerged, had completely disappeared from sight.

★

Walking a few steps behind Wry and Cara, Isabella allows them some privacy. She guides her sights away from the couple, but moments later she returns her gaze toward them once again. The two, walking arm in arm, share their private thoughts, relishing in the adoration of each other. Their deep attachment is enviable. Isabella's thoughts drift onto her own future as she considers the possibility of affection for herself. Impulsively, she turns her head, looking backwards at the trough to see Aaron, but instead, a most unexpected sight greets her.

"Stop Cara, Wry stop," she called. "He was right, Aaron was right. Look, watch the water trough, it's flooding!" Cara and Wry stopped. For some moments, all three stare at the flood of water flowing from the trough, not knowing what to do next. Cara broke the silence. "Why did we doubt him?" A rising joy along with bewilderment pulsed through their bodies as they took brisk steps toward the phenomenon. Their wonder turns quickly to fear as the ground beneath their feet begins to shake.

"The earth trembles," urges Cara. Wry quickly grabs Cara and pulls her down to the ground, urging Isabella to do the same, but she did not. Instead, Isabella continues forward.

"Where is Aaron?" she shrieked. Isabella ran, using the full force of her legs, despite the ground shaking mightily. Moments later, another obstacle presents itself against her, more perplexing than the last. The surrounding air, though still translucent, carries with it more substance. With this larger mass, it weighs more and Isabella feels the pressure of it, pushing at her body, making any high speed impossible.

"I will not give in," she said as she pressed forward against the resistance. It was then that her eyes fell upon something so peculiar that it caused her legs to buckle. The water that was previously contained in the rustic trough is still spilling out, and sloshing over the ground in copious amounts, but now, and more curiously, the water is rising upward, climbing the air, and reaching a peak that stands almost as high as the quarry walls. Once at the pinnacle, the water tumbles down, over itself and back to the ground, forming a waterfall. When the spray from the waterfall touches the land, it carves out a place to gather the waters and turns the dried out surface of the quarry into a large gushing hot spring.

At the base of the spring, new growth sprouts and rapidly forms into grasses and flowers once native to the land. Shrubs form in little mounds, and veins of mineral become visible on the grounds. What once was barren and harsh is now breathtaking and inviting. With transformation complete, the land ceases to tremble. Still crumpled upon the ground, Isabella wonders if she had fallen and fainted and is now caught up in a dream.

Wide eyed, and heart thumping heavily, she intends to proceed. Pulling herself up into a crouched position, she whispers, not expecting to be heard, "Aaron, where are you? Look what you have caused." Wry and Cara are quick to their feet. They soon arrive at where Isabella is crouching and help her to stand. They walk together, still slowly, to the edge of the hot springs and survey the waterfall with great fascination. Removing their footwear, the three test the water with their toes. The heated water embraces them.

Unusually invigorated by the warm spring, they cross the shallows and venture into the deeper parts, nearing the mist-clothed waterfall. Wry, driven by curiosity, takes in a few large breaths then enters the water in search of the trough. Surprisingly, the waters under the falls continued down far below the surface level of the quarry. Wry looks about the place where the trough should have been, but instead of the trough, all he could see were multitudes of tiny air bubbles concentrated within a large circle, popping then returning to the surface to renew their supply of air. Wry drew closer.

To his astonishment, there, upheld by the bubbles, lay Aaron, hanging underneath the depths. His state was suspended, but his face displayed unequalled contentment. Wry, not knowing if his friend was dead or alive reached into the bubbles and took a firm hold of Aaron's arm.

There was no resistance as Wry pulled Aaron's listless body back to the surface, and still no movement as he swam him into the shallower places. Wry held his friend, and puzzled over the look upon his face. His body still lay limp upon the bubbling water, but his face had increased in expression, for now, he held to a look, both queer and ecstatic.

Wry, tried to understand if this expression on Aarons' face was good or bad, or if indeed it was any indication of Aaron's well-being at all when Aaron let out a melodious laugh from the back of his throat. Then he spoke, as though in a drunken stupor, "Can you believe this? Can you believe this? Water flow," again, he laughed. The sounds of splashing water increases as the much relieved Isabella and Cara push their feet through the shallows to where Aaron and Wry sit.

The four marvelled, chattered, and then sought to hear from the invisible should it want to talk to them, but it did not seem to. Isabella purred, "I could stay here for quite a while" then hastily reconsiders, "but that jumping boy; he may be back, looking for more provision, or worse. Perhaps he will sell his information to a slave master. There would be great recompense for him. This could be treacherous for us."

As the group discuss their quandary, a lone man sits unnoticed, upon a rock by the side of the spring. He quietly traces the ripples made by a dragonfly skimming over the surface of the water with his finger.

"I suppose we must go then," Wry sighed. "But, let us take one last," his voice drifts off into a mumble as his eyes fell upon the stranger. Subtly, he points his finger toward the man though too subtly for the others to notice immediately.

Wry stares at the man, and makes an evaluation. The man looks harmless enough, gentle even. Obviously, not from the Land of Slaves, for his attire is both clean and bright. Muttering under his breath, Wry conveys his concern, "How long has he been sat with us? Why did he not introduce himself? And why is he here?" he whispers.

Isabella, Aaron and Cara startle at the man's presence. "Usually, I would be friendly, I would greet the man politely, but I am not sure to do that in this instance. It is unnerving," spilling her words out quickly, Cara places her hand upon Wry's shoulder as she always did to help her confidence rise. Now quiet, Cara listens to the Invisible within and makes her own assessment. *This situation is somewhat unusual,* she supposes, *yet we do find ourselves in quite an odd position. This man poses no threat to us; in fact, with our meeting I can feel only gain.*

Aaron however, was not so convinced. *This tranquil stranger sitting by us seems to bring nothing of ill intent. Without a weapon, and lacking caution, he looks at peace with himself and the environment around.* He sighs, his heart finding ease. Suddenly, Aaron's protective nature rises up and presents him with a fear concerning his friends, his Isabella and himself. *Things appear well, but there is a great deal at risk in us trusting the wrong man.* Aaron, requiring another view, allows suspicion to arise and argue its point. His mind is now cloudy with overrunning notions; he leaves actuality, and enters inside the reality of his imagination.

As new scenarios play out on the inside of his mind, his fear grows. Drawing energy up from Aaron's body, the fear enlarges and fortifies its territory. Aaron experiences it as an uncomfortable tugging sensation deep in his side. He winces, briefly forgetting his train of thought.

Isabella looks upon the man, and her heart fills instantly with happiness, almost as if she had seen a long lost friend. Without further thought or regard to her companions, she calls out to him in a merry voice and surges forward through the spring in his direction. "I am sure that I have seen your face before, are we acquainted, or am I mistaken?"

The man slid off the rock and into the water, stepping toward Isabella. "Yes", he replied, "we are acquainted, in fact, I know you very well Isabella from the Volcano Island." The stranger smiled widely and Isabella was glad. "What is your name, you are familiar, but only vaguely." The stranger, not seeming to hear her question embraces her warmly, and then turned his attentions to those in her company. "Cara," he lowered his head toward her in high regard, as though he was acknowledging her nobility. Then, he repeated the same action towards Wry.

Aaron, remembering his concern, looked at the stranger and spoke. "We do not have the time to talk with you here, for it is not safe for us anymore. Nor is it for you, I suppose. You must have overheard us talking about the boy that is sure to give us away to the slave masters. The boy looked half starved, and would certainly give us away for better treatment. If you are a friend of Isabella, then you are welcome to come along until we can take you to your safety, but, we cannot carry you any further for we do not have the room."

The stranger raised his hand slightly and revealed a gentle smile then brought his reply, "Aaron, I have come with some relief for you. You are correct in what you say; the boy has given you away. Already, a trap has been formed, and, without intervention, not one of you will remain free."

The man looks around at the concerned faces staring back at him and continues. "Aaron, you listened to the Eirtherol and followed their directive. It was you that called the waters to flow. In that, you did well." He smiled at Aaron with paternal approval, yet, he appeared to be of similar age. "This wellspring is a gift from the Invisible to all of you. It is a place of rest, a safe haven, but only for a short while. Aaron, go, bring you sledge close to the edge of the spring, and then re-join us in the waters."

Aaron followed the stranger's instruction and then wades back into the warm and bubbling water where his friends lay in wait. The stranger proceeds, "This spring, and its immediate surroundings have been made invisible to the eyes of your enemies. So, be invigorated by the energy that it gives out, and relax in its security, for you will need to spend more than one turning of the Greater Lights here before it is safe for you to take your leave."

It was clear that the stranger is not an Eirtherol; however, his words resonate with the authority of truth, just as the Eirtherol's did. Isabella, Cara and Wry, trust the stranger implicitly though Aaron remains unconvinced. While remaining guarded, Aaron contains his anxious thoughts and takes the man's words seriously.

★

Much later, as the Greater Lights recede, the quarry, once still and quiet, now echoes with the sound of many voices. At first, the voices are no louder than a whisper, their purpose obscured in quietness, though quickly, and with gained volume, their intention becomes apparent as the source of the voices draws nearer. "This is not good," sighs Isabella as tears well up in her eyes. The Chosen, now exceedingly alarmed, gather in a silent huddle.

A rabble of men appears on the horizon, both slaves and pirates, joined together in pursuit. Commissioned by the slave masters, the amalgamation uniformly hunted for treasure that would bring many advantages to all that took part. The females, considered valuable as women from the free lands, will be traded to Kings and rulers, or kept for the sport of the traders themselves, whereas the men, quickly executed, as their mere presence posed the threat of invasion.

A young boy was carried upon the shoulders of an enormous man. The huge man was running at a vigorous pace, ahead of the rest, leading the way. The boy called and yelled and pointed, and caused the entire rabble that followed to dart one way, then the other.

The Chosen stood very still, with barely the ability to breath. "That is the little boy whom we fed," whispered Wry. "He has given our position away." The Chosen watched on in unbelief. Their tension only increased as the rabble spouted raucous songs with tuneless voices. Through their second-hand rhyme, they allowed liberation to every pent up negative thing that they contained.

The Chosen watched on as the little boy scoured the quarry. Soon enough, a smile crossed his eager face as he remembered the exact location. His head quickly turned toward the direction of the Chosen. Though he was still a distance away, it seemed as though the young boy was looking straight at them, and directing his focus into the face of Aaron. Isabella spoke, barely moving her lips, "We have but one hope, and that is that the boy will remember our generosity toward him, and have mercy upon us." Cara was quick in reply, "I think it too late for him to change his mind now."

The rabble stopped their singing and let out a collective roar, then ran a direct route to the spring. "I can take this no more, we have a better chance if we run, so, RUN." Just as Aaron let out his command, the stranger in their midst, approached them from behind. He slung a prepared weave of vine around their shaking bodies and held them captive. Their hearts sunk. The stranger quickly spoke, "Reject the fear, and do not follow its command, for it will lead you astray. Instead, believe my words to you, for then, you shall remain in safety."

Isabella, Aaron, Wry and Cara, knowing the man to be right, began to fight a most desperate battle. "We will not be led by fear," Aaron yelled, fortifying his decision as he did so. "This is a safe place, given to us by the Invisible, we must stay in it," followed Isabella, reminding both herself and her friends.

The wailing from both parties reached a fevered pitch as the rabble were just feet away from procuring their game. Just then, the stranger spoke again, "Watch the boy." They watch. The little boy's eyes change from open and alert to narrow though his mouth still holds a controlled smile. He looks to one side, and then the other, then back again. The boy lifts his outwardly stretching hands and rapidly drops them to his sides. Looking from side to side once more, he forces his smile to stay, while fighting the evidence of newly forming tears in his eyes. With quivering voice, he declares, "They were here, here. The trespassers must have escaped."

"Poor little mite, he will be made to pay dearly," Cara whispered. "Poor little mite?" replies Wry, "I will afford him sympathy Cara, but not just now." The Chosen continue to watch on as the rabble collectively let out cries of disappointment. The mob rustles along, up, and over the other side of the quarry, and past its boundary.

The stranger releases the vine. The Chosen, dizzy from the fight, say nothing. Wry, quickly embraces Cara as she releases the tears that she had held onto, while Isabella and Aaron, pale with fright, retreat to their own company for a while.

★

Avril and Calamity stand together again in the In–Between Places. "Rabble-rousing," spat Calamity, "One of my great passions," she utters with pure sarcasm. For Calamity, along with many other Lesser Princes, had ridden upon the backs of the cold-blooded throng. Both guiding their thoughts, and increasing their fury. "The outcome was not as I had hoped for though we have secured many from that horde in a prison of their own making."

Avril's reply is void of emotion, "These men have been prepared from their ancestry to receive all the violent repetition of thought that we could inject. How then, can you possibly take any of this toward your own acclaim? You failed at the simple task entrusted to you."

Calamity's eyes glint with mischief though her face remains unmoved. It excited her to know that she could incite the correction of Avril. "That mob will continue to feed upon the threads of thought that were offered to them. Undoubtedly, they will expand upon our patterns by their own means, and their own volition; thereby giving us more weaponry to draw upon. I would not call that failure.

Yes, the prey remains undetected, but, we have increased the amount of hatred in that rabble of men significantly. They will be looking for some relief from it, and, you know as well as I that they will be soothing themselves with the lives of others. Perhaps still, the very ones we have momentarily lost!"

"But, that is not yet conclusive," Avril slights her antagonist. "Now, to the point, if the Grovels are left to the devices that they have chosen, they will cause much damage. We cannot allow them to continue. Already, they must have gone further than we have anticipated. It is most likely that they are growing in stature upon each of the Realms." Avril waited briefly for a retort from Calamity, and receiving none, she continues. "Before you returned, I sent Harshaw to the Highest Ranker Denken, He will instruct us further. Harshaw, what has been decided?"

Harshaw appeared from behind the two, drawn from his mistaken belief that he had returned unnoticed. "Well," asks Avril. "Firstly," he began, "The Grovels have been hidden from our sight with the aid of those who dwell in the Invisible Realms, Denken can't even find them, and if he can't, I don't know how a gathering of Cambrasian's could have."

"And secondly, Denken is of the same opinion as you Avril. Now is the time that we must strike a severe blow before the Grovels cause some major damage to our plans. Denken has proposed that we take from them the strongest. It is doubtful that the others will keep on in this futility without him."

Harshaw handed to Avril a rolled parchment, which she quickly unrolled, read and acknowledged with a stamp of her signet. She handed the paper to Calamity to place her own recognition upon it. The information that the parchment contained made the steps of the Lesser Princes perfectly understandable and clear. "The preparations have been adequate, making this plan almost definitely fool proof. So, let us go take the life of Aaron."

★

Aaron standing apart from the others at the edge of the spring watched through peripheral vision as his friends indulged in the comfort of each other's company. Aaron takes stock of his feelings. He was glad that Isabella had found a confidant in Cara. He was also pleased with his meeting Wry. But, as they travelled together, he had grown weary. His body was heavier somehow, as though he carried a great and unsolvable weight. Mostly, he considered that it was the pressure of the added responsibility that he felt for his friends, so generally, he had shrugged the matter off. Nevertheless, when time permitted, and he pondered his quandary, his suspicion was that this weight was neither right nor necessary.

Aaron groans inwardly and sits down at the edge of spring in attempts to understand the dilemma. His thoughts weighed so heavily that he did not notice the impulses that arose from his inner being. Nor did he perceive the prickling sensation running across his arms, trying to bring him a message.

For, only a few steps away, stand Avril, Calamity and Harshaw, and though they cannot see Aaron or the spring, they can feel the intensity of Invisible. The Princes meticulously examine the site enclosed by the Invisible and notice a definite inconsistency. Harshaw proudly reveals his findings, "Black is to white. Can you feel that vibration Avril? The little creature swelling within the Grovels side is sending us a message. It reveals a great discomfort and begs for release." Calamity's vulgar laugh rings out gleefully, "Oh Aaron, your position has been given away."

"Create your little vacuum; fear filled creature," lulled Avril, "Let him think that your confinement is his own. Do your task, and I will promise you a place, full of compression, unable to be opened for many a natural lifetime." Doing all that they had set out to do, the Lesser Princes returned to the In-Between Places.

★

The Lesser Lights dominate the skies, and throw their enigmatic glimmer upon the quiet oasis, inviting Aaron to return. Tired of the internal battle, Aaron accepts the call and wades back into the serene waters. The warmth and life within the spring quickly dissolve his anxious thoughts, although it does not seem to remedy the building pressure from within his side.

In the quietness, a voice rings out. "Aaron, Isabella, Wry, Cara, I want to thank you for your hospitality toward me. You have trusted me in a most difficult circumstance, and that is to your credit. But now, it is time for me to leave you for there is something else I must do." The stranger pauses for a moment, his eyes brim with tears as he prepares himself for what he was about to say.

"As you know, the waters that surround you are a gift from the Invisible Places, a further protection for you in a time to come. Do not move from here, do not leave the waters until the Lesser Lights return to the position that they are in right now. While you wait, benefit from the spring; allow it to increase your strength, in your body, in mind, and, in rapport with each other. Hold to your memories, and use them as a reminder if you begin to falter. If you listen to my words, then, you will benefit from a safe passage," he pauses, "However, forget my instruction, leave prematurely, and you are sure to die." After a quiet moment, the stranger smiles, "Let peace stay with you all. We will meet again at a later time," and with that, the stranger left.

The Lesser Lights retired, and the Greater Lights poured out their dense red colouring. They moved across the open skies, throwing their varied radiance over the silent quarry. They pass upward, through to the centre of the heavens, and continued over to the opposite side of the Sphere. Though almost spent their glow remains fierce. The Daystars, not yet ready to give up their dominant position.

★

The Chosen, now replenished with health and energy, prepare for the journey ahead. Each one grows in eager anticipation regarding the developing partnership that they share with the unseen beings, along with newfound confidence about the direction that they are to take.

Aaron stood with Isabella in the depths while Wry and Cara frolic under the falls. "The time for us to leave is almost here. I think it wise to scan the lands and ensure a safe departure, for, though we know the direction to go, we are all unfamiliar with what lies ahead." Aaron speaks with great certainty.

"Aaron, recall the words of the stranger, his warning was very clear to my ears. Do you think his judgement is lacking in merit? He compelled us all to stay until the Lesser Lights have long taken the skies, they are close, but they are not even present yet," voices Isabella with concern.

"Oh Isabella, I heard what he said as well," Isabella's words felt like a reproach, *she does not trust me*. First sadness is present, next anger, and then blame, with thoughts of each racing through his mind in a blink. Yet Aaron hides behind language of tenderness, "and yes, I do hold value to his words. But I am not leaving; I intend only to look past the quarry walls in the direction we are to take. I will not be gone long, and we all stand to benefit from it."

Isabella remains unconvinced, but respectfully, she accepts the choice of Aaron. After all, it was only a short time ago that she doubted him though his instincts were correct. "If you feel you must, then you must." Aaron puts his arms gently around Isabella's torso and places a tender kiss on her lips then speaks his parting words, "Tell Wry and Cara not to worry for I will be back very soon."

Aaron walks from the deep to the shallow, and then, steps out of the spring as Isabella watches on. After running his hands down his clothing to remove some of the wetness, he returns his shoes to his feet. The hot breeze dries him further as he walks hastily across the flat of the quarry. Isabella approaches Wry and Cara to inform them of Aaron's choice and by this time, he is far-gone. Having made his way up the quarry steps, Aaron was out of sight.

Moments later a screeching and sinister voice bounces across the barren quarry, "Get him, get him." Just two breaths later, more words ring out, but from a different source. "Execute the command. Do it." A single shot rings out, whistling away the silence and following, a loud and raucous cheer made up of a multitude of voices.

Isabella, Cara and Wry stand frozen in unbelief and fear. They watch silently as the fighters make their way back through the quarry, past the spring, up the ramp and up over into the horizon. Three of the mob carries a large sack over their heads, throwing it up into the air, and then catching it unceremoniously. Others of the crowd sang songs of celebration and took turns in mocking the contents of the sack. Soon, the rabble was out of sight and eventually, the sound of their voices dissipated off into the twilight's skies. The Chosen stood, encased with a numbness that defied their own strength.

A loud cry finally broke through the bitter silence as their hearts confirmed the suspicion. Isabella, Wry, and Cara knew that it was Aaron carried away in the sack. "My heart, my heart has been torn from my chest. All, and ever after, has been tainted by Aarons departure." With tears overflowing from swollen eyes, Isabella's strength failing her, she fell, sinking underneath the spring's water.

★

Avril, Harshaw and Calamity stand in the In-Between Places once again, gloating over their tremendous victory. Each Prince considered their personal contribution to be the most significant though each Prince knew the foolishness of voicing such a position.

"Highest Ranker Denken will be notably pleased with the subjugation of that pitiful Grovel, and what he approves of, he rewards. Not one, but four of those dreadful beings, crippled in one simple deed." A maddening glint flashes across Avril's brown eyes, belying her stony-faced impression. "The one from the Volcano Isle has taken such a blow that the probability of her maintaining any innocence is most unlikely, she will not be able to hear from the Invisible with all that bitterness rising up in her grief inflamed heart. And, the two for ones from Malcarve, they ride upon her dream, they have not yet cultivated one of their own to follow on with."

"So, is it accomplished?" questions Calamity. Avril replies, "It is not entirely sure, no. We have not been released from our duties toward them just yet." Harshaw brazenly interrupts the other Princes, "Perhaps you are right Calamity, but perhaps you are not. Either way, a reward still awaits us nonetheless." Once the conversation had finished, a force, outside of themselves, takes them to another place within the In-Between.

"Denken's reward," Harshaw stretches out his pale hand toward the prize. "Ruins, these are remnants, from the time of the greats. Our surrounds have been left, completely untouched for the longest of times. It predates the three-day battle, and was devised by men of great cunning, men that freely gave their own aptitude to the Lesser Princes, and accepted the Lesser Princes influence in return, a collaboration of much, now lost, knowledge." Calamity nodded in approval, whispering her reply, "Before the Cambrasian race had lost their understanding of these connections. Oh, their arts were so much stronger then."

To the unknowing, the ruins appear quite benign, just the remnants of a decrepit building, left to its own devices. However, to one with understanding, it is a proverbial treasure chest, a footprint from a different time, one harnessing another type of intelligence altogether. It held secrets, long forgotten, and wielded a great and extraordinary power.

"The Grovels from that age, the Chosen, did not bother to sweep it clean though they could have, and what is more, not one of them since has even noticed it! See, they lack the aptitude, the most heedless of fools." Avril, repulsed by their lack of diligence, felt the burning rise inside her and quickly moved her speech to another place. "There are specific details of elemental manipulation here. Elemental manipulations unused and forgotten for the longest of times. The favour that Denken has displayed surpasses all of my expectation."

The Lesser Princes place a flimsy fabric across the central part of the ruins. They collect coal and clay from a nearby area of the Tactile Plains and bring it back to the In-Between. They place their collection into a small cavity situated near the ruins and submerge it into an amber/bronze liquid, pulled from a well in the In-Between. The materials gel together quickly, and, as soon as it does, the Princes remove it with their hands, and smear the mixture across a stone that lies in the centre of the ruins, and underneath the fabric. Imprints of ancient strategy transfer from the rock, and onto the fabric. The Princes path now revealed.

"The way is now so obviously apparent," whispers Avril. "We are not to subdue them; we are to wipe out their very essence. For, indeed, what do we care if their bodies survive or not? Undoubtedly, they will perish without our facilitation; and anyway, their bodies are not what hold them to the course. Still, let their frail receptacles be stripped of anything remotely Invisible, and instead be filled with the abundance of gifts that we have to bestow." Avril, uncharacteristically, laughs, taking Harshaw and Calamity off guard.

"I can see now, the shrewd calculation of Highest Ranker Denken. That is why he is our superior. He has no intent on allowing the three remaining to pursue their destination any further, no matter how small their chances of succeeding. For, though they have been deeply crushed, we also need to consider that the ancient ones aid them, and we must never underestimate that influence upon them. Our current purpose is to make their end painful and demoralising, so, if word of their journey escapes, any simpering hope will be quickly extinguished, for no other Grovel would be willing to continue in their footsteps for fear of the shame. In fact, if we do it correctly, they will be dismissed altogether on the grounds of insanity."

★

Eleneke, Althai, Darien and Asher leave the Invisible Places and quickly gather around the Chosen in the spring. They had witnessed the cloud of mourning settling over their little friends and, quickly moved by compassion, they returned to the Tactile Plain sooner than they had first intended.

Eleneke wraps her arms underneath the arms of Isabella, and supporting her weight, lifts her face above the water's surface. As Wry and Cara huddled together, Darién and Asher place their arms around them both and hold them as one. Althai looks on, and all seven beings wept deeply.

The Chosen could feel the presence of the Eirtherol all around them, but this time, there was no comfort. With their vision, tactile and invisible, impaired by grief, the Chosen are unable to function, as Chosen should.

"This will not do," said Althai. Lifting his arms from his sides, he throws his powerful hands up into the air and claps to release a swelling musical sound from his body. The sound causes intense vibration to both the In-Between Places and the Tactile Plains, and concludes with a thunderous crash, producing a split between the realms. Eleneke, Asher, Althai, and Darién's forms change as they shift between the realms. For now, the Eirtherol appear almost Cambrasian in size, density, and visibility.

The vulnerable Chosen, though surprised, immediately recognise the Eirtherol and allow them absolute trust. The Eirtherol, continuing to hold tightly to the mourners, give them strength enough to sustain. "Isabella," Eleneke whispers with noticeable amounts of gentleness and compassion, "You are entering into a deeper sorrow, and there is time for that, but, in a short while, not just yet. You and your friends, should you stay here any longer, are in much danger, for the time of safety in this spring has come to an end. You must leave now."

Isabella, with a swollen tearstained face, could only nod in agreement. Althai and Eleneke stand either side of Isabella. Surrounding her with their arms, they guide her forward to the edge of the water, and out of the spring. Darién accompanies Wry while Asher guides Cara.

"Leave the sledge and all your belongings. Most were bought by Aaron, and by them, you will be easily identified as his companions," Darién informed. "Of course," replies Wry, and with that being clear, all seven leave the spring area and walk through the quarry in the dwindling light, to the same side that Aaron had left for earlier. With legs as heavy as their hearts, the Chosen scale the steps, observing them as a memorial dedicated to Aaron. The whistling of the wind through the quarry strangely reflects the Cambrasian's feelings of emptiness and loss, their loss of hope and their loss of Aaron.

The way of their journey was not complicated in itself. The residents of the quiet towns lay exhausted in their modest beds after a long and arduous day of toil. If, by chance, any of the townsfolk remained awake, they would not risk involving themselves with the strangers for fear of punishment to them and their families.

Once the sombre group had passed through three towns, Darién broke the silence. "This next town is where you will take some rest. You have but a few turnings of the Lights to deal with the worst of you grief, then, you will need to prepare yourselves for the journey forward." Darién's tone of voice though filled with understanding of their suffering, held an underlying tone that Isabella, Wry, and Cara, recognised to be a command.

Wry, though weary, hungry and confounded, did not hesitate to reply, "For all the things that have caused me pain and confusion on this journey." Noticing his rising pitch, Wry pauses, gathers breath, swallows down the mounting lump in his throat, before continuing, "I know, that in the fullness of conscience, I cannot turn back to where we have come from." He quickly turns to observe Cara's reaction to his statement. "Though I crave the comforts of our estate and the safety of our love in private, I know that we are treading the right path."

Wry and Cara looked toward Isabella. Still tearful, her reply was limp, "I ache all over, both inside and out. I cannot yet think more than one step at a time." All present understood that it was Isabella who had suffered the greatest loss. Cara quickly responded, "Oh my darling friend, I shall be your eyes and ears, and guide you until yours reappear. That is, should you allow it?" Isabella forces the corners of her mouth to upturn slightly at the kind intentions of her friend. "I allow it," she whispers.

A short time later, they arrive at the outskirts of the next town. The flittering of lanterns draws their attention. Althai is the first to see, and addresses the other Eirtherol with a mixture of relief and pleasure, "Look, there they are, with their lanterns, they have managed to stay undiscovered, yet again." "They are the Al'paires," he continues, widening his address to include the Chosen. "Those are the ones who will provide you with safety. Trust them as you trust us." With that, the Eirtherol disappeared from sight.

★

The occasional flash of colour through the darkened skies leaves no doubt that the Greater Lights were eager to take their turn. The quickened pace of Isabella, Wry and Cara is equally matched by the unknown Cambrasian's who made strides toward them. Once united, the residents of the land pull the hungry and spent visitors firmly to their sides, and, bearing much of the weight, hurry on to the refuge.

It wasn't long before the new partnership of Cambrasian's arrived at the unassuming residence. One of the Al'paires guides Wry and Cara into a private room. He gives them both an herbal beverage and asks them to take in some rest.

An Al'paires, treating Isabella with much delicacy, shows her to another room. She hands Isabella a drink and asks her to take in some rest. A woman, much older, accompanies Isabella also, and stays in the room while the wounded girl sleeps, and sobs, and sleeps again. The woman remains busy scenting the room with the fragrance of floral waters, soaking beautiful materials in briny liquids and then warming the materials by the open fireplace. She picks up the fabrics and tests its temperature against her soft, unlined cheeks, then uses the warm damp cloths to wipe gently over Isabella's face and neck when needed. At other times, the woman placed her hands on Isabella's back and released whispered words from the Invisible Realm.

The words caress and strengthen Isabella's being throughout her sleeping times. The scents mingle and intertwine with any memory of Aaron that she replayed, and carefully the two become bound together. The woman takes the developed scent and places it in a tiny bottle, to give to Isabella later on. It will become a comfort to her in times of loneliness ahead, a reminder, and a soul-salving recollection of the love that Aaron had given her.

The woman whispers, "His love is not lost to you Isabella; his love has built something precious. It could not have been made by anyone other than him."

Over the next few cycles of the Daystar, Isabella remains separated from Wry and Cara. It was necessary for the couple to spend time with each other to process the past events and grow stronger in their love and understanding. Isabella, though not begrudging them the love, would find the strength of it upsetting, for it would be a constant reminder of the promised love that she had lost.

Once the most intense time of mourning had passed, Isabella, Wry and Cara, led out from their confinement, and into a common room where they are again reunited. They were all delighted and relieved to be together with each other, and embraced for some time. Though no words were spoken, it was obvious, the bonds of love that they had toward each other had grown richer.

The room was encumbered with furniture from all over the sphere. Some were simple pieces pulled from any commonplace market while other fixtures were exquisite, expensive and exclusive. The varied array of colours and textures clashed with the paintings that hung upon the papered walls, in both hue and fashion.

A heady aroma from terracotta bowls filled with cut flowers clung to the air and mixed with the fragrant spice baskets set about upon the tables. It left a warm and exotic ambience throughout the cold stone room. The three watch as a woman walks to an enormous black fireplace near the entrance of the room and lit kindling. As the flames begin to flicker, she places on larger pieces of lumber and watches to ensure the licking flames are high enough to engulf it. The sounds of the flickering accompanied the airborne aromas and filled any empty space that was left unfilled.

Isabella, Wry and Cara look for somewhere to sit. The woman who had lit the fireplace now busies herself by tightly closing the heavy curtains and blocking out any external light. Once satisfied, she ignites torches, candles and lanterns that hang throughout the room. Each source of light releases a pale blue glow. The dancing colour softens the jumbled room and brings a point of similarity throughout. What once looked mismatched and gaudy now appears charming, otherworldly even.

The woman, acknowledging the surprise of her visitors, laughs as she holds the last lantern. "Every strange thing can fit together if it shares the same light." The woman, much older than the Chosen had a surprising countenance for one of that age. Her face held innocence that radiated with joy.

Thirteen others sat in chairs around the room. Clearly, they were not from the same land, but it was equally as obvious that they were a close-knit family. First Isabella, then Wry, and finally Cara, found a place to sit, all curious to what was about to happen.

"I am Halvo, Halvo of the Al'paires," a mature man seated near the open fire introduced himself. "I hope that we have brought you some comfort in this time of your substantial loss," he pauses to consider. "We had received the Eirtherol with whom you travel, and they told us what we needed to understand about your circumstance, so, if you prefer, you need not go into lengthy detail." A younger woman interjects, "It can be hard to speak of some events over and over, bringing the freshness of it into your minds." Suddenly, remembering her manners, she smiles, "Veeta is my name."

The Chosen were relieved at the Al'paires understanding. Halvo spoke again. "The Eirtherol were very clear in their directive to us. We only have a short time with you, and already, our first instruction has been followed. The haze of mourning that surrounded your heads has been evaporated. The loss of Aaron will, of course, still be felt; however, you will have strength enough to bear it until you reach your next place of safety.

The Eirtherol also shared with us some unusual occurrences. You are precious, so loved. For your sakes, there are things moved, and things held back, impossible things, both here and in the In-Between

Places, all for your inclusion. Even with this generous increase, there is only a small passage of time left, allowing you to get to where you want to go. Though they, and we, are hopefully convinced that each one of you will indeed fall into your future venture."

"That does bring me comfort," answers Isabella, "and, I am grateful for your attention to us, but, there is something that I fear you do not understand. I had a dream that has guided me along on this journey, and we have taken its direction. Cara and Wry had it placed into their hearts too, and even the Eirtherol confirmed it. If the dream is right, the one I am following in it is Aaron, he was to bring us the compass. How can we achieve the end if we cannot follow the directions?"

"Isabella, he did. He did not bring you the compass. He led you to the compass." Halvo gently informed, smiling from ear to ear. "Al'paires means the pointer of the way," he pauses to examine her unresponsive face, "or compass, we are known as the compass. It was not the best way to our meeting, there was another way, a preferred way, but, it was not chosen," Halvo spoke quickly, sensing the hurt that radiated from Isabella's confounded heart. "But Aaron still fulfilled a significant part of his destiny, and, he led you into a major part of yours.

It would have been better should Aaron have listened to the man in your midst, the one at the spring, yet, that will not be held against him. For, he meant to protect the three of you, most especially you Isabella, he loved to his death, and that speaks of the quality that was stored in his heart more than the misinformed decision that he made. He will be remembered for his love, not his mistake."

The matter settled in the air, and, after a small pause, Halvo began to speak again. "Open the curtains again my love, I want to show them." Veeta, being seated right next to the windows, stood up and drew back the curtains. The outside light poured into the common room once again. "Once you have adjusted your eyes, I want you to take notice of what you see. Look first at the natural places, and then, from the Invisible. Speak out what you see, for you will not offend us."

Cara's curiosity getting the better of her, she replies immediately, "Clearly, you do not come from the same place, for you are so different, different colours, some tall, some smaller, and yet there is a similar quality to you all." Then, after a speedy reflection, it occurred to her what the similarity was; yet, she was reticent to speak of it. Quickly, she looked downwards.

A young woman, around the same age as Cara, was accustomed to this reaction after having seen it many a time before. She spoke, "Oh Cara, you are so lovely to see, with your long dark hair and fair complexion. You carry such a beauty and grace. You are noticed in an instant, wherever you go, even sought after for the things that you carry, things that you have always carried. For my family and me, we were not made that way; we are plain to the sight, seemingly unremarkable, each one of us."

Cara appeared uncomfortable, but the young woman, not deterred, continues. "I invite you to look at us again, look into the Invisible and see us." Veeta drew the curtains closed once again and began to sing a haunting and wordless song.

In the atmosphere of the Al'paires, it was very easy for the Chosen to enter into the Invisible Places. As soon as their focus pulled away from the visible, in their minds eye, pictures started to form. Firstly, they saw a baby girl, lying down upon a pillow; clearly, she was intended for perfection, for goodness, for all time. The baby began to grow, and as she did, words, written upon materials, some for her good, and some to her detriment, flew about the child from the mouths of those around her. The words were trying to dress the little baby in garments of their making.

As the child continued to grow, the material words joined themselves with images, and, as time passed, they collected unspoken things that existed around her too. Soon, she was again older, and the manifest words pressed heavily upon her and strived to force their way inside. The child resisted but instinctively knew that eventually, the weight of it would be too much for her to contest.

The child, closing her eyes, called for aid. At that moment, she identified another source of words. Just as a mother feeds her unborn child, these words continually flowed from the parent source and into her belly. She examined the words carefully, and, recognising their goodness, allowed them to travel through her, and penetrate, first her heart, and then her mind.

The words strengthen the little girl's resistance until she easily rejects the pressure gathering and conspiring against her from the outside. Though the material tried to bind her from the outside, she paid it little attention, and instead noticed the words that flowed and increased within. They grew, layering kind, upon good, upon good.

Then, the girl matured further, and, something extraordinary took place. The words that she had allowed to form on the inside, these upstanding and broadly cast lyrics, developed and relinquished little words of their own, words of particular design toward the child, words that only she could carry.

These words, with their pictures and emotions in accompaniment, endeavour to shape and cover her little body. They swirled around and around and guarded the girl in an extreme and unusual handsomeness. The girl, now permeating with purity, dazzled. Just to be in her presence was a privilege.

A voice interrupted the vision, "I am Avera." The Chosen open their eyes and quickly recognise this plain girl as the child from the vision. Isabella grasps for words as she processed, first, the revealed sight, and then, the concept disclosed. *I am embarrassed that I did not notice your exquisite beauty and strength before. I feel as though I should bow in your presence, knowing this about you. You are truly a Queen. I had judged you a pauper.* Isabella looks at Cara, opens her mouth to speak and, words failing, pursed her lips and placed her attentions back toward Avera.

"This is our sacred cord, the thing that binds us together as a family, and, the agent used for our change, our maturation, our, perceived lack," Avera laughs. "It is also our very plainness that allows us to go about entirely undetected, unchecked, and even ignored," she laughs again at the irony. "Ones as lovely as you cannot go unnoticed."

"But you are adorable," spoke Cara with tears in her eyes, the vision still impressing upon her mind. She had always been susceptible to beauty, and what she had just witnessed overwhelmed her. Blushing, Veeta giggles, "We are all lovely of course though we are all made for different purposes."

Halvo qualifies, "We were each selected for our merits, joined into a family, and send from the place that you are now heading to. Our calling is to direct and aid those that desire to walk toward that same path. We are to give courage and point you to your destination until the Invisible has become your entire truth too."

Halvo looks directly into the faces of Isabella, Wry and Cara, said, "You have done well to come this far." He smiles a wide grin and continues, "In this next cycle of lights, we will take care of your physical needs, and strengthen you with our words and our understanding. You will be given directions to where you are headed, and sent off for safe passage. It is our privilege to do so." The meeting concludes.

★

The trio spent their remaining time well, taking full advantage of the hospitality offered them as they prepared for the way forward.

They searched out the wisdom of their hosts over appetising meals, relaxed in the contained gardens and bathed in the fragrant, warm water tanks.

Isabella spent time in the confinements of her room, inscribing her thoughts onto parchment and wrapping them tightly in the scented material that reminded her of Aaron. She placed her fresh flowing tears upon the seal that she used to fasten the parchment and kissed the paper as though concluding a ceremony. For, though the tragedy of Aaron remains painfully close; she had found her way to move forward.

The time to leave had arrived. The Chosen assembled in the tiny vestry, waiting to depart. Halvo's deep voice preceded him, "So, now is the time for you to leave." He and Veeta appeared at the end of the corridor, with hands full. "We have prepared satchels for you to take. Only the necessity, for it is not our intention to burden you with excessive weight, but there is certainly enough for you until you reach your destination. I doubt you will have the time to want for anything else."

Halvo handed each Chosen a map and a compass. "These will point the way for you," he continues, "your destination is no longer hidden, so, regardless of what transpires, do keep your course. Divert only, only, if you are in dire need, and then turn back, as soon as you are able, to your direct route."

He pauses, "It will be difficult for you; I can assure you of that, for you will not get there without hostility. Most have found the last leg of this journey to be the most gruelling." Halvo breathed out a deep sigh as he spoke this to them, knowing of the severe hardships that they have already had to face.

Halvo had released a second sigh before he gave them this warning, "Just before your destination, there is a place where the lines between the Tactile Plains and the In-Between Places are confused. The

Lesser Princes of Barren will take full advantage of this fact. Their stained consciences do not hold them to any code of honour, well, none that we understand; they will challenge you most unfairly. In fact, they will try to put an end to your life.

We are disadvantaged in yet another way, though, in the end, it will not matter. For, we do not know the weapons that they will choose to use against you, so there is no full assurance that we can bring to you. They are unscrupulous beings. So, hear my best advice, hold fast to your destination, and look only to the Invisible Places, for both the In–Between and the Tactile Plains, will delude you."

With this warning, the trio stands tall, almost military as they girded themselves with the internal strength required for combat. "You are all upright and healthy," spoke Veeta softly, "and you have made it this far, you have been proved for the journey." With smile radiating reassurance, she added, "Everything that you need does surround you."

Holding to the comfort placed within Veeta's words, they said their goodbyes and left the shelter of the Al'paires.

★

Within the In–Between Places, an orchestration of immense proportion had begun. Avril, Harshaw and Calamity, understanding their degree of advantage, took no chance of failure by employing the services of other experienced Lesser Princes. They would need these additional services to execute an assault in a manner that would be noteworthy for many a time to come.

Calamity strides across the site that holds the rebuilt ancient ruins, her long feet trampling heavily atop the ground. She barks out orders, as her long red hair snaps about like a whip, cracking in every direction. Not one attendee paid her any attention. Her voice increases in both volume and ferocity. The Lesser Princes hear the sound, and thinking it to be a pack of snarling dogs, look over the expanse to view them. With no dogs in sight, the source of the sounds is quickly evident. Her orders now fell upon the intended audience. The vile agitations that they contained reached in toward the Tactile Plains and hung about in their designated areas, growing fear and confusion, and increasing the capacity for mischief.

Harshaw stands in an elevated position over the partially rebuilt ruins inside the In-Between Places. This view enabled the Prince to observe possibilities that may otherwise have gone unnoticed. He was careful to take into account the skills of his opponents, and, in this light, regarded all of the probabilities that lay within his grasp. Once Harshaw thoroughly explores all of his options, he makes a choice. Pulling upon the atmospheres, he manoeuvres through time, space and matter, to accommodate cunning reality.

The Lesser Princes situated below, held, upon each long finger, a long elasticated band. Following Harshaw's instruction, the Princes begin pulling the bands tightly and securing them upon particular points. The action speedily accomplished produces a well-defined structure.

Avril watches as the connections form a tight grip and link up to one another. The reestablishment of this genius that her predecessor's displayed struck veneration into her heart. "I will take vengeance for you, oh ancients," she whispered softly. "For it is here, where you lend me your knowledge, that I will rule the skies and I will tear them apart. It is here that I will cause the winds to rage, and the Lights of the skies to dim, and it is here that I will cause the wild waters to flow. I will wash them away, and harm all that they represent. I have the plans now thanks to you, and, I have the permission."

★

Isabella, Wry and Cara spent most of the time of light walking according to the map and compass given them by the Al'paires, allowing for only small breaks of refreshing. Even with this season extended for them, they were still unsure of its length and were not prepared to risk longer.

It helped that their feet were clad in specially fashioned shoes given to them by the Al'paires, although their bodies still felt the weight of the trek, both physically and otherwise. Isabella walked most of the way behind the others in quiet reflection, intent on keeping her focus ahead of her, and not behind, whereas Wry and Cara, appealed for levity within, and chattered to take attention away from the gravity of their circumstances.

As they continue to walk, the air grows thick, darker somehow, and uneasiness rises up around them. "We must have been walking for longer than I had anticipated, for the darkness is already growing. Or perhaps Ento has come into play though I did not think the spell of Numa had come to its conclusion." Wry allows his thoughts to leave his lips. He had not intended to bring any apprehension out into the open, only speculation.

Though the three try to ignore this growing concern, it continues to play upon their minds, and, as it does, the uneasiness around them increased. In a vain attempt to disguise her anxiety, Isabella reiterated their position, "Well, whether the time of Ento or not, we are at the edge of the river, and it is at the edge of the river we are to be."

Uneasiness continues to elevate, and though they attempt to focus their minds in a more positive direction, their very bodies betray them. Goosebumps running up and down their now chilled bodies indicate that it was now the time to take notice. Something was happening, something odd.

Just a few footsteps away, a small and unusual collection of cloud began to formulate at knee height. Each cloud painted in various shades of grey, swarm in circular and opposing directions. As the clouds churn, they cause a force of rotation absorbing the different clouds into one intensified mass of greyness. In no time at all, this dark grey mass grew wider and wider until it invoked its own small, yet hard, thunder and lightning display.

"I don't like it. Is it common for these parts?" asked Cara, her voice rising in alarm, "Let's keep walking, faster. Pass it by. What do you say, Isabella?" Isabella answers, releasing a surety that lay within her, "I believe it has but one purpose Cara, and that is to raise our agitation though I doubt it can do much more than that." Cara shudders, "Well, maybe so, for it has been successful, my anxiety is certainly raised. Hurry, Pass it by!" Isabella and Wry eagerly comply with her request, and though the cloud soon passed, their fear only intensified.

★

Just a few steps beyond the cloud, the heaviest of rains begin. Cara delivers a proposal, "This has begun heavily, and so, perhaps it is best for us to walk away from the river for a while. The banks have become rather slippery, and it will not be long before they start collapsing." "There is merit to your suggestion, but, is it the right way?" reminds Isabella softly, "Do you not remember the parting words of Halvo and Veeta? We are to keep the course as much as possible, and, the river is our course."

"Yes, Isabella, I remember, but what of his other advice to us? He said that if we must detour, then we must, as long as we return to the course as soon as we possibly can." Isabella sympathises, "Cara, I am probably overly cautious, yet this I ask, let us walk near the river for a little longer at least. Aaron was snatched from us for not following a warning," tears flood her eyes, and though Cara could not see them for the rain, she could hear the pitch of Isabella's voice rising. So, in sympathy, and against her better judgement, Cara agreed.

The banks of the river were quickly broken with the sheer volume of water that blanketed down from the open skies. The walkway at the side of the river had become so soft with the soggy soil that even the lifting of their feet became taxing. "It is with blurred vision that I navigate my unsure footing," laughs Cara nervously, trying to belie her most apparent intimidation. While overhead, the skies grow more active and begin to crackle and to moan. The hairs stood up all over Isabella's body, and before she could respond to Cara, the ground beneath them started to give way.

Cara closes her eyes as the fear that she contained began overtaking her heart. "Those rods of fire and electricity gather to throw themselves at us with such striking force." Wry takes her hand and squeezes from her knuckles to her fingers repeatedly, "Cara, I know, I remember what happened, what you have told me, and that history will not be repeating itself, just keep going forward." With each crash of the rolling skies, Cara's tension rises. Near inconsolable, she forces out the breath from her lungs and wonders if she has strength enough to carry her through until the end of their journey. Isabella allows some space between herself and the couple. Through partly obscured vision, she watches Wry attempt to calm his disconcerted lover.

The storm grows furious above their heads, its fierce winds forming huge gusts that draw in debris from many sources and throw them around, obstructing the vision of the Chosen even more. The lightning draws closer, and eventually strikes the ground hard, opening it up. Now unable to see her friends, Isabella is quickly separated from them and blown off course.

★

Avril was pleased with the progress. "Calamity, you have an aptitude worth my compliments, keep up the wailing, for the atmosphere you create is conducive only to anger, fear and doubt. It seems, though, that we shall not need your immense talent on Cara, or Wry, for we have gutted the Grovels by finding a surprising weakness in the female. The lightning is certain to be her end. She draws it toward herself. Pathetic, wretched creature! Serenade instead over Isabella; let her feel your guttural tones. I want you to fill her reality with your existence, so much so, that she is not able to remember one single good thought of her own."

Avril watches with delight as Isabella Grovels along the muddy ground, searching for some place of respite. Avril voices loudly her intentions for all Lesser Princes present, "The mind of that Grovel will quickly remember its confusion over the death of her beloved Aaron." Avril silently joins Isabella and begins whispering her caustic melodies into Isabella's ear.

Struggling against the chaos of the storm, Isabella retreats into the words of Avril, finding them a safer place than the tempestuous squall about her. Quickly, and almost gratefully, Isabella accepts the whispering of Avril as though they were her thoughts, and becomes consumed with the unanswered questions circling within her head. "You can do this all by yourself, I am sure of it," whispers Avril, "I am quite convinced that you will finish what I have started. Continue, destroy yourself!" Avril then returns to the In-Between Places.

Not quite understanding how she had made it this far, Isabella silences her tortured mind and realises her geographical location. Now, standing at the bottom of the foothills surrounding the region, she was quite a distance from the river. The weather, still brutal, had only increased in strength, but, through the slight protection that the hills offered her, she could make out a small opening ahead.

A cave had been hacked out of the rock, whether by Cambrasian, or by natural sources, Isabella did not know, nor in fact, did she care. Without any need of convincing, she crouches down lower to enter the small opening, and briefly forgetting about her tormenting thoughts, she breathes a deep sigh of relief. The dark, dry cave proves adequate protection from the tearing winds and violent hail. Isabella presses herself up against the rough wall and briefly relaxes into the sense of its extra security.

Suddenly disturbed, Isabella realises that she is not alone, and although she could see no evidence of company, she feels the presence of life. She speaks aloud, hoping to draw it out, "I hope you are not a wild animal though I am sure you would be kinder than the outside of this cave. The storm is so harsh; I feel I have sea legs." There was no movement, nor any reply.

After a while of staring blankly into the darkness, Isabella's thoughts turn toward Wry and Cara. Taking some comfort in the fact that they have remained together, she wonders about their condition. *Cara must have suffered some awful tragedy to feel such mad panic at the weather. She could barely keep herself contained within her skin. Still, they are both remarkably capable Cambrasian's in their ways. Wry will be a stabilising force for her when she is in need of it.* Her thoughts played with their images for a short time before turning her attention toward her position.

Isabella opened her near ruined satchel. In most cases, the bag would have proved waterproof but not in this instance. Even its excellent quality could not stand up to the ravages of the rage-driven winds. The map, now completely illegible, dissolved under the pressure of Isabella's wet fingers. Though previously having memorised its content thoroughly, she was quick to dismiss its loss.

Surprisingly, the compass was still in perfect working order and added to the much-welcomed sense of relief that she experienced. She placed it down on the floor and searched the contents of the bag further. The satchel contained what was necessary for her physical wellbeing, bandages, small bottles with medicinal contents, a knife, a torch, a flask, a light blanket and a handful of other useful things. Removing the flask, Isabella takes a frugal sip of its nourishment and places it down on the ground next to her. Finally, she removes the light blanket and covers herself with it.

It was remarkably warm for its weight and bought Isabella to a comfortable temperature quite quickly. In quiet contentment, her thoughts turn, once again, toward Aaron. "Aaron, how I wish you were with me. I can still feel your kiss, the one you placed on my lips the last time I saw you." Her fingers, stroking her lips as tears rise into the frame of her eyes, "I wish I had you for longer Aaron," her voice breaks as the sobbing escapes from her lips. Then, to her recollection came the bottled scent with the memory of Aaron contained, and she wonders if the Al'paires had packed it. Fumbling, urgently through the satchel, she is relieved to find that they had. Isabella opens up the little bottle and relishes in his memory, consoling herself with his imagined company. Shortly after, out of sheer exhaustion, she fell asleep.

★

No longer was accuracy required in the In-Between Places, for the fear that Cara discharged from the Cambrasian Sphere incited the violence of the unnatural lightning toward her. Clearly out of control, she stumbles around the slippery ground, trembling with fright. With every scream that escapes from her lips, a lightning bolt strikes closely, and often about her person, yet Wry, her only stability, holds her tightly to his side.

"With her torment, she invokes of its power; we could not separate her from the bolts if we tried." Harshaw, bemused over the feeble attempts of the couple, shakes his head. "Why does not the perishing male fool let go of the ninny to save his skin, for she is, of course, the bolts prime target?" "Harshaw," Avril replies, "it is because the idiot still holds to a belief that love will serve him well." In answering his question, a burning sensation rises up into her throat at the mere thought of it.

"Cara," shouted Wry, hoping his voice would be heard over the abysmal noise that terrorised them. "Hold on to me Cara, do not let your nerve take you. I will find us a place to rest until the storm subsides. I will Cara, just hold on." Cara was quick to respond, "I cannot take control of my anxiousness any longer, for it seems that all self-control has left me already. My eyes are burning from the flashes, and my ears pound with the boom of its manifestation. Even the pelting of the rain upon my skin causes my body to jolt inwardly. It feels as though all chance has slipped away from me; I can do nothing more to console myself."

Avril watches carefully, "Be vigilant Harshaw. The release is almost here. For, Cara can no longer feel or hear anything other than our influence, and Wry, well, though he still holds on to his own balance, he no longer affects the atmosphere around him. The shot will be clean. Be ready to take it."

Under instruction, Harshaw took hold of the pliable chords and manoeuvred the unnatural lightning to a single point of precision. Avril lifted both arms as if she was about to conduct an orchestra, and made her prediction, "Two will fall, not one. We will break her heart with the elements, and his, he will break himself." Avril lowers her arms with artistic triumph, one reminiscent of her former splendour. Harshaw's line of sight, now divided between Avril and his mark. Even with his shared focus, he could see a slight squint in Avril's eyes, indicating the tremendous pleasure she experienced at this most pivotal moment.

Checking his trajectory one final time, Harshaw pulls tightly upon the chords to release any slack, and lunges backwards to release the bolt. The charged rod pierces through from the In-Between Places and heads directly toward the intended target on the Tactile Plains. Each Lesser Prince stands in silence, watching the result of their preparation play out before them.

Then, impact. Cara, seeing only a bright light, felt her chilled body instantly warmed. Briefly, she imagines that Eirtherol has come in force to save her, but then, her mind turns to stillness and she knows nothing more. Left utterly aghast, Wry is powerless to do anything other than watch as her limp body falls hard upon the sludgy soil. As the lightening still crashes and the rain continues to fall, the winds, unrelenting, howls like a maddened dog around him.

"That is as far as our permission grants us; regretfully, we cannot use them for sport," Avril said revelling in the well-accomplished mission. Then, she issues a command, "Let the forces extinguish themselves. Though, do take your time oh reckless tempest, then return to rest once you have drawn to your conclusion. But for now, and for us, our instructions are to gather together the necessary forces and move up to the farthest gate to catch any residue of Grovels that may still pass over the line, for that time, has most certainly come."

★

The unnatural storm began drawing to a conclusion when the last of the lightning hit the beaten ground. Isabella wakes from her slumber, and still groggy, sits up to lean against the wall of the cave. Sensing the hidden presence yet again, she warily calls out to the mysterious being, but still no answer. "I know you are here, I can feel you," she speaks slowly. "Hear me, I have no wish to take anything from you, I only want to share this shelter until I can return to where I came from." Again, receiving no answer, Isabella sets about as though she was alone.

Firstly, Isabella prepares to bring some sustenance to her famished body. She pulls out the tiny candles that are in her possession, places them securely in small holders and lights them. The hand carved candles are exquisitely detailed and the scent of the wax, lined with a prepared fragrance, evokes the promise of hope. The smell quickly permeates the harsh atmosphere of the cave, and Isabella's contemplation falls upon the thoughtfulness of the Al'paires once again, "Of course they did; of course, they see beauty as a necessity also."

Taking out the container of dried fruit and a small cake of bread, Isabella begins eating her meal, staring dreamily into the candles flame as she does so. Behind the flame of the candle, a face emerges, one that Isabella is quick to recognise. "Why did you hide from me?" Isabella questions. "Sorry Isabella, there was somewhere else that I needed to be. I did watch you, though, whenever I could."

Eleneke's manifestation upon the Cambrasian Sphere is only partial. Her present form, appearing like light, dims then brightens as she slips in and out between the Tactile and In-Between. Isabella's eyes receive the Eirtherol's form in both intensity and dullness, and in both ways, her features were easily recognised.

Staring intently at Isabella for a short while, Eleneke examines her condition. "Isabella, you have been looked after well by the Al'paires. They have restored some much-needed strength to your body. Also, they have led you to the releasing of grief and the gathering of peace." "Yes," replies Isabella, "They did as much as anyone could have, and more so." Eleneke looking at the satchel, asks, "May I." "Of course," Isabella gestures to the buckled satchel.

Isabella exhales to release the tension holding her body rigid. With shoulders now drooping and stomach relaxed, her frame reveals the despair hidden within. Eleneke, still examining the satchel, addresses one concern, "This weather is like nothing we have seen, at least, not for many a Cambrasian lifespan," and with these few words, Eleneke understands why the storm had become so fierce. "You have done well to withstand it Isabella, but this satchel did not fare so well as you." Eleneke opens the satchel and pulls out the silken material bathed in incense used at Isabella's healing. Isabella's lips start to tremble at the sight of it. Then, the scent besieges her. "Aaron," she softly sobs. "Yes Isabella, Aaron. You have bound up your grief enough to continue, and you have excelled in the matter, but our will is to give you a greater release now, a greater freedom, and more understanding. Aaron's absence will always be great loss to you, but it need not be your torment."

"Forgive me Eleneke, if my passions should rise, for I am quite raw in my thoughts. But, I will not hold back for if I did, nothing would release at all." Eleneke nodded. "Why, Eleneke, did you not prevent his death?" Isabella asks, her voice rising in tone with each word, and with the same intensity, she continues. "Are we not giving our lives for your cause, we stand on the same side do we not? Where was your power to save him?" Isabella pauses, expecting an answer, but was met only with silence.

Isabella continues, "Aaron called forward the waters from the trough to rise and the water did rise, and the effect of his foresight became our reprieve, our advantage. Cara, Wry and I also heard the same words come out from the Invisible Place, the words about the waters flowing, though only Aaron persisted. He even persisted while we teased him. Aaron was the one with the bravest heart, and we were saved by his conviction. Why then was he dealt such a strong blow?" Pausing for a moment to collect her thoughts she resumes, "Was it not you, Eleneke that spared me from my own death. Remember, the deck of the ship at my journey's beginning? If you could save me, then how is it that you could not save him?"

With pain clearly etched upon her face, Isabella's eyes plead for Eleneke to answer. Eleneke, holding out her hand, waits for Isabella to take it. Isabella, observing the gesture, obliges. Quite quickly, warmth transferred through to the hands of the Eirtherol and into Isabella. The heat runs through the very core of Isabella's body, warming her from her head to her icy toes. Within a few moments, her dampened clothing was thoroughly dried and her being refreshed with exuberant life. "I can feel your goodness Eleneke," discloses Isabella softly.

Eleneke's smile releases peace out from her being and into the cave. "There you are, my lovely Isabella, breathe it in. It is far easier to hear the truth when you no longer war within, or without for that matter." The tenderness in Eleneke's voice made her love for the Chosen obvious.

"I was honoured to watch your formation, even before you had entered the Cambrae Sphere. It was there, in that privilege, that I got to know you from your very foundations, each aspect of you before you ever were. I attended on the day of your arrival to the Sphere, the day you were released from your mother when you flung into your father's expectant arms. The joy present that day was glorious, and you were the reason for its release. You, Isabella, have been a constant delight to me since. Sturdy and soft, curious, and full of surprise, you have caused me no end of laughter."

Looking deeply into the eyes of Isabella, Eleneke continues, "You came from the Volcano Isle, a place that held little confidence in things unseen, and still, you heard the smallest of hopes, and trusted in what you could not see. You believed in the goodness of the Invisible places, a goodness that was not, and still is not, disclosed fully to you. As you followed this small hope and left the comfortable and sure existence you were born to, you took a great personal risk. For this reason, Isabella, you existed within a fervent grace, one that permitted me to intervene. It was grace that rescued you."

Isabella takes it all in as Eleneke continues. "Aaron, both brave and bold, would give anything for you and your safety. Isabella, his love for you was great, as was his loyalty toward Wry and Cara. However, Aaron allowed a place for fear, one that generated suspicion and mistrust. You and Cara have both seen it. Isabella, you gave him the warning. Influenced by fear, Aaron stepped out, thinking he understood, and trusted, not in the direction revealed by the Invisible. No, instead, he walked directly from his own counsel, and lost his life by trusting a misinformed decision. I, nor Asher, have the power to stop one who insists in such a way."

"I know Isabella, that in your heart, you are already aware of this. I just bring you the confirmation that is needed, confirmation to settle the matter within your heart." Isabella, forcing a tight smile across her lips gently nods. Teardrops tumble down from her sodden eyes and course hotly across her flushing cheeks.

"I am thankful," she replied, nodding again as she attempts to subdue the lump in her throat with a swallow. Wiping the wetness from her face she continues, "For this cave, the storm, even the separation from Wry and Cara, though I hope we do not remain separated for long. For, it has stopped me from commanding my attention toward other directions; forced now, to look only at my thoughts, I can release the truth to them; those truths that they need to receive. The tumbling of them all, around and around in my mind, was tiring Eleneke, but now, my mind has been stilled, settled, a shroud has been lifted."

Taking another deep breath, Isabella clutched Eleneke's hand tightly, relaying her gratitude. "I can hear my own heart again. I can hear it." The relief was notable, even in the tone of her voice. "It is time for me to go." Isabella packs up her things and prepares to leave.

★

The force of the wind tore at Wry's clothing, his face stung with the cold and his ears long since had any feeling at all. Cara lay unresponsive in the grip of his arms as he carried her to a nearby tree that had retained its standing position. He lays her down under the shelter of the tree and holds his coat above her face to shield her though she had gone.

The weight of emotion lay so heavily upon the heartbroken man that he found fervent comfort in thoughts of joining his beloved one, wherever she may be. Wry falls to his knees and yells his mind into the winds, "It would be so very easy. The river is now without banks, and it carries a great deal of debris, it would only take a moment to be dragged underneath it." Wry, releasing tears upon his breath has barely enough energy to breathe in again. "I am hollow, empty," he wails.

Suddenly, another opinion enters his mind. Wry takes control of his breathing to hear it. As he gives the notion his full attention, the notion gives him strength. Wry pulls himself from his knees and looks again at Cara's lifeless body. "You and I my love, have a promise given us. We had seen it in the invisible places, assured of the promise even before we began this awful journey. My love, we will see the fulfilment of that pledge. You need not leave me yet." Wry opening his mouth straightens Cara's neck. Filling his lungs with air, he transfers the breath into his lover; again, and again. Nothing! Not accepting defeat, Wry places his hands over Cara's heart, and presses, and presses. Still nothing!

Wry, almost screaming, yells into Cara's unresponsive body. "We have a promise Cara; you have the right to come back." Wry closes his eyes in search of clarity. *I will deal with this, I can. I will take on the full force of pressure against me. I will bring it answer. I will silence it. I will.* Wry listens to threats and fears revealed by the storm then answers it. *You are without power and influence over the Invisible Places. You are not its master, nor are you mine.* The intimidation toward Wry from the storm becomes silent. Wry moves on. He speaks to the voice of reason and logic. *Stop presenting me with facts and equations as you see it for you cannot see, nor do you know, all things. Your aid is no use to me at this point. Be silent.* The voice of reason and knowledge within Wry is now quiet. Then, Wry goes deeper still and acknowledges the presence of terror that threatened permanency to Cara's state. *Be silent, for there is nothing helpful or useful to you at all.* Terror obeys. With each of his fears now silenced, he listens.

With fears quieted and hope raised, Wry broke through into the realm of the Invisible. Tiny bubbles from the Invisible Realm rise up from his belly. Bursting open, they release peace along with understanding. Wry, now still enough to recognise them hears his answer. "Speak to her, cause her to awaken again, for you are able."

Wry lay down beside Cara. He pulled his body close to hers and, tenderly caressing her face, he whispers into her ear. He tells her of his devoted love for her and reminds her of the truths that they had learned in each other's company. He speculates wildly upon the future that lies ahead of them, the future that is further on than the place of the storm, and off into the land promised to them. Wry continues his whispering through an entire light cycle. The winds and rain slowly lessening around them, the lightning now ceased, and even the sky appeared normal again, but his darling Cara was still gone.

Wry hears another instruction. "Light a fire, for when she wakes she will be cold." Without hesitation, Wry takes a combustion cake and some matches from his satchel placed it upon the ground and lights it. The tiny flames grow quickly into a small bonfire, bringing warmth into the immediate area.

Having done all he knew to do, Wry was satisfied and sat down to wait. "I refuse to back down," he mutters under his breath, reminding himself. He waits for further instruction though none came. Yet still he sits, waiting for his soul mate to awaken. Wry, having become so sure of the outcome, fell into a light sleep until an icy hand gripping his shoulder abruptly awakens him. A familiar voice softly complains, "Wry, I am freezing."

Wry held Cara tightly by the firelight for the longest of times. With equal measures of exhaustion and elation, the pair fell into an illusion of suspended motion, as the Sphere seemed to slow down around them. The Eirtherol aiding this sensation from the In-Between Places causing the Chosen's celebration of victory to linger as they rebuilt, refreshed and fell in love, more deeply.

★

"**W**ry, something quite thought-provoking has happened to me while I was away from here. I saw Aaron." Cara gently cupped Wry's face with her hands and looked directly into his eyes as she spoke. "He was being comforted by the stranger that we met, the stranger that held us to the spring. Aaron was concerned that he had bought them disappointment. He seemed quite distressed, as though he had ruined their plans.

You should have seen the expression upon his face, my love when he heard the stranger's reply. He told Aaron that no one was disappointed in him, not in the least. He said that in fact, it was quite the opposite; they were happy to receive him, and were proud of what he had done. A celebratory gathering was being prepared, in Aaron's honour. It was to be held in a place called the Province of Kings. Aaron is a king! Wry, we were traveling with a king, and we did not know it."

"But, that is not all I have to tell you Wry. As Aaron and the stranger continued speaking, Althai came to me to relieve my fears. He said that upon the Cambrae Sphere, death is considered so final, so severe, as though the Tactile Plains are the pinnacle of existence, but it is not. We do continue, just not as we are accustomed to.

Althai also revealed that we have not the need to panic, for, although we believe ourselves to have deviated from our course; we most certainly are not. In fact, he says that we are instead further, for the measure taken against us has only served to strengthen our resolve, and, also the determination of Isabella. Once Althai had finished speaking, he placed his hands on his chest and made a noise that caused incredible sounds. The noise cracked the very space around me. For a moment, I thought it to be electric bolts again as I could not see, but it was not. In the next moment of my awareness, I found myself lying on the floor, alone, with your coat covering me."

Wry and Cara holding each other near the sizzling fire in silence, quietly waited, and listened.

★

Isabella recalls with precision the directions from the chart destroyed in the storm. Carefully reconstructing its outlined paths, she traces landmark to landmark in her mind, until her course is entirely clear. Once completed, a significant question poses in the front of her mind. For though she has stumbled far from the course, it has not been to her disadvantage; for, from this position her final destination is much closer that it had been. However, if she chooses to take the shorter route, she may never be reunited with Wry and Cara, nor know how they have fared.

Fond affection for her friends erupts from inside her heart, making her way forward rather obvious. Despite the frugality of glimmer thrown down from the Lesser Lights, Isabella hastily works her way backward towards the river. Although the landscape is dramatically changed, the form of the waterway promptly discloses her whereabouts.

The winds had all but ceased and the only rain to fall was shaken from the surviving trees as Isabella passed under them. Her body, cold and uncomfortable, she preferred instead to concentrate on an inner security that told her everything was going to end well. She marches forward with redefined purpose, holding her own hands and smiling to herself. As she walks, she considers recent events, *Even now, even after such pain, such loss, and if it were possible to do so; I would again choose to leave the Volcano Isle and the safety of my friends and kin. For I have been enlarged so much. Without this leading, this experience, this journey, I would not be capable of this understanding.* Invigorated by her thoughts, she walks with quickened pace. With heart rate increased and breathing deepened, Isabella relishes the challenge of life.

Up ahead, Isabella sees light flickering in the distance, the welcoming flush of a blazing fire. Once closer to the fire, she could make out the figures of two Cambrasian's, one male, one female, and presently, Isabella, Wry, and Cara were reunited. The Chosen spend the remaining time of darkness relaxing by the fire and recounting stories from their separated journeys.

Chapter 5

ENTO

A stream of light, pouring from the Invisible Realm, enters into the being of Eleneke. She ponders.

Ento's time has come. She desires to brush aside the ruddy skies, intent on flushing things clean. Her violet glow colours the atmosphere, calling out for the rain clouds to wash, purge and freshen in preparation for the return of Acar.

Ento, though you ready yourself to banish the redundant, making room for the new, you are not free to perform your duty just yet. For as unnatural events unfold, in the skies, and on the land, you can be confident of restraint. Though do not despair, for your time may yet come.

The Greater Lights climb the recovering skies, announcing that the time of Ento is indeed now present. The unmistakeable depth of colour paints both land and sky with its familiar beauty. Despite the crisp breeze, Isabella, Wry and Cara, struck by its unmistakable qualities, stand still to take it in.

The ground ahead is bare and sparse with little vegetation left. Nevertheless, the unperturbed trio press on. Planting each foot down firmly with every step, they incline their bodies in the direction they were heading, but as they continue forward, an unnerving awareness begins to germinate.

Cara, needing answers, plays with possibilities in her mind, and is compelled to present some of her reflections aloud, "I cannot tell if this land is peculiarly silent or whether the storm has had a detrimental effect on my hearing." The Chosen confessing her question as she presses her ear gate with the palm of her hand. Isabella quickly responds, "I do not think that your ears have been damaged Cara, for this noiselessness is bewildering. Though, from my inner ears, I am experiencing something quite different, a humming buzz, like electricity escaping out from its source." The trio stopped walking to listen.

Wry breaks the silence, "I think you are right about the quietness," he agrees, "but we are so close to our destination now! I care only to ignore it and stay on the path that we know to follow. Surely, if we take much longer, we will miss what we mean to find. We have come too far now, and I do not want to risk it. We have already taken many costly choices, and I do not wish to take them in vain."

Again, the trio face toward their anticipated objective, hastily making strides in its direction, but this time, they place their focus upon the invisible and receive from the steady stream of knowing that freely presents itself. The impressions translated contradict the silence and spoke instead of an atmosphere charged with intensity, so much so, that the Chosen's skin tingled and their jaws clench in response. Yet what they began understanding internally was not yet manifest in the external.

Parting from the river is now distant memory as the trio trudge on through the dry land. Ento, now governing, reveals its violet hue, generously spraying the colour across the now chilly land, though all is not as it should be, for the air is not damp, and the breeze is not blowing, as is typical during the season.

As the Chosen progressed, the sparse vegetation upon the ground had progressively diminished until nothing living is visible. The barren terrain, dresses instead with dusty colours of red and brown, were adorned with strange concentrations of clay in varying sizes speckled over the top. The horizon lying above flushes a soft pink where the colour variations of sky and land converge.

Cara, disturbing the silence, sighs lightly, and then speaks, "As we get closer to the compass point directions, those globules of clay on the ground have increased in size. It looks as though the ground suffers pilling as much as my woollen coverlet does." Cara laughs in direct contradiction to any experience of disquiet she hosted. Isabella and Wry acknowledge Cara's wit with smiling eyes, but their mouths remain closed.

Knowing their target is nearer, the Chosen instinctively walk faster and faster, requiring more airflow into their beings. The stagnating air, void of wind and movement, pester their wanting lungs. With supply lacking, the trio becomes increasingly light-headed and weak.

★

Mockery sits comfortably in his wheelbarrow while Ridicule and Flattery push his cumbersome frame. The three Princes, presenting anecdotes of the misfortune of others, laugh together shamelessly, relishing the insensitivity of their company.

Drifting around the lesser-known realms, they locate information that would further their craft. From their vantage point in the little-used realms, the Lesser Princes are privy to certain dimensional benefits and perspectives that are not possible to ascertain elsewhere, and as they did so, the trio had heard about the recent deaths of Aaron and Cara.

"That Aaron, he humiliated himself all by himself, clever Grovel, he did not need us to help him at all," Flattery spat with laughter. She could never understand the foolishness of the Cambrasian race. "Stupid, nothing more to say other than stupid really," replies Mockery as he joins in with his own raucous laughter. Ridicule, the less astute of the three, pulls his bellowing back to a covered mumble and attempts to be heard, "Betting you have an idea Mockery, bet you do," his eyes widening in expectancy.

"That was a well-placed bet Ridicule. I think we are to celebrate such a momentous occasion, though how the death of a mouse is momentous baffles me, truly, I don't understand it," they laugh again, harder this time. Although laughter frequently interrupts his pace and clarity of speech, Mockery continues regardless, "Humiliation is a gift that is meant to be shared." Mockery's eyes stream with tears as his obnoxious gaping mouth dribbles.

Wiping the spit away from his mouth, Mockery almost settles his laughter. Grabbing a hand of Flattery, he squeezes tightly and continues, "That forlorn Lassie and the two-for-ones need to remember of their humiliation. Oh, they deserve to. Who is it that they think they are anyhow." Beginning to explode again with laughter, Mockery takes a moment to settle once again. Attempting to divert his attention from ridiculous thoughts, he squeezes Flattery's hand and continues, "Highest Ranker Denken wants them shrouded so heavily in shame that they walk with drooped shoulders. He wants the ever-present light that flickers in their ignorant eyes to become dull and even peter out. Denken, at very least, wants them so dulled that no one would ever afford them, or their ideas, any respect. Therefore, we have reason to forge a plan against them. Shall we begin?"

As Mockery, Flattery, and Ridicule plot, the other realms feel a shudder. All tied to the Chosen and their destiny, both from the Tactile and the In-Between, experience it. With the air of growing restlessness pressing in upon them, they all make a petition, unbeknownst to each other, requesting a meeting with the other beings involved.

With permission granted the Cambrasian's now enter quickly into the In-Between Places. There they gather with Eirtherol, Returned Kings and the little Ones that Chose Not to decipher the growing discontent. "Do not worry about losing time, little Cambrasian's, for it is of no value here, and you will certainly not have lost any upon your return. I remind you of this to take a moment to congratulate you for your personal devotion to our common cause. For, whether you know it or not, I wish to refresh within your thoughts, that sometimes, you are the only ones alerted, and you are the only beings that can take the first action. Keep in mind that you have access to great power. Much more power than you realise. That being said, you cannot do all this on your own, so, our forces band with yours." The assembly of beings settle into deep repose and join to enter the Invisible Realm together.

★

Mockery and his staff, unaware of the attention they drew, traversed the multiple layered realms, gathering strategies and many other useful ideas. Then building them together into multidimensional pictures, they intended to influence any possible space left open to them within Isabella, Cara and Wry. Having discovered areas of discontent left disclosed by many over the ages, it was easy enough to do. "With these offerings, we do not have to be inventive at all. Never was my forte, inventiveness, never my forte," Ridicule mumbles. "Pilfering, much more my thing is pilfering." Mockery smiles widely, his eyes squinting further. "Those Cambrasian's, silly creatures, they don't even know to sweep up their messes. They believe no other being can see it. Forgotten messes, not by us, there is nothing forgotten by us. I would not have it any other way. How convenient it is for us, how convenient indeed."

With the plan now in place, Mockery and his accomplices returned to the Tactile Measure of Time. Flattery carefully whispers into Mockery's ears, interpreting all that she thought valuable while Ridicule pointed out to Flattery anything missed on the periphery. In this way, they watched and waited, understanding that the opportunity to assault was not necessarily immediate. The Princes looked for an opportunity after the death of Aaron. They witnessed the three surviving Grovels leave their respite with the Al'paires, but seeing the level of protection over them, they knew they were not free to attack.

After that, an opportunity to attack opened, but before they could start, they saw the birth of the monstrosity that was the unnatural storm and watched as it waged against their intended victims. Uncertain that the storm would be effective, they stayed within the Tactile Measure of time and witnessed the separation of Isabella, Wry and Cara and the inexplicable occurrences that unfolded. Not wanting to encounter the Grovels on a high, they waited a little more.

The opportunistic group watched on with interest as Isabella, Wry and Cara regroup at the fire once the storm had concluded. "We will leave here in a very short time," Mockery announces, "for, if we wait for longer, our opportunity to damage them will be diminished, and frankly, I want to give them a smashing wack of our goods. Leave them heaving in self-distain. Look ahead, just a little way down the track, someone is waiting to steal our gratification should we hesitate."

They pressed through the layers of the lesser-known realms quite smoothly until they reached the last realm before the In-Between Place. This realm presented a problem. Ridicule accepted the resistance posed as a challenge, and continued forcing with all his might, yet something unknown held him back. Mockery called for Ridicule to use him in his wheelbarrow as leverage, so they, and Flattery, joining efforts together, press, push and knock all the harder, yet they could not force their way through. Utterly perplexed, they hesitate.

"Reformulate after a rest," just after the words left Mockery's mouth, the reason for the resistance became evident. For as they tried to break out, something was trying to break in.

A startling light seeps through the boundaries toward them, soon over towering their significantly built frames. With it, the stench of sweet freshness pervades. Mockery calls for Ridicule to pull him backward as Flattery turns her head over her shoulder, attempting to avoid the smell.

"What are you doing here Eirtherol, you are far from welcome," spouts Flattery, the back of her hand now covering her nose. "I have permission to go where ever it is that I please, and now, it pleases me to be here. Do you have the power over me to change this?" Althai contradicts the arrogant Prince. "No, you are severely outranked," he reminds. Flummoxed, Mockery, Flattery and Ridicule fall silent. Althai continues, "You will remain silent in my presence, and you will listen, and you will comply with my instruction. My word holds you all prisoners here until I decide you released.

Mockery, Flattery, Ridicule, you have been found guilty of planning an unlawful attack against the Chosen within my company. Others within my company, beings from the Cambrasian Sphere, have discovered your impending attack and you are subject to our will now.

We have been fighting you for quite some time though you have remained unaware. Your plans now, completely dismantled, all content used has been located and destroyed, on every plain and realm. My team were thorough. There is nothing left in your arsenal toward Isabella, Wry or Cara, and you have no further leeway to search out for anything new." The disgruntled Princes, squirming as they listen, pull their faces into contorted representations of disdain in defiance. "I refuse your resistance," Althai's body hums and whistles, revealing the pure power that he contains. The Lesser Princes, now reminded of his authority, stay still. Althai continues, "Now, you will leave those three Chosen alone, and you will set no one after them to do your bidding." With Althai's words still ringing in their ears, Mockery, Flattery and Ridicule, now drained of any power to leave, remain suspended in places within.

★

Eleneke, Asher, Darién and Althai, now upon the Tactile Plains, had been walking with the Chosen for quite some time though they remain unseen and unheard. On occasion, the benevolent Eirtherol vigorously stir the air around the stifled little beings to increase the oxygen flow, allowing them a small break from the stale air, but other than that, there is no contact made.

Althai considers aloud, "Is it time? Is it time? Yes, it is time," Speaking a little louder, he explains himself. "An intense time of testing is here for the proving of the Chosen. They must not sense our help or our presence, yet still accept guidance from the vantage point of the Invisible. If they fail, then they fail, and we will bring our aid and prevent their destruction. However, if they hold on to what they have learned, they will be stronger, many times over. So, remain hidden," Althai, pleased to have reached this point, smiles a broad grin toward Eleneke, Asher and Darién. Then, opening the cavity of his mouth into full capacity, he draws in copious amounts of air until his chest can expand no further. Once full, he thrusts the air back out again, causing aerated whistling sounds to escape and vibrate into the surrounding atmosphere.

The released sounds from Althai's body and the sympathetic vibrations from the Tactile Plain swirl around Isabella, Cara and Wry in large, loose, and undetectable circles. The rings spin faster and faster, decreasing in size, but increasing in mass. Once the circles settle into their predetermined speed, they continue on, persisting in this way until one recognisable Cambrasian word forms. "Awaken".

Isabella, Wry and Cara notice the spinning word but experience it only as an irritation. Thinking it to be airborne sand, they trio rub their eyes and blink to rid themselves of the itch that suddenly invaded their person. It did not hurt but felt peculiar nonetheless. Within a short while, a substance like tissue fell from their eyes and the discomfort eased.

Isabella cupping her hands places them over her eyes and blinks rapidly to clear away any remaining irritation. Then, running her fingers over lids and lashes, she reveals, "Peculiar, my eyes, whether I close or open them, they feel different, as though something is missing. But I have checked and cannot feel a change." Cara also rapidly opening and closing her eyes pulls at their corners, forcing tears to flow, "Odd, at first I thought it to be dirt drifting into them, but this cannot be, for there is no wind. It is possible I suppose that we have disturbed the ground with our feet. Even so, as you have said, it is as though something left, not entered." Wry, releasing his face from his hands, looks out at the horizon. With voice now mumbled and weak, he asks, "Open your eyes, Cara, Isabella, look around you."

The once clearly defined landscape now appears as vague shapes and muted colour, shifting and moving quickly forward and back. The trio with no clear vision feels the panic rise up. As hearts pound and questions rise, the trio brace themselves, preparing to battle the confusion. "Here we go again," mutters Cara, "and I am only just over the last." Wry and Isabella grip her hands and stand close. In the next moment, the landscape became well defined again. Grateful for their returning sight, the three release an audible sigh of relief.

The pathway forward is still the same reddish brownish broken clay earth, but now instead of peculiar little pebbles strewn around the landscape, boulders of varying proportion rest in their place. The air remained cold and unmoving, but now an extra element had joined to it.

A pale and ghostly form intruded upon the typically violet skies though it paraded as tangibly as the landscape itself. "Look, in the sky at that ominous cloud. I know it; I have met with it before. However, now I see it for the first time with my tactile eyes. Each time I had sensed its presence, I am presented with a warning, one alerting me to become aware of my surroundings, and search out for what requires my attention." Isabella quickly discloses to her companions, though they are already aware.

"Isabella, Cara and I have been exposed to this before, though, I think it stands as a representation of something rather than a being in itself. Undoubtedly, we are walking into danger." Wry answers, and then holds his arms out to prevent Cara and Isabella from progressing forward. "I do not have even the slightest inkling of what the repercussions of our decision to continue may be though I know our decision is right. Let us restate our intention, and to that intention, be resolute. I am recommitting to the vision of our hearts, and to each other, and I intend to follow on to complete our journey, regardless."

"I am always with you Wry though I still experience tremendous fear," replies Cara with dampness gathering in her eyes. "Our path has been long established within my heart, and I will not turn from it either." Isabella only nodded her agreement. For in her heart, something else took precedence. A scent, a smell, reminiscent of something, though she could not recall, emerged from nowhere and danced about her person. Then before she recognised the bolstering scent, it hastily dissolved. Isabella quickly decides to keep the occurrence to herself until she could explain it.

Cara again checked the position of the compass and pointed in its direction. All three, with face set forward, pressed on. As they trekked on further an unidentified sound drew their attention. In, out, in, out, swelling and collapsing, rising and falling, suggesting life, though there was no life to see and certainly not life sizeable enough to elicit that kind of measure.

With sound increasing, the Chosen stop once more. Carefully they scrutinize the land for the source of this rhythmic breathing but could only see parched and exposed terrain. "What do you think has happened? I see what I could not see before, and now, I hear nonsensical things. What are we to make of this?" Isabella speculates. "This is real," Cara replies, "though I cannot pretend to understand it either."

Starting to walk again, Isabella, Wry, and Cara continue to reason and debate, finding the distraction a comfort from the ever- present respiration noise. Sometimes, it sounded behind them, and sometimes in front, frequently varying in volume. With debate no longer enough to distract, the Chosen move in silence, their eyes darting in all direction, as they move quickly forward. An irregular pounding begins, quietly at first, then louder and louder with each passing moment. Isabella and Cara's bodies flinch, while Wry suppresses his own fear enough to sound courageous in his words, "I wish it were not for me to say, but I can see the source. It is the rocks, they are moving." Disgusted at the thought, Cara replies, "Do not tease us Wry, for it is a quake or something like it." Wry insists, "Cara, I do not jest. Walk faster; let us see if we can avoid this altogether." Their bodies, still labouring under the stagnant air, move faster. "What other dread lay in wait for us?" cries Cara quietly, "I still nurse the scarring from my last battling." "Yet, here you stand", Isabella reassures.

The boulders edge from side to side with increasing violence until the sheer force of vibration shatters the spherical contours. Shapes of oversized bodies break free from their restrictive confinement. Their frames, the same reddish brownish colour of the stones, stretch out to reveal towering beings with distorted limbs and bodies. This continued until an army of stone rose up around the Chosen on all sides.

The transformation continues as the creatures stretch out their stone cold limbs and fingers. Deposits of minerals from underneath the earth spring up and crack through the stony bodies, into the legs and feet of the creatures, spreading and branching out all the way to the top of their heads until a network of pulsating veins fills the In-Between beings with tactile life.

Isabella, Wry and Cara turn their heads, and then their bodies, struggling to comprehend the horror that engulfs them. "What is happening, what is happening, what is happening?" Isabella repeats to herself. Cara places one hand into the palm of Wry, and one into the hand of Isabella, and squeezes while releasing her words, "Oh, my skin is creeping. Look, they pay us their attention. Wry, Isabella?" she questions. "Let us walk forwards and on the course, stay together and try being quiet," whispers Wry out of his bewilderment.

Before the transformation of the beings had finished, Isabella, Wry and Cara could hold their nerve no longer. The frightened trio, requiring every bit of energy that remained, sprinted as far as their legs could carry them. Soon, the breathing sounds of the rock life forms gives way to utterances of abuse, first in an unknown language, and then into the Cambrasian's own dialect.

The hateful abuse continued to rain down intimidation and humiliation onto the Chosen. It spewed its vileness out incessantly, threatening to crush the Chosen with fear and embarrassment. "Try not to listen to them, for they are ancient beings, well versed in malevolence, just keep running for as long as we can," roars Wry.

Without slowing down, the Chosen turn their focus toward the Invisible Realm; though they make many attempts, they cannot connect to its safety. The Chosen, then appealing to the Eirtherol for assistance but cannot locate them either.

Without the Invisible Realm, and without Eleneke or Aaron, Isabella agonizes over the sense of isolation and loneliness that she felt. Wry and Cara were the finest of companions, but they belonged to each other, and she belonged with no one. The thoughts plague her mind and rapidly squander her energy. More afraid of what was within than what was outward, Isabella crumpled, "I can run no more."

Broken at the waist and holding onto her knees, Isabella catches both breath and thought. Wry and Cara, though confused by Isabella's lack of stamina, stopped running also. While Isabella prepares an explanation, she detects that familiar fragrance in the air once again. It again dances around her face, further then nearer, for the tiniest of moments, increasing in strength and then backing off again. "Sweet fragrance, if you do not linger, then I cannot place you," she voices in exasperation. Nevertheless, it is too late for the scent had already subsided.

Wry and Cara stood near Isabella while keeping a watchful eye on the abusive vein filled rock creatures. Wry pleads, "Isabella, please come on, you need not run if you cannot. You can walk, though, can you? We must move forward, there is a limit to our time. Push on my love, push forward. You can tell us of your thoughts later." Wry laid his hand upon the small of Isabella's back, directing her forward while Cara reinforces her from the other side. "I am sorry. I have no wish to hold us back," replies Isabella as she freely complies.

Continuing to walk forward, the discourse sent from the rock creatures intensifies. Their threats and intimidations grow more menacing, divulging personal weaknesses of the three Chosen. Fact injected with fiction spewed forth, causing their untold secret shame to be openly identified. Isabella, Wry and Cara silently cringing inside at the information the creatures had revealed, fixed their eyes ahead and continue walking.

★

With their essence now inserted inside of the rock formations, Avril, Harshaw and Calamity look ahead at the flat and natural ground. Finding their altered form to be rudimentary and vulgar, they take no pleasure in such conformity but understand the necessity. "I do not like this thick, unyielding form, it is too restrictive. Isn't gravity and time enough to suffer under?" complains Harshaw. "Tell it to Denken," replies Calamity with equal measures of distaste.

Avril ignoring the inept chattering from of the other Princes remains silent. She was much more interested in making out the identities from a group of Grovels that quickly approach. "Harshaw, Calamity, stop your banter and lend me your eyes. It is taking longer for me to adjust than I had expected. The Eirtherol must have laid something in the soil to hinder me." Avril's new body creaks as she lifts a hefty arm to point out the group. Harshaw and Calamity look off into the distance to see. "That group of Cambrasian's ahead, they look like the feeble weeds we snuffed out. See, the one on the end, she looks like the dead one, the screaming and mindless idiot, the Grovel that attracted the attentions of the lightening to her."

Harshaw and Calamity study the Grovels for quite a while. After testing their sights in another direction, they confidently offer up the unanimous verdict. "Avril there is nothing wrong with your vision; you can see clearly," replies Harshaw, "Just look at the other two with her, isn't that Isabella, your assignment, and her companion Wry, the incorrigible Wry. Somehow, Isabella has found the road back to them. I did not deem her that capable, she must have received help."

Even through the casing of her solid body, Avril could feel the burning rise up through her centre and settle in her throat. "That Grovel is too vacuous to survive us!" she screams. Fuelled with utter fury Avril launches into a fervent dance. Stamping her huge, heavy feet upon the hard ground Avril causes the dry soil to open and split with each thud.

The many other Lesser Princes in the vicinity take her cue and launch into an angry romp, aiding what they envisaged to be an elaborate display of intimidation. The clamouring mob now unusually excited by the result of their physicality upon the Tactile Plain became louder and more forceful in celebration.

Avril excited about the chain of events basks in her influence. *Many are choosing to follow me; interesting. Denken will be pleased. He may believe it was through my planning.* Heartily laughing inwardly, the Lesser Prince, losing her focus for a moment, misses something of great importance.

★

An unlikely voice addresses the Prince from behind. Avril hauling around her cumbersome body holds it in a position of defence though not enough to face the one speaking. Then, ceases her roaring, she listens. "Avril, what made you think that you could measure the importance of these little ones?" Eleneke inquires, "You do not know the hearts of the Chosen, or indeed the heart of the Invisible at all, do you?" Her questions met with silence. Eleneke, pauses for longer than is comfortable then, asks another. "Did you not know that each of your contributions, every single one, directed them straight toward the Invisible, and closer to their greater good?" Again, no sound passes from Avril's gaping mouth. Eleneke, receiving no answer, continues, "In fact, I feel the need to thank you, Avril, for you have helped me in my purposes. For, had you not stirred up such dissent from the unnatural weathers toward the Tactile Plains, Isabella would not have had sufficient opportunity to settle her embittered grief this early on. That bitterness was in all truth, the only force strong enough to conceal her rightful destination."

Avril, manoeuvring her bulky frame around, intended to meet the artful strike head on. Having selected her counterattack, she eagerly prepares to direct the inflammatory statements upon her foe. The Lesser Prince readying the laborious body encasing her, opens the jaw wide, and moves the information from her essence and onto to the tip of the tongue. Avril further expands her body to its maximum capacity and adjusts her eyes to face the intensified glare seeping out from the Eirtherol. However, much to her surprise, there stood four beings, not one. Shocked and disgusted, Avril's stare latches upon one.

Unwanted memories trickle into her unprepared mind, reminding her of a time that she preferred to forget. The memories left unattended for eons, carry with them the full sorrow of her loss. Energies now changed from anger to hurt, Avril recalls.

Before to the 3-day battle, she had watched this majestic being from the outskirts of the Invisible Realm. His beauty and innocence had captured her imagination, and she aspired to know him. The highest from the Invisible Realm saw her strong desire and generously granted the hope. Avril, mesmerised by the beings quality, visited him on many occasions and the two developed a close and loving rapport.

Around that time, the Barren Prince grew restless for reasons of his own. Wishing to stir up dissension toward those in the Invisible Realm, he develops a fabrication, one designed to draw an army to himself. Avril believed the lie while the beautiful being that she adored did not. For a while nothing much changed in the Invisible Realm as the Barren Prince was permitted time to separate those that could be separated.

Once he had identified those loyal toward him, the Barren Prince, develops his band of Eirtherol, assigns tasks toward the more powerful beings, the first of those being Denken. Denken, immediately accepting, receives the charge to separate bonds of love.

At the hand of Denken, Avril, along with others, were quietly provoked into jealousies and hatred, and then presented with other previously unheard of concepts. Ideas born from fear and lack, introduced into the beings, contorted their thinking, and prepared to do the same to their bodies. Once the process takes hold, the infected Princes were required to prove their loyalty.

With his screeching words, Denken releases direction, "No longer will you be known as Eirtherol. You are under the ownership of the Barren Prince now, and your new name will reveal this to all. For now, you are the Lesser Princes of Barren, and as Lesser Princes of Barren, your order is to battle the Invisible Realm and all that it stands for. You must stand against the Eirtherol, most notably the ones you share history with." Unaccustomed to anything but goodness, Avril shook inwardly at the blatant hostility pouring from Highest Ranker Denken. She knew her path was set for now, she was a slave.

Unaware that all Eirtherol knew of the impending attacks, Avril complies with the wished of Denken and attempts to enter the high places to make battle with the Eirtherol. Still possessing all of her beauty, she went to step into the highest of places in the Invisible

Realm. "You cannot enter here any longer Avril," spoke the voice of a guarding warrior. "You have made your choice." With that, the warrior picks her up and hurtles her bewildered body down toward the lesser places. Suddenly understanding what she had done, she screams forward for mercy, pleading for the one she loved to help her, but he did not come.

"Althai, why are you here?" Avril, besieged with pain as her tender affections resurface, remembers her personal weakness. "Quiet now Avril, It is my time to speak. Look back at the Chosen, you too Harshaw and Calamity." With the command, they shift their bodies as rapidly as possible. "Do you see the emerging blue flame that surrounds them?" Avril replies reluctantly, "Yes, I see it." "You know full well of what that is Avril, and shortly, they too will understand."

The three Lesser Princes watch the Chosen as Althai continues. "Very soon your stand against these Chosen will stop, and then you must return to Denken with your reports." Althai stares at the unsuccessful trio. "Avril, even with all your brilliance, you cannot win. Do you not yet understand this?" With these words still humming around the Lesser Princes heads, the Eirtherol take leave from natural sight.

Even with energies fading, Isabella, Wry and Cara, continue taking sizeable steps toward their destination. Refusing the vile onslaught from the thousands of Lesser Princes, they enter their inner place of personal refuge. Even though the three greatly desire for this ordeal to be over, it is evident to themselves and all who witnessed, that they would reach the compass point, or die trying.

After a few more steps, the mysterious fragrance joins Isabella, and dances around her being, but this time it lingers. Isabella draws this beautiful fragrance into her being and with each breath, the scent grows more potent. Isabella excitedly speaks, "I know it now, Cara, Wry, and I know it to tell." The couple, sensing a confidence in Isabella's voice, pay her strictest attention. "When the storm had finished, and we met up again, I have been experiencing a rich fragrance around us. It has been flitting about, teasing my senses, yet, until now, I had not been able to identify its essence."

Lifting their heads higher, Wry and Cara sniff around, searching for the buoyant aroma. "It is the very essence of the scent released over me in my time of greatest need after Aaron left." Pausing for a moment, Isabella inhales again, "Wry, Cara, it is upon you now also. The Al'paires, they are with us and they have sent us their strength. They have joined with the Invisible on our behalf."

Relief falls down upon the trio while laughter rises up as the new information becomes real in their minds. "We do not walk alone; the backing of many surrounds us. These rock creatures, they freely torment us, but what is it that prevents them from destroying us bodily." Isabella laughs again, "It is they that are afraid of us."

The blue flame around them expanded and strengthened, and though they could not perceive it with their natural eyes, they grew in understanding of what was taking place. Their path, no longer obscured, lies open in front of them.

As the intensity of scent and brightness continues to build, the Lesser Princes move away from the light, as fast their cumbersome bodies could carry them. For even through their unpractised tactile vision, the Princes could see the essence of many more powerful than they are, spreading out in every direction. Other Chosen walks together with Returned Kings, Eirtherol, and beings not yet released, each one lending their strength, binds to the destiny of Isabella, Wry and Cara.

Avril stares in horror at the nauseating sight. Calamity, seizing the opportunity, speaks condemnation, "That is it Avril; they walk in the clear confidence of belonging to the Invisible. There is nothing we can do now." Focusing on Avril's unmoving and stony face, she continues. "We were ordered to return to Denken and tell him of your failure. We must go," Calamity asserts.

As Calamity's words leave her stony lips, the trio, hoisted immediately from their stony forms, find themselves in Highest Ranker Denken's chamber, though Denken is not yet present. They stand in silence, expecting at any time, a sudden and painful chastisement from the Highest Ranker, but it does not come. Instead, a sound, echoing through the darkened chambers of Denken's office, draws nearer. The sound wheezes out in high frequencies, changing pitch three times, and then stops.

A masculine voice calls out impatiently for Denken. The slow and drawn out words, accompanied by the sounds of deep and hollow wind instruments, chill Avril, Harshaw and Calamity to their cores. Knowing now, of who speaks, the terrified Lesser Princes, not looking up, fall down to the ground. It was the Barren Prince.

Denken, shaking, enters the room. He assumes the position of the much lower rankers, and unwilling to look up, apologises profusely for his tardiness. "Shut up, shut up, you are spared. Stand now." Denken stands on command, holding his head as close to his chest as possible. Ignoring the presence of the Lesser Princes, the Barren Prince continues, "They are to be taken from their position, stripped down publicly, and placed back upon the tactile plains. There, they will start again, from the beginning, gathering and logging information. That is it. They will be restricted in their access to the In-Between Places, and, should they need to change position, they will need a Grovel that is willing to carry them. Assignments with any particular chosen are now, cancelled. Tell them." The Barren Prince disappears.

All four Lesser Princes, no longer hearing the whistling of the Barren Prince's body through the outer chambers, stand up straight. Denken, stretching his neck upward, releases his fury driven voice, "You heard the Barren Prince. Go."

Avril, Calamity and Harshaw, accepting their fate, leave for their public undressing. After all, their failure was immense, and all failure is deserving of great punishment.

★

Though breathing was still uncomfortable, and the landscape remained emptied of life, the three Cambrasian's continue unperturbed until the desert is far behind them. The Chosen walk close together in a slow rhythm, meaning to preserve energy for unforeseen circumstances though none presented.

Directing their steps, Isabella recalls accurately all of the markings on the map that the Al'paires had given them. "Look," she points to a narrow dirt path, leading right to the top of a cliff. "We are almost there." With their destination close, Isabella, Wry and Cara abandon all sense of reserve and increase their pace, eager to arrive at their destination.

★

The smiling trio stood atop the summit and held hands. "Well Isabella, here we are, your dream has led us to this place. What is next I do not know, but right at this point, I do not care either." Breathing in deeply, Cara savours the moment, before bubbling out more words of excitement. "We have seen so much change in such a short while. The contrast is quite extraordinary. Even bodily, we are changed; both strengthened and bruised by the vile storm and such like. However, and most significantly I think is that, we have been introduced to real wisdom, and our unseen eyes have become considerably sharper. We have found another way, both exhilarating and profound."

Isabella, Wry, and Cara, with lightness and thanksgiving flooding their hearts, dance unreservedly, relishing in the joys of celebration. Nearby Eirtherol, attracted by the innocent display, gather around. The invisible beings take small colourful packages from their robes and, removing the contents, pour the substances onto the Chosen in generous proportions. Peace, expectations, triumph, along with other useful gifts increase the fervency of celebration, as the anticipation of hopeful things grew.

Eleneke, Asher, Darién, and Althai stay atop the summit and watch while Isabella, Wry, and Cara meet with other Chosen familiar with the way forward. Now walking toward a narrow staircase carved into the cliff face, the Chosen, standing tall, appear regal, though still somewhat bedraggled. Quickly navigating the stairs, the three are ushered into a large village filled with many thousands like them. The Eirtherol stand quiet and peaceful, listening to the passionate applause escaping from the village. After taking a moment to digesting the fullness of what had just happened, Eleneke speaks, "For, after what has seemed like endless ages, the final allowance of Chosen has arrived. The Daystars will soon meet."

Althai, positioning his body to receive the tactile air, releases the sound of many trumpets and then responds, "These ones are emerging into an extraordinary occasion, for they are tottering on the tip of one era and falling into the brink of the next. The time has come for their release, my friends, let us go and watch this unique unveiling from another angle." After his announcement, all four Eirtherol slip off from the Tactile Plains and return to the Invisible Realm.

★

Isabella surveys the unfamiliar land, taking note of the many other Chosen gathered. There were young, old, and every age in between, from all over the Cambrasian Sphere. "It looks as though some have been waiting a great while for us to join with them," Isabella observed, laughing inwardly as she added, "I had felt so alone throughout our journey, most especially after the time of Aaron's departure, as though no one could ever understand me. But now, now I can see the foolishness of my thinking, for many, many, have walked a similar path."

Wry collected Isabella under one arm and Cara under the other. "Now we are all here, Isabella, you must be sure of this, Cara and I have no intentions of letting you far from our sights. Our love is with you and always will be. We are your new family, and you are ours."

The mood, electric and jubilant, heightens as a tall, grey-haired man wearing a purple poncho, stands upon a pedestal. He motions for numerous others from varying parts of the Sphere to join him. Surrounded by a collection of pipes ranging in size, he addresses the attentive crowd. His amplified rumbling voice booms out alongside the rich, melodious and resonant tones from the pipes, closely followed by the voices of interpreters, speaking at the same time.

"As Acar, Numa and Ento move together in these next short moments, all three Greater Lights will sit in such a close proximity that, they will melt into one another and appear as one, united in both shape and colour. Never has such a thing happened, and as far as we can predict, it will not happen again. This is the extraordinary first sign to us that our path forward is clear and open.

Each of us has been charged and equipped to take the things of the Invisible Places and establish them, here upon the Sphere. Everything we need to this is already in our possession. We can turn these lands back to the original intention. By love, we will pull down old arrangements, and by love, we will build up new ones.

From this moment on, we will be the recipients of novel ideas and unfamiliar concepts that will have a significant impact on both land and inhabitants, and as agreeable as that sounds, it will present us with challenges, ones that we cannot even begin to prepare for or understand. However, do not be anxious about this, for reasons you are already aware. First, fear clouds our hearing and second, we do not stand on our own.

Keep this in the forefront of your minds also. We are the first of many and, as the first, it is certain we will make many mistakes as we navigate through unfamiliar territories." The man, taking a step backward, lifts his head toward the skies, then gasping in expectation. "Look up now and watch, for the moment has arrived, the spectacle in the sky begins."

All Chosen, without exception, turn their heads toward the heavens. Many hold their breath while others release sighs and squeals of excitement. Ento and Acar, side to side with Numa approaching underneath, their colours mixing, changing and brightening, produce countless shades. The Daystars overlap, their glow intensifying until darkness covers the land. Whispered and mumbling voices resound from the crowd as the Daystars swallow each other's individual form to become one.

A dazzling white light sparking from the united stars shatters through the darkness, revealing the makings of the Sphere down to its core. The beams pulsating at high speeds, reach deeper through the Sphere and higher in the sky with each flash. Turning their attentions toward the bodies and land around them, Isabella, Wry and Cara, with mouths gaping, explore further.

Bodies of Chosen, though still holding to shape, are no longer the dense, fleshy containers they had been. For now, small and opaque circling coils of sounds, breath and written word held the beings within. Curious to understand, Isabella looks toward Cara, scrutinizing her form.

Tiny bubbles from the Invisible rise up from the depth of Isabella's being, and to her mind, whispering, "Look into Cara's ears." Immediately, Isabella looks, observes the swirling patterns making up Cara's physical form, and identifies something peculiar. While most of the breath, word, and sound spun around at constant speed, a small number of them did not. "These variant strains threaten to upset the balance," the whisper continued, "You are able to fix it."

Isabella, remembering the trauma from the storm that Cara has suffered, breathes in deeply. Repeating the whispered word of the Invisible in her mind, she moves closer to her friend's ear, *I am able.* "Reverse," she whispers directly into the ear, "Damage, reverse." The words reform as a spinning coil, enter Cara's ear and stop the inconsistent movements. Inspecting further, Isabella sees a word, unlike the others, lodged in the centre of the halted coils, and realising it does not belong, she calls it out, "You do not belong here, go; leave." The word spins out from Cara's body, dissolving completely.

Hmmm, now there is a gap. What do I do? What do I do? Isabella puzzles. The Invisible, hearing her question, whispers the answers into her being, "Ear, receive peace." Isabella looking down at her own body watches as a word forms inside her. Then, traveling upward, the word stops, settling on her tongue, ready for release. Isabella, moving closer to Cara, opens her mouth and releases the words into Cara's ear. "Ear, receive peace, all is well." Immediately, the halted coils, along with the new addition, begin spinning at the rate of the others. Cara gasps, "I am well; in my hearing I am well."

By this time, all gathered in the village knew what to do. With each injury and affliction dismantled, shrieks, sobs, and grateful noises pour from the lips of giver and receiver alike. Once everyone is fixed, the excited crowd move their attention toward the land, quickly restoring it to perfect order.

As the Daystars continue their path, the white light diminishes, and darkness covers the land. Soon enough the stars colourings separate, becoming increasingly lighter until all returns to normal. The Chosen fall silent.

The grey haired man takes a step forward on the pedestal and looks down to the awestruck crowd, and motions for the interpreters to join him. "The Invisible and the Tactile, always intended for each other. We were made for beauty, and from beauty." The crowd, first releasing unbridled cheer, become collectively quiet again. The man continues, "Everything we have seen and done and experienced while the Daystars hung in unison, are things that we can still do, and see, and experience, with the guidance of the Invisible, through our inner vision. You are equipped. Be confident, and go in love."

A light rain starts to drizzle as the enthusiastic band, following their inner vision, leave the village in their thousands. With countenance shining brightly, they forge ahead into the unknown, unsure of their destination, yet guarded by faith and wisdom.

Isabella walks behind Wry and Cara, watching as they banter and cheer. Alone, though not lonely, she spends time reflecting on her travels over the period of Acar, Numa and Ento, *What a funny thing, for after everything I had searched for, and all that I have found, it is now blazingly clear. I have now, only just reached the beginning.*

The anticipated age has begun.

Made in the USA
San Bernardino, CA
07 December 2015